A dark fantasy
LGBTQIA+ anthology

Of Fire and Stars

EDITED BY S.O. GREEN

EERIE RIVER PUBLISHING

OF FIRE AND STARS

CHRIS BANNOR

NEEN COHEN

GEORGIA COOK

MORGAN ELEKTRA

K. B. ELIJAH

ANGÈLE GOUGEON

S.O. GREEN

DONNA J. W. MUNRO

MCKENZIE RICHARDSON

FRANK SAWIELIJEW

WYNNE F. WINTERS

Contents

FOREWORD

BY S.O. GREEN

This is a book about fae. Some of these fae are gay. Some of them are lesbian, bisexual, transgender or queer. While this isn't necessarily a book that depicts fairies as an allegory for the LGBTQ+ experience, every story contains LGBTQ+ characters, and every story contains fairies. The rest was up to the authors.

In these pages, you'll read stories about characters who lose their voices, characters who have to hide who they really are, characters learning how to love, characters struggling just to survive. Some are fae, some are human, but every single one of them is interesting and real.

The stories also had to be dark. Fire and stars are so much more enchanting in the dark, aren't they?

We're lucky to be living in a time when there's so much diversity emerging in the fantasy genre, and when representation matters to so many

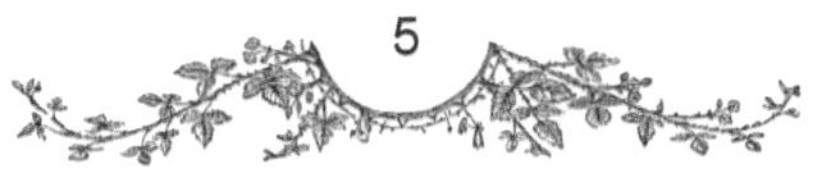

people. During the Pulp era and 'Golden Age' of speculative fiction, queer characters were only ever villains, if they weren't entirely absent, or at least hidden.

Even during the New Wave, when LGBTQ+ themes started to gain traction in the genre, it was a slow uptake. So many publishers were worried about offending their primary demographic, and writers brave enough to openly confront the issue suffered for it.

It's a far cry from the era of myths and legends that stories of the fae originate from, a time when sex was powerful but borderless, and gender was second to the business of living through the day. Gods and heroes could be either and neither and everything in between, and so could the mysterious creatures in the wild spaces of the world.

When early humans anthropomorphised nature, they imagined beings much like themselves. Fierce, but capable of kindness. Petty, but willing to be appeased. It's not a surprise that many of them were also queer.

Maybe that's why an anthology combining LGBTQ+ themes and the fae seemed like such a perfect fit. We're paying homage to our mythological roots. After all, fae can be anything and everything they set their minds to. It's a freedom everyone should enjoy.

This book is at the intersection of sexuality and gender identity, mythology and modernity. Sometimes sexy, sometimes sinister, sometimes heroic and sometimes harrowing. It's beautiful and eclectic and different, just like life. Just like all of us.

It's a book about how queerness is in the bones of the world, in its forests and streams, in its myths and legends, as natural as any other force of nature. As natural as fire and stars.

~ Simone

The Voice Stealer's Song

By McKenzie Richardson

Whispers come from the forest on the darkest nights when the moon is full. The people of Littletown have gotten good at ignoring the ghostly invitations. But every now and then, someone goes into the forest.

More often than not, they never come out again.

Olive's eyes were nearly blank, they rolled so fiercely, only the whites showing. "Come on, Deja. You don't really want to go to that stupid dance, do you?"

Deja cocked an eyebrow skyward, face stern. "I just thought it'd be fun. You know, cheesy music, getting dressed up, sharing a slow dance..."

At this, a lump formed in Olive's throat. A slow dance. That was what this was really about. Olive and Deja had been unofficially dating for nearly

six months now, though they'd been friends much longer. Their 'unofficial' status had less to do with the question of exclusivity and more with Olive's hesitancy to announce their relationship to friends.

"But wouldn't it be more fun if we just hang out at my house?" Olive tempted.

"That's all we ever do. We've never actually gone out."

"That's not true. We got ice cream last weekend."

"With all your friends. That's not a date. That's just a bunch of people hanging out."

A sigh escaped Olive's lips as they nervously itched at their ear, where the RIE hearing aid rubbed against the skin. They'd been wearing them since childhood and were used to the sensation, but heightened anxiety often made the itching impossible to ignore. Detecting the disappointment in Deja's eyes, Olive's heart lurched.

"Fine. We can go to the dance."

The eruption of light that burst from Deja's expression was worth the uneasiness in Olive's stomach.

Thank you, Raincloud! Deja signed. Touching her fingertips to her thumbs in the shape of an O, she flicked her hands downward to mimic rain.

Yeah, yeah. Anything for you, Sunshine, Olive signed back. They created a D-shape with the thumb and index finger of one hand then flicked their other fingers toward their face like rays of sun.

Olive had received their name sign as a child for their stormy eyes, but it also reflected their reserved personality. When Deja secured her place as their best friend, Olive had bestowed her with a name sign that matched her bright temperament, the perfect balance to their own.

Sweeping them up in a hug, Deja squealed giddily, before dashing off to pick out an outfit.

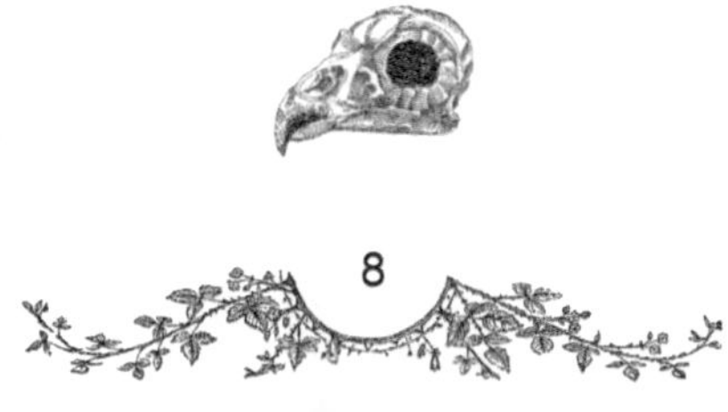

When Olive opened the door, Deja struck a pose, decked out in a floor-length gown the color of dewy cherry blossoms. Intricate braids wound round her head, and there was a slash of bronze across each cheekbone, giving her dark skin a metallic gleam.

Olive's stomach dropped into their shoes, the ones they wore for track practice. It wasn't until Deja tapped Olive's chin that they realized their jaw had dropped. It took all their control not to take Deja in their arms and press their lips to every inch of her.

Behind them, Olive's mother gushed how elegant Deja looked.

"Thanks, Ms. P. I think I clean up pretty well." Deja's laugh was contagious, that sunny disposition always seeping into whatever space she inhabited.

Olive's mother fiddled with Olive's hair, knotted at the back of their head. Then she ducked her face into Olive's range of sight. While not exceptionally skilled in lip-reading, it was easier to follow conversations, especially those that involved their mother's high-pitched voice, when Olive could see the person's mouth.

"Couldn't you have done something with your hair? It's finally grown out and you just throw it back all the time. All the boys are going to be drooling over Deja."

Olive couldn't meet Deja's eyes, but felt them boring into their face, waiting for Olive to set their mother straight.

Instead, Olive disappeared upstairs. They kept the dark blazer and black jeans, but exchanged their dirt-coated shoes for a pair of black ones that looked a little more formal. As they headed downstairs, conversation drifted from the living room where their mother and Deja were talking. Or rather their mother was talking to Deja, who appeared too stunned to speak.

"It really is nice you girls are going to the dance together. I'm glad Olive has someone to go with. She's just so shy around boys. I'm sure she'll get a boyfriend one day, but it's nice she has such a close friend."

Olive rushed in before Deja could reply. "Well, Mom, we should be going. Don't want to be late for the dance."

Hooking an arm through Deja's, they said a final goodbye and escaped into the cool darkness of the night.

The silence in the car was unbearable as they drove the road that curved with the tree line of the forest. Olive wanted to say something, to apologize, to explain, but words felt useless in the presence of the anger radiating from Deja in waves.

"Deja, I'm sorry," Olive began. They knew it wasn't enough. Deja just stared out the window in silence. "Come on, talk to me."

"You said you were going to tell her."

"The timing's just not right."

Olive's eyes darted to Deja's face then back to the road. The low frequency of Deja's voice was easier for Olive to hear, but sometimes it rose with emotion and seeing her face made it easier to clearly understand.

"Olive, you haven't even told her to use your correct pronouns. I know it bugs you."

"It'll just confuse her. I—"

"Well, at least give her a chance. How is she supposed to know if you don't bring it up?"

Olive made no response. Instead, they concentrated on the road. The center line reflected the headlights in a hypnotic pattern.

After a tense pause, Deja licked her lip. "Olive..." Her voice was so soft, like moth wings shivering. "Will you dance with me tonight?"

Olive scoffed. "Of course I'll dance with you. Just like every other dance we've gone to since middle school."

"I mean...with me." Deja stared at the dust gathering on the dashboard. "Like a slow dance."

Olive's foot rose from the gas pedal, as though slowing the car would help their mind process Deja's request. Their gaze did not leave the road, staring straight ahead, unable to meet Deja's eyes.

"Deja, I—"

It was too late. They'd paused too long.

"Just let me out here."

Olive's body complied despite their mind's protests. Gravel rumbled under the tires as the car pulled over, settling at the point before the road twisted away from the forest. The passenger door flew open before Olive could find the words to object.

It took Olive a moment to collect their courage before hurrying after Deja. By the still-lit headlights, Olive followed Deja's silhouette toward the tree line.

"Deja, wait!"

The rubble along the side of the road lurched beneath Olive's feet, sending them to the ground. Bits of rock cut through their jeans. Olive winced, but was up and moving again, ignoring the blood beading at their knee.

A hedge ran along all sides of the forest, dotted with moonlight-hued blossoms. It acted as a boundary, a six-foot buffer between it and the trees.

Deja had reached the faint edge of the headlight's beam where the brightness gave way to the unknown. There she paused, like she was thinking better of her course, the bone-white flowers catching the faint light like a warning signal. Then her body stiffened, her head cocked to one side as though listening to something far off. She glided forward, movements slow and sweeping like a ghost. Olive tried to catch up, but the throbbing in their knee slowed their pace to a steady limp.

Deja broke through the line of white flower bushes. Olive called out again, repeating the warning they'd heard all their lives.

"Don't go into the forest!"

Deja slipped into the darkness—there one moment, gone the next—like sinking beneath obsidian waves. Olive stopped at the line of white flowers. They stared at the point where Deja had disappeared. They had to go after her. They knew that. But their mind pushed against the declara-

tion, fought with the well-known warning.

Standing at the hedge, Olive stared at the inconceivably dark forest. They thought of the stories they'd been told of people disappearing into its depths, how it whispered in the night. Pulling their phone from their pocket, Olive selected a song to stream through their hearing aids. They didn't know if the forest really whispered, but if it did, they did not want to hear its voice.

Then, Olive flicked on the phone's flashlight. With a deep breath, they pushed through the curtain of darkness, calling after Deja.

Even with the flashlight, the dark was like a physical presence, its blackness creeping into Olive's vision. They yelled Deja's name, listening carefully beneath the low rumble of the melody playing in their ears.

A few feet in, a flash of movement caught Olive's eye. The shadows shifted, tiny slivers of darkness glistening in the flashlight's glare. Taking a step forward, Olive nearly jumped out of their skin as a raking sob cut through the night, overpowering the hum of the music.

Olive dove toward the shifting shadows as the darkness burst into a flurry of feathers, so black they were nearly imperceptible from the night. Stray plumes rained down, littering Deja's crumpled form on the forest floor.

"Deja! Deja!"

The girl did not move. Olive closed the distance between them, taking Deja in their arms. They had to get her out of the forest, away from whatever had caused the storm of feathers.

Lifting Deja, they turned up the music and raced away from the fluttering mass. They burst through the tree line, mouth open but mind too numb to recognize if they were screaming or not.

At the flower line, they collapsed, cradling the motionless Deja in their arms in a mockery of the slow dance she'd wanted all along.

The moonlight overhead illuminated the bronze streaks still decorating Deja's cheeks. Olive shook her, trying to pull her back.

Hands appeared from nowhere, rippled with wrinkles. Olive looked up into kind eyes.

"We need to get her away from the forest," the woman said, in a rasping voice.

Together they carried Deja to a little house a few yards from the line of white flowers. Inside, they set her on a low couch. Olive's eyes never left Deja's face as they squeezed her hand, trying to will her awake.

A moment later, the woman returned with a mug full with green, steaming liquid. She pressed it to Deja's lips and coaxed a few drops into her mouth. As the warm liquid coated her tongue, Deja opened her eyes. Golden-brown irises stared blankly ahead. She didn't respond to Olive's voice. In desperation, Olive signed Sunshine over and over, but it was as though Deja was unaware of anything around her.

"She must rest," the woman declared, pulling Olive away.

She gestured for Olive to join her at the circular kitchen table. "My brother went into the forest. He never came out. That one's lucky to have a friend like you."

She nodded toward Deja who still stared blankly at the ceiling. Despite the old woman's admiring tone, the word 'friend' felt like a slap to the face.

"What happened to her?"

"By the looks of it, she had a run-in with Madrigal herself." At Olive's lack of recognition, she continued. "Leader of the Rhyth fae, the most powerful one I've heard of. She collects sounds. She's particularly fond of human voices."

"So, she took Deja's voice? But she should have responded to my signs. It's like she didn't even see me. It's like she's..."

"Blank? Yes. Madrigal didn't just take her voice. She took the part of her that can produce language. Signs are words like any other. Madrigal has taken her ability to communicate, even within herself. That's why she feels so empty. Without language, without thoughts, what is a human after all?"

Olive's brow set in firm resolve. "How do I get Deja's voice back?"

The old woman's eyebrows crept up to her hairline, then a thin smile spread across her lips. "A brave one, I see. Your connection runs deep. I can feel it now. To retrieve the voice, you must face the Queen Rhyth herself."

"How do I find her?"

"That'll be the easy part. Follow the voice. Once Madrigal adds a new one to her collection, she wants to use it. Follow her song and it will lead you right to her. But keep your wits about you. Madrigal can be tricky. I'll take care of this one," she added with a glance toward Deja. "You must go, before it's too late. When the moon's light extinguishes, her voice will be lost forever."

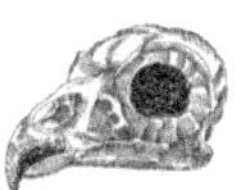

Olive had never set foot in the forest. As children, they'd challenged one another to get as close to the tree line as they dared. Olive hadn't even made it to the white flower buffer. Even Philly Everdear, who'd jumped off the shed roof to prove she could fly and broke her arm in the process, had only managed to get within a foot of the closest tree.

When she'd returned to the safety of the lawn, Philly's face was pale. Her hands trembled despite her play at bravery. She'd said the forest had whispered to her, said it spoke with her grandfather's voice.

Olive stood at that line of flowers, glowing with pale light in the full moon. Picking the moonlit blossoms, they filled the pockets of their coat. Their ears strained for any sound as they faced the forest. From the darkness, a murmur emerged. Its sound rose to a whisper, a recognizable voice. Then it became a song.

Olive knew that low, soothing voice. It was the one that had whispered to them behind closed doors, the one that had shared a lifetime of secrets, made promises and confessions of love. It was the one that made their heart flutter at the mere thought.

It was Deja's voice, but it was not Deja who spoke.

Olive clenched their eyes shut and urged their foot forward. Every muscle in their body flared, every nerve telling them to turn back, to run, to cower in the safety of the real world. But then the image of Deja's blank gaze crept back into their mind, the hollowness of her features, like the life had been sucked out of her.

When Olive opened their eyes, their feet were firmly planted at the tree line, the boundary between the mortal world and something else entirely. A ghostly whiteness danced before their eyes, slithering in midair through the trees. It was like starlight on vapor, the tendril of a bioluminescent jellyfish, will o' the wisps leading the way to a faerie realm.

With a single step, they entered the forest. Every few feet, they dropped a flower as though adorning the aisle of a midnight wedding. The blossoms gleamed by the starlight that slipped between the trees.

Olive may have been too old for fairy tales, but if the stories had taught them anything, it was to take precautions. They followed Deja's stolen voice deeper into the forest, a feeling of dread creeping close behind.

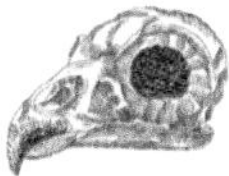

The voice wound between the trees, the song tracing a roadmap through the shadows. In the darkness, everything looked much the same. It was impossible to tell one tree from another.

Despite the signs of life around them, there was little noise aside from Deja's song. Even the sticks snapping beneath their feet sounded muted and dull. Olive tapped at their hearing aid. They'd been fully charged in preparation for the dance, but as Olive whistled a shrill tune, the sound barely resonated.

Olive dropped another flower, sparing intermittent glances back at the reassuring trail. The light of Deja's voice spiraled and swirled, so at odds with its eerie surroundings.

The deeper they went into the forest, the darker it became. As they walked, another sound joined the tendrils of the voice. This one did not have a physical presence, but it rattled in Olive's ears, sending a shiver down their spine.

Ahead, the light of Deja's voice halted its forward motion. It zigzagged through the air, dancing around something hanging from a branch.

The brilliance of the voice illuminated the source of the rattle. A skel-

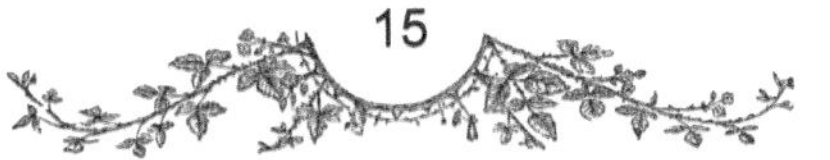

eton hung from the tree, bones picked clean. Olive jerked back, lurching away from the macabre decor. In the spaces between the bones, twisted vines clung, holding the pieces together. As the wind rustled, the skeleton shook. The bones clicked and clacked, like a set of deathly wind chimes.

The wisp of light danced, swiftly weaving itself between the ribs, climbing out the skeleton's sternum, all the while singing in Deja's soulful voice. It slipped between the broken-toothed smile, disappeared for a moment inside the cranium, then emerged once more through the right eye socket.

Disgusted, Olive took another step back, wanting to put as much distance between themself and the bones as they could manage. A sharp crack split the night, followed by a rattling like beads clinking together. Before they knew it, the forest floor slipped out from under them, and they were falling backward into blackness.

Olive woke to an insect biting their ear. They made to slap it, but found their arms tangled.

"No snacking, Riff!" a piercing voice screeched.

Olive winced at the volume, amplified by their hearing aids. They made a second attempt to lift their hands, this time to shield their ears, but whatever was wrapped around them prevented movement. When their eyes adjusted, they found themself in a sort of net.

A band of dark figures scuttled nearby. By the filtered moonlight, all Olive could make out clearly were four pairs of glowing eyes.

"Snack, snack," one of the creatures said, hopping about in a way not quite human.

Though their limbs were bound by the net, Olive managed to rise onto their elbows to get a better look at their captors.

Four impish creatures surrounded them. They reminded Olive of hunched over treble clefs, though their edges weren't well-defined. Their outlines were wispy, like black smoke. Long snouts sprouted from spindly necks, and big, round bellies gave way to thin tails that ended in a sharp flick. Each looked exactly alike, their bodies so black they nearly blended into the surrounding shadows. From each of their heads sprang a protrusion, with a wisp at the end like the flag on an eighth note.

One of the creatures bounced in front of Olive. "A human, a treat! Mistress will be pleased!" it said in a cheerful tone, its bright voice at odds with the darkness of the forest.

"A treat, a treat."

"Better show Mistress. Hop to it!" the loud one yelled.

"Not so loud, Forte," the first snapped, shaking its head as though the sound had gotten stuck in its ear.

"Oh, Major, be nice. You know he can't help it," the fourth and final imp-like creature said. Its tone was the polar opposite of the one it addressed, dark and melancholy where the other was bright.

"Fine, fine, Minor. But let's get going."

"Get going, get going," the second repeated. Tiny drops of blood flecked its squashed mouth, and Olive's stomach gurgled at the realization *it* had been the thing nibbling at their ear.

"Shh, Riff," Major snipped.

Then the four creatures began to strum the chords atop their heads. Muted waves of colored liquid streamed forth. One blue-gray like the sea before a storm, one red-brown like dried blood, one green as the shadows of the forest, and one a murky yellow like jaundiced skin. The suspended liquid bubbled and warped like hot tar as it wrapped around the net that housed Olive, sweeping them into the air.

Olive sucked in their breath as they were hoisted upward. Where the musical liquid touched skin, Olive felt buzzing, a purr that ran through their blood, like the vibration in teeth when humming through a clenched jaw.

"They're sound waves," Olive breathed, fascinated by the way the liquid moved to the tune the imps played.

Deja's song was fainter now, more an afterthought than a melody.

No, not Deja's song. Simply her voice. Olive had to keep reminding themself of that.

As they journeyed through the forest, a tower emerged, its composition only discernable from the trunks of its wooden neighbors by its stone-gray hue. They passed a vertical arrangement of water-filled pots and pans, droplets cascading down like a fountain, singing the melody of a rain shower.

As the creatures paraded onward, one separated from the pack to scurry ahead. The imp yanked a beaded cord near the tower door. A clacking sound reached Olive's ears, but it wasn't until they'd arrived at the base of the tower that they saw its source. Attached to the cord was a deer skull, bleached white as the moon. When the string was pulled, the petrified tongue of the deceased animal rattled inside like the ghost of a bell. Olive fought down their revulsion and tried to focus.

From above, a voice beckoned. Deja's voice.

"What is it, my sweets?"

"We've brought you something, Mistress," Major said, pride in his voice.

"Oh, good. What a lovely night for surprises. Bring it up."

The band of shadow-creatures pushed through the door and proceeded up the winding staircase, their tune still carrying the confined Olive.

At the top, they entered a one-windowed room. A chorus of rattles and plinks drew Olive's attention to where the shadow of a figure stood. The cloaked being stepped aside to reveal a small bowl filled with white stones, like a collection of tiny moons. As the stones rolled between her fingers, the women let out a sigh of satisfaction.

"Sweet as honey," she said, before turning her full attention to the new arrivals.

At first, Olive thought it was an animate skeleton beneath the cloak, reminiscent of the eerie chimes they'd encountered earlier. The face was a skull, recognizably human, all sharp corners and white bone. The ivory covering gave way at the mandible, ending with a long, flesh-covered neck. Two pointed ears poked out beneath a wave of long, dark hair—proof of a living occupant behind the mask-like exterior. From each side of the figure's head sprouted a spindly antler.

The woman's hair swung as she walked, reaching just below her waist. Within it were thin braids, objects woven into the strands. Olive made out the shape of a bird skull, a ring, a seashell, a pocket watch, and a tiny key carved with thorns and roses. As the woman moved, noises sounded. A child laughing, bones clicking, drums beating, scissors snipping, and the distant hum of a lullaby.

"Ah, a new pet," the woman said, in Deja's voice. When she spoke, the skull's mouth did not move, but Olive found they could easily make out the words. They seemed to appear directly inside their head rather than having to travel through their ears.

Olive's eyes locked on the figure, heat rising to their cheeks.

"You've no right to use that voice. It's not yours."

The woman laughed, dropping Deja's voice for a moment. The familiar tone was replaced with a sound reminiscent of the rubbing together of insect legs. At her feet, the little creatures hopped and hissed like cats dancing on two legs.

"All that enter this forest are mine to claim. What are you to decide what is and is not for the taking?"

"Here, here!" Forte yelped.

"Quite right," Minor droned.

"Yes, what right have you to decide?" Major called in agreement.

"What right? What right?" Riff chanted.

Olive did their best to keep their eyes trained on the woman's face, but the empty sockets of the skull gave no hint of emotion. Staring into those holes felt like falling down a well. Olive feared, if they tipped over the edge, they'd never find their way out.

"Such a pretty thing," the woman continued, once more using Deja's voice. "But what secrets you hide."

A hand reached out from the folds of the cloak, the flesh somewhere between every color and no color at all. As it drew closer, Olive spewed a glob of mucus onto Madrigal's chin, which slipped down her neck onto flesh. She wiped away the spit as the little creatures at her feet barked reprimands.

"That's enough, my little Rhyth," Madrigal said. "Why don't you all go play?"

Having been dismissed, the creatures slunk from the room, disappearing into the shadows outside the door.

Turning back to the human, Madrigal cooed gently as she pulled the net away.

Olive had expected her skin to be cold, as surely warmth could not flow through a creature so dark, but when the fingers grazed their cheek, they were surprisingly warm. Without realizing it, Olive leaned into the touch. For a moment, listening to the voice felt safe, like everything would be okay. Madrigal's thumb brushed Olive's hearing aid and they pulled back.

Their thoughts felt scrambled. It was that voice. It was *Deja's* voice, but this was not Deja. Olive had to remind themself of that. The fae were full of tricks. This wasn't real.

Fingers traced circles across Olive's face, along their jawline, and down their neck. Muscles aflame, Olive squirmed, trying not to give in to the touch.

"Don't shy away, little one. A lover's voice, a lover's touch. It's all the same."

Deja's voice wrapped Olive up in its soft embrace, caressing their skin as hands followed the lines of their clavicle. Caught up in the moment, Olive let out a soft groan before they could snap themself out of the trance.

A small blue light escaped from between their lips. Madrigal plucked it from the air as quick as a snake, rolled the light into a ball, and delicately wove it into one of her braids. When she flicked the strand, the orb's light intensified, Olive's groan echoing from it.

"Such a treat," the dark fae said, rolling her neck as she enjoyed the sound.

Olive's mouth opened, panic flashing through their eyes.

"Don't worry, little one. You've still got your voice. That was just a taste." She flicked the orb again, listening to the groan. "Ah, tastes like fresh-turned soil, the way it coats and pulls."

Olive stared at the woman, unsure of her words.

"But I suppose a human wouldn't understand. You spend so much energy on your senses, parsing them all apart behind your eyes. Sight, sound, taste, smell, touch. It's all so complicated. But the Rhyth, we've found a better way. We only hear. We see, touch, taste, and smell sound. We sustain ourselves on it. And there's nothing better than a fresh, new sound, especially a voice."

Olive shuddered.

"I heard you before, in the forest. Heard you call out to your love, the one I took this voice from. I could hear the sadness in your blood as it touched the leaves." She glanced at the dried mess of Olive's knee. "It was that desperation that let you out of my forest. But now you've come back to me. I won't let you slip away a second time."

"What do you want?" Olive whispered, afraid if they used their voice too much, the villain would pluck it away.

"Just company," Madrigal admitted. "It's not every day I get a visitor. Not to mention two in one night. I was hasty with the first, unable to control my hunger. But you..." Madrigal reached toward Olive, but they shuddered away. "There is strength in you. I hear it. How boldly your heart beats, how fiercely your blood pumps. So unsure of yourself, but so powerful in your own right. Every inch of you calls to me."

A moment passed, the air thick. Madrigal lit a candle against the gloom, sighing as the matchstick scraped against the skull-face with an audible scratch.

"I invite you to stay with me in my home, as a guest of sorts. I can show you such wonders."

Olive stared hard at the empty eye sockets, unable to detect what secrets they hid. "And if I refuse?"

"You saw what became of the other human who ventured into my forest. I'd hate to see that happen to you."

Olive didn't know what to say. They did their best to hide their thoughts, but Madrigal chuckled as though reading them as easily as the pages in a book.

"You miss the one whose voice I don. I hear it in your eyes. You love her. How sweet. But I can be all she was and more. I can give you whatever you wish."

From beneath the folds of her midnight cloak, Madrigal retrieved a pale object looped through a silver chain that hung round her neck.

Its surface was snowy-white. The object looked to have been carved from some massive bone, roses and thorns etched along its edges. In the center was a single, carved appendage, like a hand on a clock. All along the edges were tiny doors. Near the bottom was a small hole that looked as though it fit a key.

"I can be anything you want," the dark fae said, in Deja's voice. "Anyone."

Madrigal pulled at the bone-key wound into her hair and fit it to the keyhole. Then she wound the clock.

"Do you prefer this?" Madrigal asked, in a man's deep tone. "Or this?" She turned the key again, and this time the voice was high and piercing. The pitch was nearly imperceptible to Olive, as though it belonged to some small, inhuman creature. "What about this one?" The next voice was slow and heavy, suggesting it had persevered through many ages.

Each time Madrigal turned the key, she took on a new voice. Reaching its starting position, Madrigal assumed Deja's once more.

"A fun trick," she said. "But I've a feeling this is the one you prefer. The way it tickles these little, human ears of yours." At this, she traced the swirl of Olive's hearing aid. "You wouldn't need this with me."

Madrigal pulled them from Olive's ears and examined the tubing that connected the microphone to the dome-covered receiver. Though they'd gotten used to the hearing aids over the years, it was always more comfortable to go without.

"What oddities you humans create for yourselves."

All the while Madrigal had been cycling through her collection of voices, Olive had been thinking of escape. Madrigal blocked the path to the door, but the open window lay just behind them. While Madrigal toyed with the hearing aids, Olive slowly edged toward it, sliding their feet soundlessly along the wooden floor.

"You really ought to conceal your intentions if you plan on tricking me," the fae advised, setting aside her trinkets. "Your face speaks for itself. I hear the truths you try to hide."

Before Olive could dart out of the way, Madrigal was upon them, wrapping them in the folds of her arms. Olive pushed back, stumbling into the table where the candle still flickered. The lit wax toppled, catching a ream of paper aflame. Now Madrigal stood before the window, the moonlight beyond illuminating her outline. Olive's eyes darted from the flames to the fae, who appeared to bask in the sound of the burning paper.

With all their might, Olive threw their shoulder into the fae. Madrigal's skeletal expression did not waver as she lurched through the window. The cloaked creature fell into open space. There it stopped, suspended in air for a moment, before spinning faster and faster, hair whipping wildly. When it seemed it could not gather more speed, the sphere burst into a wave of raven's wings.

Olive slammed the shutters against the feathered cloud and hooked the latch. A pounding resonated from behind the wooden panels. Olive threw open the door and rushed down the stairs, snatching their hearing aids and carefully securing them back in place.

The band of Rhyth blocked the way down as they scurried up the steps to investigate the noise. Taking them by surprise, Olive swiped at Major while turning the bend. The cheerful imp slammed into Minor who tipped onto Forte who crashed over Riff. The lot of them collided in a chain reaction like stout, black dominoes. As the four imps rolled down the stairs, Olive leapt over them, away from whatever pounded on the other side of the shutters.

At the bottom, Olive burst out into the moonlight, a sense of freedom catching at their heart. But when they looked to the sky, the flurry of raven feathers descended, drawn by Olive's heavy breath escaping their lips in white puffs.

Olive ran, toward what they did not know. Their only thought was to flee the creature that lurked in the darkened sky. They could feel the presence behind them, pursuing them into the tree cover. Branches and brambles streamed past their vision. All the while, the distance between them and the flurry of feathers dwindled.

When Olive glanced over their shoulder, their sight filled with black feathers. They turned just in time to avoid smacking headfirst into a tree but lost their footing. Sensing its prey's vulnerability, sharp talons stretched toward Olive, snagging their shoulders. Brittle tips pierced Olive's flesh.

The claws yanked them into the sky. Flying higher and higher, they pushed through the twisting branches in a rain of leaves and twigs. When Olive peered down, it was like seeing the world from space; everything looked so small. Then came the falling. Talons released their catch and Olive hurtled through the air, tossed by the wind, flipping head over heels toward the lush greenery below.

Before impact, Olive clenched their eyes shut and waited for the end. But it did not come. Instead, claws caught once more as the feathered mass snatched them from the air, like a cat toying with a mouse. The feathery storm wove through the air, descended slightly, then released Olive.

This time, it let them crash to earth. One of Olive's shoes snagged in the tree cover, tumbling after them. They landed hard on the impacted earth, the thorns of a bramble bush slowing their descent.

As Olive crawled from the bush, a black cloak rippled before them.

"There's no escaping my forest," Madrigal stated, once more using Deja's voice. "I will always find you. It'd be much easier if you stayed willingly."

Olive emerged from the brambles, yanking off the other shoe.

"Never," they whispered.

The shoe hurtled toward the dark faery. Madrigal stepped aside and the projectile collided with a dull statue tucked away in the shadows.

"Pity. It was nice keeping you alive. But I suppose you'll make a fine addition to my silent collection."

The two had landed in a clearing bordered by a low hedge. White moths dotted the bushes, a ghost image of the blossoms along the forest's perimeter. Perched at intervals within the border were looming figures of stone. There were recognizably human faces and limbs among the group, but also unexpected elements. A pair of delicate wings sprouting from one's back, a waist that gave way to a scaly tale; goat legs and horse hooves, donkey ears and winding horns. Olive stared at the lifelike statues, their expressions hauntingly blank, stone eyes staring. They were so realistic, but their emotionless features gave them away as merely stone replicas.

"Welcome to my garden," Madrigal said, waving a hand toward the cluster of statues. The dark creature drew a silver knife that caught the moonlight on its blade. Fear filled Olive's eyes as they scurried just out of reach.

They were up and moving, limping across the clearing toward one of the statues, a man's torso bulging from a horse's body. They ducked beneath its muscled legs, hoping for some cover as Madrigal lashed out with the knife. Olive dove just in time and the knife clicked against the statue's hindquarters, a sliver of stone separating from its host.

"It's easier if you give in," Madrigal cooed. "Though there is a bit of fun in the chase."

Olive circled the statue, attempting to keep the massive rock between them and the dark faerie. The tip of the blade found purchase along Olive's shoulder and a bloom of crimson sprouted along the skin.

With one hand, Olive staunched the wound while the other pressed against the petrified centaur for support. They were surprised to find it warm to the touch, its body textured with coarse strands of hair. Only then did Olive give in to their suspicions. No hands could craft such careful detail. The creature's essence beat beneath their fingertips, alive but trapped, calcified but present.

This was the final result of Madrigal stealing away what gave it breath.

Olive's heart tightened, imagining the same fate for Deja.

Madrigal lunged again. This time, Olive threw their arm up in a defensive sweep, catching the faerie off guard. The knife flew from Madrigal's hand as Olive's fist met the skeletal face. A single tooth dislodged, dropping to the ground like one of the pale moths.

"I knew there was fight in you," Madrigal chuckled. "There's strength hidden beneath those folds. I'll give you one last chance. Stay with me willingly, feed my soul, and I can give you wonders beyond anything your imagination could dream up. Stay, little Raincloud. Stay with me."

Madrigal's voice was so soothing, so tempting, a part of Olive wanted to give in. If they stayed, they'd never have to tell their mother about their real feelings for Deja. They'd never have to seek acceptance from their friends. They'd never have to open up to the world about who they truly were and risk the resulting rejection.

But as Madrigal's words repeated in their mind, the pet name lodged there. They'd never even told Madrigal their name. Realization hit. The dark fae hadn't only taken Deja's voice, it seemed. She'd taken her memories.

Olive's response was past their lips before they even had to think. "No."

"Suit yourself."

Madrigal dove, pinning the human to the ground. Olive squirmed out from under the folds of the cloak, desperate to escape the garden of shadows and lost souls, to get away from this dark creature. They were able to slip from the tangled mass of limbs, but Madrigal's hand shot out and grasped them by the ankle.

With all their strength, Olive kicked at the looming skull with their free leg. Their bare foot connected with an audible snap. Pain radiated up the limb and into their hipbone. Madrigal shrieked, a cross between a sheep's bleat and a cat's snarl, throwing her hands to shield her face.

Blood poured from Olive's foot, a jagged shard of bone protruding from it. At first, they thought they'd broken their own foot, but when the shard came out easily, they noticed the other fragments on the ground.

Madrigal's skull-mask lay in five distinct pieces, coated in Olive's dripping blood.

"You beast," the dark fae snarled, dropping Deja's voice. "You wretched, wicked thing."

As Olive gazed at the fae, Madrigal lowered her hands. Olive could not suppress their gasp.

Where Madrigal's face should have been, there was only a patch of blank skin. No eyes, no nose, no mouth, not even a depression of features. All that could be seen were long, pointed ears emerging from the twines of midnight-black hair.

"I thought to keep you as a pet," Madrigal admitted, voice echoing in Olive's head. "Your sounds are so lovely. I'd have kept you like a songbird to sing me to sleep. But you've done it now."

Madrigal straightened to her full height, looming over the human. As she moved, the objects in her hair let out their songs as though fearing her fiery wrath. Within the cacophony, Olive caught the sound of their own voice, the pleasured groan captured earlier. It was so soft, but so pure, a repressed urge finally giving in to desire.

Up until then, Olive had thought if they remained quiet, the fae woman could not use their voice against them. But perhaps it was time to change tactics. Perhaps their voice was precisely the weapon they needed.

Pulling their hearing aids from their ears, Olive opened their mouth so wide it cracked at the corners. Then, Olive screamed. The air rippled with the sound. As the waves reached her, Madrigal lurched back, hands involuntarily clamping over her delicate ears.

Olive screamed again and again, wordless noise soaked in anger and fear. They screamed as loud as they could, belting out the frustration that had been mounting for years.

They thought of their aunt's prodding remarks that if they just dressed more feminine, they'd find a boyfriend. They thought of their mother's refusal to let them cut their hair, despite their pleas that it only got in the way. They thought of their middle school principal, who insisted they wear a dress to graduation. They thought of the boys on the track team who said a girl who couldn't hear would never run as fast as them.

They thought of every person who'd ever told them who they were, what they should be.

And when all the hurt felt as though it were too much for their heart to hold, Olive thought of Deja.

Of how they'd never taken her out on a real date, never told anyone they were together, never said they had a girlfriend, never held her hand in public. The world had been so unfair, but what made Olive the angriest was that they hadn't been ready to fight it. They'd kept to the shadows, hoping to go unnoticed, hoping to escape the ridicule, the names and the taunts and the bullying. They were angry at all they'd missed out on because the world had told them no. But most of all they were angry they'd listened. They were angry at what they'd allowed Deja to miss out on because they hadn't been prepared to face the truth.

But they faced it now.

In an attempt to stop the noise, Madrigal lifted one hand from her ears and snagged hold of Olive's hair where it had slipped from the elastic at the back of their head. She gave it a tug, pulling the human toward her.

Out of the corner of their eye, Olive spotted the discarded knife. They swept it up as the fae yanked them closer like a fish on a line. The hair pulled taut, Olive sliced at the strands, which fluttered uselessly in Madrigal's boney fist.

All the while, Olive screamed.

Losing her grip, Madrigal fell backward, hands over her ears. She cowered against the powerful noise of the human who had turned out to be not quite what they'd seemed.

With a final surge, Olive let out the last hints of a rasping voice.

"I am Olive Pesca and I love Deja Green. You wretched witch, give back my girlfriend's voice!"

Olive pushed themself to their feet and approached the Rhyth woman. The faceless creature shrunk away as Olive snatched the exposed bone-clock. They jerked the chain, which broke away from Madrigal's neck. Throwing it to the ground, Olive pried open the tiny bone doors one by one.

Inside the first was a yellow orb that tittered with laugher. When the door opened, the orb whizzed through the sky, bursting like a firework. The next revealed a purple flame that trickled from its cavern with cool light, bathing Olive's hands in frost.

Still writhing on the ground, Madrigal screamed, voice shifting from male to female, old to young, high to low. It rippled through its changing voices as one after another escaped their prisons.

Olive ripped open each door until the bone-clock was empty, releasing the countless voices of generations of lost souls. Then they raised it above their head and sent it hurtling to the ground. They ripped off the bone hand and stomped the clock's face, speckling it with bright blood.

Madrigal's arms flung from her body, fingers gnarled, but no voice emerged from her. In the silence that followed, she spun around, hair whipping into raven's wings. She took to the sky, voiceless and empty.

Panting, Olive collapsed next to the shattered remains, watching the lights of the voices dance overhead, looking for their way home. They could smell the flames consuming Madrigal's tower, overtaking the fresh scent of the forest.

Their throat burned and they knew they wouldn't be able to speak in the morning. But they had not lost their voice when they'd gone into the forest. It had not been stolen. They had used it for themself and for their love. They had given it willingly.

Hearing aids back in place, Olive trudged through the forest, following the trail of pale flowers in the approaching dawn. They were surprised to hear it filled with sound. Leaves rustling, birds warbling, fauna scampering, insects buzzing. Above the trees, the sky was brightening, and the forest lit up with its song.

At last, Olive emerged from the tangled thicket. Beyond the line of flowers, a pair of silhouettes waited, one with arched back, the other a youthful spine.

With the last of their strength, Olive ran toward the pair. Deja met them halfway.

"Olive, my Olive. There you are."

Deja's mouth spoke the words. There was a warmth in them that

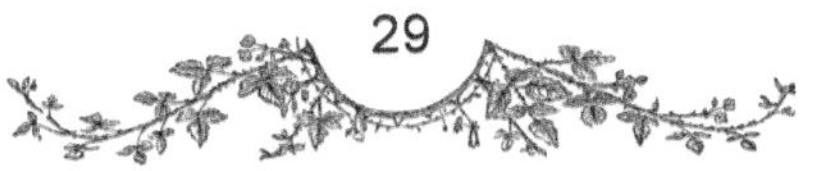

Madrigal had not been able to replicate. Olive's heart ached for it. The pair embraced, Olive leaning heavily into Deja, gladly receiving the kisses along their brow.

"You did well," the old woman said.

Then Olive's eyelids fluttered, and they gave in to the calling blackness.

Olive swallowed the lump in their throat. Beside them, Deja squeezed their hand.

"Deja and I are more than friends," Olive said. Though it had been a few days since they'd stumbled out of the forest, their voice was still hoarse. "She's my girlfriend."

Olive's mother's eyes darted from the couple's intertwined fingers to her child's face.

"So are you...? Are you a...?" She bit her lip, unsure of the words.

"I don't really know who I am right now. I'm still figuring it out." Sensing Olive's vulnerability, Deja rested her head on their shoulder. "But I'll be using they/them pronouns," they continued.

"Right, right. I've heard of that."

Though their mother was slow in processing the announcement, Olive was relieved to see she was receptive. They hadn't known how she'd react, but she was trying.

The trio talked a few moments more before Deja and Olive stood. "The movie starts in an hour. We want to have time to get something to eat."

"Of course, of course," their mother answered, walking them to the door.

As Olive stepped out into the dusk, they sensed Deja stop behind them. Olive glanced back to see their mother holding Deja by the hand and pulling her into a hug.

"Thank you for everything," Olive's mother said. "It's nice to know

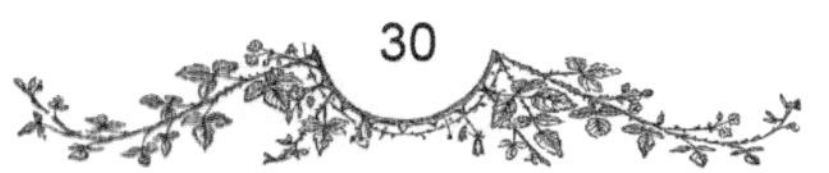

she...*they* have someone like you to help them."

Olive's chest warmed.

"The pleasure's all mine, Ms. P," Deja answered, glancing at Olive. "They've always been there for me."

The two walked to Olive's car. As they unlocked the door, Olive glanced at the edge of the forest. They hadn't heard it whisper in the night. They hoped it never would again. But if it did, they knew they could handle it.

Ready, Sunshine? Olive signed.

Ready, Raincloud.

Olive slipped into the driver's seat, kissed Deja on the cheek, then started the car and headed out on their first official date.

Sweet Enchantment

By Georgia Cook

Nothing changed in Faerie. Sometimes things affected the appearance of change, but they quickly grew bored, began to fidget, and reverted back to their original forms.

Lessons sat unlearned, stories repeated themselves endlessly through the twisting hills, and every song sung was the first ever heard.

It was always midnight in Faerie, always balmy midsummer, the sky filled with stars frozen in position for thousands of years. The forests were deep and full, the shadows black as ink. A flock of brightly colored starlings fluttered above the treetops, avoiding the grasping branches, swooping and diving against the backdrop of a high, bright moon. In the distance, a hunting horn rang out, accompanied by an inhuman shriek.

Nothing so long-living as a Faerie survives without a fair-weather memory, and nothing forgets faster than a fairytale.

All was calm. All was still. All was exactly as it should be.

Cressida slipped through the trees, skin pouch hanging securely at her side. Pale eyes stared mournfully from the shadows, rough bark mouths drawn over wooden teeth, summer-decked fingers twitching and shuddering. No birds sang in these woods; no lost animals survived longer than an hour. The trees devoured everything.

Nothing dared snatch at Cressida. She, with her silver knife and circlet of leaves. She, who walked freely and with purpose through the grove. Keeper of the Border Forest. Mistress of the Oaks. The trees trembled as she passed.

Little Faerie, Little Faerie, they whispered. *Where are you going? What are you doing?*

Cressida ignored them.

Few knew the precise location of the borders between Faerie and Beyond—the spaces where the air became thin, where sunlight and changing seasons slipped through the cracks. Sometimes, animals wandered through by accident—drawn past the veil by music or trickery or simple misfortune—but here the gap was narrow, lost to all but those who knew where to look.

Cressida paused in a grove of shifting apple trees. The air here was still, sat in perpetual waiting, hunting horns and faint leafy whispers stilled between the winding trunks. A small, iron gate stood in a tangle of weeds, unattached to any fence or wall. Twisted in vines and thick with moss, it was easy to miss, as if the surrounding woodland were trying to bury it.

Cressida tried the latch. It clattered stiffly, hinges groaning in the loamy warmth, but opened with a push.

She grinned. Quick as a shadow, she swung the gate wide and slipped through.

Immediately, the air shifted. Gone was the summer warmth, gone was the midnight moon, gone were the whispers of panpipes across the grass. The forest beyond the gate was cold and dark. The trees here were dull things. They would not dance for Cressida. They would not weave themselves into a thorny bower for her to sit, even if she whispered to them their true names. The air smelt of mud and grass. A winter chill nipped Cressida's skin.

This was a shadow place. A human place.

A winding path cut through the trees up ahead, dappled with golden winter sunlight. Cressida strode towards it, treading carefully between the human-tamed brambles and hanging branches. She'd committed the route to memory, playing it time and time again in her head, savoring every detail.

The path continued for nearly a mile, dancing and twisting through the forest, doubling back on itself in a lazy curve. Cressida smiled to herself as she walked. The path had always struck her as a nearly-Fae thing, touched by the mischief of the Summer Realms. A perfect sentry between the worlds.

After a mile, the path opened suddenly onto a clearing of twisting wildflowers. In the middle of the clearing sat a small, stone well. Unlike the Faerie gate, the well was clean and cared for. Someone had taken time to peel away the climbing ivy and scrub the stones, brushing away the spray of autumn leaves across the wooden lid.

Cressida crouched in the undergrowth outside the clearing and waited, fiddling with the strap of her skin pouch. So often she'd made the journey here, only to be met with failure, watching nothing but an empty clearing for hours and hours. Cressida was as unused to disappointment as she was uncertainty, but she had been forced to learn both in pursuit of today.

There! A movement in the shadows. The swish of fabric and a snatch of song. Cressida froze, heart pounding. Suddenly, the branches on the edge of the clearing parted, and a figure in a dark green dress stepped into the sunlight.

The girl on the opposite side of the clearing was beautiful and plump, with rich, red hair and a face full of freckles. Her eyes caught the light as she turned, blazing like burnt wood. Cressida's heart fluttered. She wanted to burst from the bushes and run to the girl. She wanted to take her in her arms, to touch her, to wind her fingers through that fire-spun hair.

Cressida had never been in love before. Oh, she'd *wanted* things; she'd stolen and eaten and broken for the sheer delight of breaking. But love... Love was something new. Love was bright and beautiful, warm in the hollow of her chest. Cressida never wanted it to end, but oh, she ached.

There was need, there was hunger, and then there was...this.

A snap of branches. The girl turned sharply. Cressida ducked, tucking herself deep between the trees.

"Hello?" The girl had a soft, honeyed voice. Cressida's skin prickled with delight. She didn't respond, but in her mind she sang.

Hello, pretty human. Hello, pretty thing. Step no closer, but love me all the same.

Love me.

The girl waited, watching the tree line for a long moment, then turned away and bent to lift the well-cover. Cressida crept closer, daring to let the sunlight brush her toes, cast her eyelashes in spun gold.

The girl was leaning over the well wall now, peering into the depths. Cressida wondered if she should creep even closer, peer over the girl's shoulder, catch their reflections staring back at them, forever entwined in a sea of inky ripples.

She could. She could...

There was a thunk and a distant splash. The well-rope pulled taut. The girl wiped her forehead and began to haul the bucket back up. Cressida blinked, shifting back against the shadows.

No. No. Not yet, pretty thing. Not yet.

The girl stumbled away through the trees, footsteps made awkward by the additional weight of the bucket of water, until she vanished completely in the golden green. Cressida waited a while longer, in case she returned, then slipped back between the trees and returned to the gate.

The air changed as Cressida crossed the border back into Faerie. She stood a moment beneath the whispering trees, savoring the swell of summer warmth, the lingering scent of apples. Then her eyes snapped open with a swell of anger.

Stupid! Wretched human!

Cressida kicked a stray sod, watching it scramble away across the clearing. Again! She'd done it again! She, who walked the boundary between Faerie and Earth. She, who tended to the living trees, who feared nobody and nothing on this side of the gate, reduced to speechlessness by a pretty human thing!

At first she'd thought the girl had enchanted her; weaved an enthralling sickness through her bones. But as the weeks passed, as the world grew stranger and brighter, as her need to simply exist at the girl's side grew stronger, Cressida began to understand the true unfairness of her predicament.

Faeries understood love— they used it often and abundantly in their own human entrapments—but they knew it only as need, as a shadow cast against a beautiful wall. To actually *feel* it was a weakness Cressida had never experienced. How did humans cope?

She took a deep breath, planting her fingers firmly against the bark of the nearest tree, letting the roughness soothe her, the low beating of its wooden heart bringing her back to herself.

She needed a plan. She needed a cure. She needed a human understanding of her plight.

In a thoughtful mood, she went to visit the Bard.

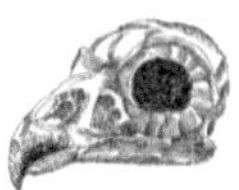

The Bard had arrived in Faerie some two hundred years ago, drawn by the call of a faerie flute. If he'd had a name before his crossing, nobody remembered it or bothered to ask. Even to himself, he was simply the Bard, and he was one of the few humans still nominally sane.

He sat on a rock in the middle of a fast-flowing stream, in the shade of a bowed willow. A small waterfall misted the air behind him, mingling with his lute music to create a watery hiss.

Light as a leaf, quick as a shadow, Cressida slipped across the grass and positioned herself amongst the reeds on the river's edge.

The Queen had not permitted the Bard to stop playing in almost a century. He'd been wearing a coat of bright, red and yellow diamonds when he'd arrived. Now the coat was ragged and green with algae. His eyes were dark and sunken, his fingers red raw and bleeding. He'd been handsome once, but not now.

"Bard," Cressida crooned. "Sweet Bard."

The Bard jumped, fingers catching the lute with a discordant twang. He caught it just before it hit the water. Cressida let out a delighted laugh.

"G-good morrow," managed the Bard, hands continuing to strum up and down the blood-slick instrument, "sweet faerie."

"It is never morrow, dear Bard," said Cressida, stretching herself across the grass. "And I am not sweet. Don't talk such nonsense."

The Bard nodded. A beat of sweat trickled down his chin. "What... What do you desire?"

"I am in love, Bard. How do I woo a lady?"

"A-a lady?"

"Yes, Bard, a human lady."

The Bard swallowed.

Cressida leaned closer, the gurgling river spray catching her throat. "Tell me," she said, "and I will allow you to stretch your legs."

The Bard's eyes darted to the water, then back to Cressida. She enjoyed the fear in his gaze, the desperate longing. "But...the Queen..." he whispered.

He had a soft, rasping voice. The voice of a man who hadn't opened his mouth other than to sing or cry in more than a human lifespan.

"The Queen isn't here," Cressida smiled. "I am. Tell me, sweet Bard, and I may also permit you to keep your tongue."

The Bard swallowed, shifting on his rock so that his sleeves rustled in the night air. "I do not recall how things were before...all this..." he began, strumming nervously. "But I recall the sensation of things. I believe I was once in love..."

"And what did you do about it?"

"I..." The Bard's brow furrowed. "I played him music..." The strumming grew softer, sweeter, almost harmonious. "I played him music, and it made him laugh. And I thought I had never heard such a sweet sound..."

Cressida considered this a moment. "Teach me a song," she said. "A human song, capable of making any woman love me."

"I don't think any song—"

"Teach me the song you played your beloved."

The Bard sighed and nodded, then played a handful of notes on his lute. The song wound out across the river and back into the trees, tinged with heartbreak and sweetness.

Cressida listened as it passed. "That doesn't sound like love to me," she said.

"Oh, it is love," said the Bard, sadly. "Love in every form. Love as heartbreak."

Cressida wrinkled her nose. "Why would I make love sad? I don't want to be sad."

The Bard shrugged. "In my experience," he said, fingers straying back to their endless strumming. "We don't get a choice."

Cressida stomped away down the riverbank, leaving the song until it vanished between the trees. Then she sat a while and pondered.

Could she charm her beloved with music? Fairy music, she knew, was a thing of predatory lure, to beguile and capture. But humans... Humans did it all themselves...

In a thoughtful mood, Cressida plucked a reed from the riverbank, cut and prodded with her nails until it resembled a crude flute, then put it to her lips and blew. The reed-flute produced a thin, hollow note, like a startled bat.

Perfect.

Seized with delight, Cressida leapt back towards the gate in the apple orchard, running and dancing, shifting like a fallen leaf through the smallest of gaps.

She would sing to her beloved! She would play her melodies, sweeter than any apple, sweeter than any Fae-spun honey. And then her beloved would love her back, with every longing owed to Cressida's heart.

The light on the other side of the gate had shifted from day to sunset. The sky overhead blazed a brilliant red, shot through with branches of orange and deepest black. Time ran differently in the human realm, swirling and curving in grooves of perception and understanding. Cressida wondered what that could possibly be like.

She walked carefully through the darkened forest. In the dark, the trees almost reminded Cressida of her own—looming, stretching things, wrapped in their blanket of shadows. If she placed a hand to one, she wondered, would she feel the flutter of breath? The weary creaking of a wooden heartbeat?

Ahead of her lay the clearing, as sacred now to Cressida as her own heart. Shadows filled the bowl of emptiness between the trees, turning it grey and cold, tinged with flecks of sunset. And in the middle, her red-gold hair tumbling about her shoulders, peering into the trees on Cressida's side—

Cressida's breath caught in her throat. Her beloved!

Had she been waiting for Cressida? Had she seen her in the shadows, small and green and beautiful, and fallen in love?

Still concealed, Cressida lifted her lips to the reed-flute and blew. The sound whistled through the undergrowth, sharp as an arrow, discordant and warbling. The girl started back with a cry, gaze darting between the trees. Cressida's heart leapt. She tried again, harder this time, but managed only the same warbling note.

The girl drew back, stumbling on the frosty ground. "Hello?" she called, in her summer-soft voice. "Who's there? I'm warning you!"

Was this love? Was this what human love sounded like? Cressida peered from behind her eyelashes, but saw only terror and uncertainty etched across the girl's face. Those emotions Cressida understood.

She tried again, harder. The reed-flute's shrill screech filled the clearing, each note tumbling after the other in a tuneless wail. The girl plugged her ears with both hands. "It won't work!" she shouted over the sound. "I know of curses! You can't fool me!"

Cressida danced and whistled until her lips bled, but no matter how she threatened or cajoled it, she could not make the reed-flute play the Bard's song. The sound was always too thin, too piercing, too utterly *wrong*. By the time she opened her eyes again, the girl was gone, panicked footfalls fading into the distance. The clearing stood empty and dark.

Cressida threw the flute to the ground and flung herself down by the well. "Cursed Bard!" she shouted. "I shall have the willows pluck out his eyes!" And felt much better for saying it.

She lay in the darkness a while, letting it wrap its calming fingers around her, breathing the scent of moss and tree bark. She would win. Whether it was the will of a stubborn hawthorn, or the heart of a time-slowed oak, Cressida of the Grove always won.

Had she not been granted ownership of the forest? Had she not been gifted the way of trees by the Forest Mother herself? Didn't she, in all of Faerie, deserve her desires?

Stupid! She was stupid! Stupid and blind as a sapling. Trusting a human with love! To think they understood anything at all.

Was there not a resident of Faerie who understood love best of all? Was there not she who had collected more human lovers than all of Faerie combined? She who danced between the standing stones and stole away every pretty little thing?

She would know.

She knew everything about love.

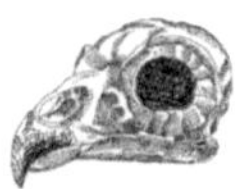

In the middle of Faerie lay a vast and beautiful garden. It spanned the length of a human country, sectioned into rows and twisting, green alleyways. Bluebells gleamed underfoot, bursting from overgrown flower beds to entwine the grass. Sunflowers twisted with leafy ferns, brambles tangled themselves around foxgloves, strangling the light and deepening the loamy shadows, creating dark, little groves of moss and trapped heat.

And through it all, as beautiful as beauty itself, walked the Queen.

As she walked, she hummed a soft, discordant melody she'd stolen from a human head many centuries ago. It was the only song she knew, and she enjoyed it immensely. She paused at an intersection between two leafy corridors and bent to inspect a rose bush, her perfect features twisted in perfect scrutiny. She lifted her hand. A pair of silver secateurs flashed in the darkness. Another rosebud tumbled across the grass. The bushes around it trembled.

The Queen stood back. "What ails you, little Changeling?" she asked, without turning.

In the flowerbed behind her, Cressida froze. She'd been crouched beneath a rampant rhododendron, certain of her own total concealment. Slowly, she extracted herself from the bush and emerged into the light. She refused to be embarrassed. She refused to feel shame.

"My Queen," she dropped a low bow, the tips of her tangled black hair brushing the grass.

"Cressida of the Border Forest," said the Queen, with a touch of familial scorn.

"Just so, Your Majesty."

"You tend the trees. "

Yes, Your Majesty."

"Why have you trespassed in my garden, little one? I have so much to tend to, and so little time for wandering Changelings."

Cressida felt her cheeks grow red. Embarrassment and love! What

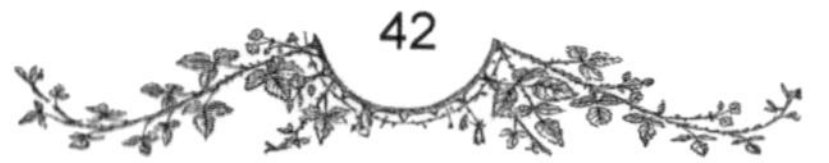

cruel tricks to bestow upon oneself. "I wish for a boon, Your Majesty."

"A boon?" The Queen's eyebrows arched delightedly. "What boon?"

"I have fallen in love."

The Queen's beautiful lips twisted in what might have been a smile. "And what have you done about that?" she asked.

"I asked the Bard," said Cressida. "He told me to play my love music, but I can't do it the way he does. Faerie music only lures. It doesn't love."

"Poor Bard," mused the Queen. "His mind left him long ago. He will say anything we want to hear. Humans are so delicate..."

"Was he correct?"

The Queen laughed, a high, delighted sound, tinged at its deepest point with something sharp and unnatural. "For himself, perhaps," she said. "But human love is so small, so fragile. It breaks so easily, and it comes in so many delightful, little forms. One is never the same as the other. I'm sure what would lure the Bard might only chase away your pretty, little beloved."

"Then what do I do?"

"Charm them, my sweet thing," replied the Queen. "Charm and keep them. It is the only way."

Cressida had seen the Queen's beautiful collection of humans, ranged around her throne room like perfect china dolls. She'd seen their glassy-eyed stares, their vacant expressions—so empty, so motionless, as unchanging as Faerie itself.

"I don't think I would like a human toy," she said, doubtfully.

"Why would you want a human for anything else? A pretty little thing, all of your own. A magpie jewel!"

"Because..." Cressida paused. Because she didn't want to see the human girl like that. She wanted conversation, she wanted merriment, she wanted to hear her beloved laugh. "Because I want her to talk to me."

The Queen waved a dismissive hand. "What fun is that?" she asked, and all the plants in the garden rustled their leaves in chorus.

Cressida returned to the boundary gate in a thoughtful mood.

Should she charm her beloved human? Keep her pale and complacent at her side? The flute hadn't sufficed, but that was because she'd used human music. To charm a human to Faerie...

Night had fallen on the opposite side of the gate. Not summer night, as it was in Faerie, but a chill winter's night. Cressida's arms prickled with goosebumps, her breath steaming in the air as she picked her way towards the clearing.

Something moved up ahead. Lamplight gleamed. Cressida froze in the underbrush, her heart pounding with uncertainty and outrage. How dare they! How dare someone disturb the clearing of her beloved! How dare someone invade their sacred space!

The figure turned.

The hood of a long cloak pulled back to reveal a familiar face, pale and anxious in the lamplight. "I know you're there!" called a familiar voice. "I heard you! Come out at once!"

The first words Cressida's beloved had ever addressed to her.

She froze, suddenly achingly aware of herself; the thorny darkness of her hair, the ivy leaves wound around her body, the lichen green tinge to her skin. She had always found herself beautiful, as all Fae found themselves beautiful, but now she had never felt so small, so strange. Was that what love did?

Slowly, tentatively, Cressida stepped from the tree line into the pool of moonlight. The girl drew back, eyes widening. In her hand she clasped something hard and cold. It glinted in the lamplight, drawing Cressida's eye—a horse shoe.

"You can't make me go!" the girl cried, lifting the shoe threateningly. "I have to step across the boundary voluntarily! I know how this works. I know the rules of Faerie!"

She knew of Faerie! Cressida's heart leapt. Her beloved knew of home! Perhaps the flute music had worked after all! Perhaps she had spied Cressida in the undergrowth, loved her for all the things Cressida loved in her beloved.

She reached out a placating hand. "Beautiful human..."

The girl stumbled back, lashing out with the horseshoe. It swiped Cressida's arm. Cressida sprang away with a shriek. The skin burned where the iron had touched, rising in angry, red welts beneath her fingertips. The night sky circled above her as she fell to her knees.

Nothing hurt as much as iron.

Cressida looked up. The girl was standing over her, clasping the horseshoe like a shield, eyes wide and unsure. "But you... You're just a girl..." she said.

Cressida said nothing. Her skin seared in agony.

Slowly, slowly, the girl knelt beside Cressida and held out a hand.

Cressida shrank back with a hiss. "It hurts!"

"I know..." The girl lowered her hand. "I'm sorry..." She shifted uncomfortably. "What's your name?"

"Cressida," said Cressida, and realized she wanted nothing more than to hear the girl say it. It would not be a real name, she thought, unless she heard it from her beloved's lips.

The girl nodded, taken aback.

"What's your name?" Cressida asked.

The girl opened her mouth to reply, but drew back suddenly. "I can't..."

Cressida nodded. Her beloved truly did understand Faerie. Usually, Cressida would bristle at losing a human's name, but this time she didn't mind. Her beloved would always be Beloved in her eyes.

"You are, aren't you?" said the girl. "You're from..." She stared into the trees on Cressida's side of the clearing. "My grandmother told me stories of the Faerie realm, but I never thought..." She turned back to Cressida with a thoughtful expression. "I've not...seen you before..."

"I've seen you."

"You have?"

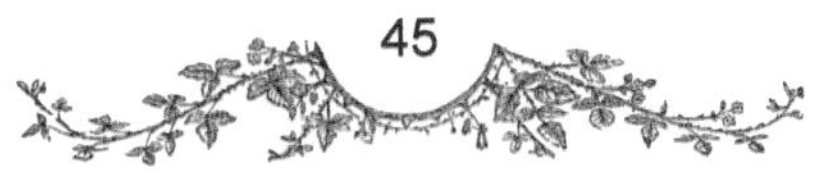

Cressida nodded. "Every day. Every time you use that well. I've been watching."

"Oh." The girl went pink. "I didn't see you."

"I know," Cressida replied smugly.

"Why?"

Cressida's face grew warm. She wanted to tell the girl how beautiful she was. How her hair shone in the morning sunlight, how the rustle of her dress against the undergrowth was more beautiful than any panpipes. She wanted to say that she would have stolen any jewel in Faerie for a chance to hear her speak.

"Because I wanted to," she said at last, and surprised herself at her own disappointment.

Cowardly Cressida! When had Cressida of the Trees ever been cowed?

With a surge of desperation, she leapt up and clasped the girl's hands. "Come with me!" she said. "Come between the trees. Let me show you Faerie!"

The girl drew back in alarm. "No!"

"Why not?"

"I know what happens in Faerie! I know the legends!"

"Not to you! Never to you!" Cressida reached out, emboldened by the girl's uncertainty. "My pretty beloved..."

The girl's eyes widened. "Keep away from me!" She lashed out again with the horseshoe.

Cressida flinched away, teeth bared. She reached for the girl's arm, but she was already up and running, lamplight flickering through the darkness, cloak flying out behind her, until her hurrying footsteps faded, and then all that was left again was Cressida.

Hurt! Hurt by her love! Branded!

The trees in the grove beyond the gate rustled in fear as Cressida

lashed out with a howl, eyes burning with outrage and heartbreak. Her foot caught the trunk of a slender apple tree, notching the bark. An apple fell from the highest branch, landing with a thud at Cressida's feet. She bent to pick it up. It was smooth and beautiful, crimson skin fading to a mossy green. All Faerie fruit was beautiful. Until you took a bite.

Cressida slipped the apple into the skin pouch at her waist, letting the comforting weight of it settle against her thigh. Looking up, she saw a dozen, hollow wooden faces staring down at her, eyes clouded and sorrowful, mouths wide in frozen supplication.

Her beautiful trees. They understood. They always understood. She was Cressida, Keeper of the Glade, and her trees were her own.

Cressida found a handhold in the bark of the nearest one, grasped it tight, and hoisted herself up. Hand over hand, she clambered between the branches, moving as swift as a sparrow, until she came to a small hollow between two overlapping trunks. She flung herself down into the tiny gap, letting the gentle rustle of the leaves and the soft whisper-moan of distant voices lull her to sleep.

Time passed, although the world remained exactly the same. Cressida opened her eyes.

Something was moving through the forest, thumping through the undergrowth with heavy, rustling steps. Cressida lay still, listening hard. Would she fly from her tree and confront the trespasser? Would she pluck out its heart and wear it as a necklace? Or would she stay where she was, stiff and bitter, and let the stranger count themselves lucky for catching her in a merciful mood?

The rustling grew louder, then stopped suddenly beneath Cressida's tree. There was silence. Nothing moved in the forest below, nothing breathed. Then...

"I sense you up there, little Changeling," came a whisper-soft voice. "I smell you."

Cressida peered through the branches. On the ground below stood an immensely old woman, bent and hunched, back bristling with branches. The hair flowing from beneath her hood was bushy and moss-like, her eyes beetle-black. In one hand, she held a vast burlap sack, slung over her shoulder; in the other, a gnarled walking stick.

"You were hiding from me, little Faerie," said Mother Forest.

"Not at all, Mother."

"Do not lie, girl," the old woman jabbed a bony finger up, through the foliage. "You were hiding. Come down and address me properly."

Cressida slunk down the tree trunk, lizard-like, and landed amongst the undergrowth, dropping a low curtsy. Nobody argued with Mother Forest, who had been here longer than anyone, before even the stars in the sky had chosen their form, before the grove of lost travellers had flourished into the forests of Faerie. Before even the Queen—who was the oldest of Faerie—a mere sapling compared to Mother.

"Good girl." Mother Forest adjusted her grip on her walking stick. She towered over Cressida, her tangled moss-hair brushing the tops of the middle branches. "Now, what troubles you?"

"Nothing troubles me, Mother."

Mother Forest drew herself up to her full height, face set and stern. "Was it not I who took you from the human realm? Is it not I who claim all Changelings? Who knows those who will grow to be wicked of heart and cheerful of nature? I know you, Cressida."

Cressida hung her head, cheeks burning with shame and sorrow. "I'm upset, Mother."

"And why so, little Changeling?"

"I am in love!"

Mother Forest's eyes gleamed. "Love, sweet thing?" she asked. "Who in Faerie has ever wished to love?"

"I do," said Cressida, jutting her chin. "I wish it more than anything."

"More than anything?"

"Anything at all!"

"Then you forget what Faerie is, child. You forget what Faerie does."

Cressida glared at the ground. Mother Forest reached out and touched a gnarled claw to her chin. "We do not comply with human wants, little Changeling," she continued. "We do not accept human wishes. All we do is in service to ourselves."

Cressida stared at the trees, at the dew-damp grass. She lifted her head to the high midsummer moon. She didn't want her beloved to become like the Bard—nervous and half-mad, picking at his lute with bleeding finger stubs—nor like the Queen's pretty, glass-eyed pets. "Then...what do I do?" she asked.

Mother Forest smiled. "Take," she said, her eyes glinting in the moonlight. "Take and hold, dear heart. Take and hold. Like a tree will swallow iron, like the sea embraces a stone. Take and hold, and never give back."

"But what if I don't want that, Mother Forest?" asked Cressida.

Something shifted in the old woman's sack. The burlap warped, as if something small were pressing sluggish limbs against it from the other side. A thin, gulping wail filled the air. Mother Forest gave it a hard smack with her walking stick.

"What do you love, Cressida?" she asked. "What has always been yours? Why are you trying to love like a human, like a Bard, like the Queen of us, when you can love only as yourself?"

After Mother Forest had gone, picking her careful way through the bracken, Cressida sat in the loamy darkness up in her tree, lost in a sea of tentative wishes.

What did she want? Of all things, in all the world, what did she truly desire?

She ran her hand across the bark around her, feeling the roughness, listening to the jackhammer heartbeat deep inside the trunk. She felt the press of the apple at her waist, unbruised and unblemished from its journey up and down the tree. For the first time in days, Cressida felt her own heart calm.

She knew what she wanted.

Oh, Cressida knew.

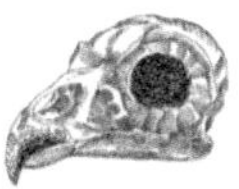

The human girl did not return to the clearing for many days. Cressida sat beneath the trees, patiently waiting, watching the moon arch unnaturally across the sky, until she began to wonder if she had lost her beloved after all.

Until one night, several days after the first, when the shadows at the edge of the clearing shifted. Cressida's ears perked, eyes flickering to the movement. There, between the trees, small and uncertain, lingered a figure, hair shining copper in the moonlight. Cressida rose from her hiding place.

The girl turned. No glint of iron this time, only the pink tinge of fear and shame across her cheeks. "Oh," she said. "It's you."

"Yes," said Cressida.

They stared at one another for a long, long moment. The girl shifted uncomfortably. "I wanted to...apologize," she said at last. "For the other day. For the iron."

"No," said Cressida. "You were correct to use iron. It is the strongest ward against us."

"Did I hurt you?"

Cressida lifted her arm to show the curdled, red mark across the skin. The girl started forward as if to touch it, but held herself back. "I'm sorry," she whispered.

Cressida shrugged, affecting what she hoped was a disinterested air. But inside, her heart sang.

"Why did you come back?" asked the girl.

"To see you," said Cressida. "You wanted to see me too."

The girl went red. "Why do you think that?"

"Because you are here also."

The girl looked away. "I wanted...to speak with you again..." she began, slowly.

This close, Cressida could see the worry in the girl's eyes, the crease of her freckled brow. It didn't matter that she didn't know the girl's name. She would happily stand here for an eternity, admiring her face, knowing nothing else.

Cressida blinked, broken from her trance as the girl reached out—gently, gently—and took her hand.

"They told me..." The girl glanced over her shoulder, back into the trembling night. "They told me that...the human-looking Fae. Those that pass as human. They were once human children."

"Changelings," said Cressida, proudly.

"How awful!"

Cressida stared. As far as she was concerned, she had the best life of all; a life dictated by Mother Forest and the twisting timelessness of Faerie. Mother Forest had been right. How could a human hope to understand? How could a human know anything?

"There will be others..." the girl continued, staring into the gaps between the trees. "As long as the gate remains here, others will be stolen. Others will be lured into Faerie..."

Cressida reached out and squeezed the girl's hand, giving it a gentle tug. "Let me show you," she said. "Let me show you, just a glimpse!"

"And then we go?"

Cressida nodded. "And then I will follow you forever."

She squeezed tighter, entwining their fingers, and led her gently back through the trees on her side of the clearing. They walked through the darkness, hand-in-hand, feet following the twisting, silver path. Cressida's heart soared. She never wanted the path to end. She never wanted to release her beloved's hand. She wanted to walk forever, savoring the touch of the girl's skin, the faint, apple blossom smell of her hair, lit by a perfect crescent moon.

Heaven and Fae combined; better than any wish.

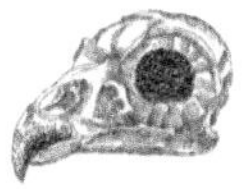

At last, they reached the place where the forests merged. The little gate looked so small on this side of the boundary; a flash of rusted metal in the midst of a winding copse, struts slick with moss, wound tight with ivy.

"That's it?" whispered the girl.

Cressida nodded. "It's protected. By the trees, by the forest."

"Why?"

"Because I asked them to." Cressida reached into her skin sack and brought out the apple. It gleamed in the moonlight, ruby-slick. "I have something to offer you," she added. "A gift."

The girl drew sharply from Cressida's grip. "I was warned," she said. "To never eat food offered by the Fae..."

"It is a gift, given freely." Cressida pressed closer. "It will let you pass into my realm. Do you trust me? Do you trust that I love you?"

The girl's eyes searched her face. Cressida noted that they were a deep, mossy brown; like the bark of an oak tree, almost black in the darkness. She knew that she would always adore her beloved, name or no name, love or no love returned. Was this how the Bard had felt? How the Queen saw her rooms of blank, staring doll-humans? Was this love to all creatures, differing only in their response?

The girl took the apple. It glittered in her hand, a perfect jewel. "It will...allow me to visit your realm? And you will protect me?"

"I will always protect you."

"A-and you will help me protect the others? Anyone who might be lured there?"

"If you wish."

The girl bit her lip. Then she nodded, brought the apple to her lips, and took a bite. Juice splattered her chin, sticky-sweet. A smell like summer honey filled the air. Cressida's heart leapt with joy.

The girl wiped her mouth, flashing Cressida a hesitant little smile...

Then she froze. The smile vanished. She gasped, stumbled, tripped, her hair trailing from beneath her hood. The apple tumbled from her hand as she stared at her fingers. A thick, rough texture had risen across the skin, dotted with cracks and splits and areas of soft, green moss. It flowed across her hands, down her arms.

She turned to Cressida, movements already stiff and uncomfortable, as if her joints had rusted together. "What's happening? What did you do?"

Cressida grasped her beloved's arms to stop her from falling. "I gave you a gift, my love!" she whispered in her ear. "A gift!"

"A gift?"

A gift forever. A gift known to none but the trees in Cressida's glade. To stand sentinel in the place where the two worlds met, where the gate would be hidden forever in the shade of twisting branches.

The girl struggled, but her feet were already frozen to the forest floor, lashing winding tendrils down through the earth. "Please!" She flung out a hand in desperation, panicked tears trailing down her cheeks. "Please stop this!"

Cressida held her tight, whispering sweet nothings until the sobbing stopped, until the tears turned sticky and sweet in her hands, until all was right with the world. When she drew back, a bowed apple tree lay entwined in her arms, shimmering silver and burnt red in the moonlight. Cressida ran a hand across the bark, felt the familiar roughness beneath her fingertips.

The tattered remains of a dark green cloak hung tattered amongst the branches. Cressida tugged it free, held it close, pressed her face against the torn fabric.

Cressida knew what she loved. She knew what she loved above all else. She knew the call of her heart, and she knew what would twist the ache of her beloved into a sweeter, more familiar form.

Cressida laughed with delight. She danced and spun beneath the silvery branches.

How kind! How clever! Mother Forest truly did have all the answers!

Now they would be together forever and ever, and she could visit whenever she pleased. She could sit beneath the branches of her truest love, and weave apple-blossoms through her hair.

What delight! What delight!

Nothing ever changed in Faerie. No lessons were learned, no paths redirected. But now, there was a new tree on the border between Faerie and the human world. A new tree to grow between the gaps of realities. For Cressida to tend and prune.

Change, of a kind. But no change at all.

Cressida reached up and plucked an apple from the tree's lower branches. It glistened in the warm moonlight, crimson and soft to the touch. Cressida held it a moment, listening for the rustle of leaves, the soft beating of an apple-pulp heart, then took a bite.

A smell like honeysuckle rose in the air. Juice dribbled down her skin, sugar-sweet. She licked it clean. It tasted of victory and promise, of a lover's embrace entwined across the worlds. It tasted like stolen kisses.

The sweetest of all.

THE WARDEN

BY WYNNE F. WINTERS

It's been two years since I set foot in my hometown. It hasn't changed.

Residents look up as I navigate my Honda down the single lane. Most people don't bother with cars. If they need to head into 'town'—the nearby village of Ashbourne, with quadruple the population at 2,000—they take the bus, which runs twice a day: to Ashbourne in the morning and back to the Fringe in the afternoon.

As I creep down the dirt path, people peer into the windows, wondering what big-city suit has dared intrude into their salt-of-the-earth lives. I can name every person I pass—they'd know my name, too, if they recognized me. None seem to. I take a bit of satisfaction in that.

My mother's home is at the far end of the village, past the end of the road. I roll to a careful stop in the grass, grimacing at the thought of the Honda's undercarriage, and head to the lone cottage, cheerful and vine-covered as I remember.

As I do, my mother's closest neighbor, a stooped busybody named Greta, just so happens to come out her front door. She gasps in surprise and holds her heart, as though she didn't hear my car engine a mile back.

"Clodagh!" she exclaims, her expression caught between admonishment and glee. "You're home! It's been so long!"

I flinch at the name. I haven't heard it for two years, but it stings as badly as ever. It's a beautiful name. A strong name. A woman's name. A name for the person everyone expects me to be.

"Clover," I say.

Greta furrows her brow. "What?"

"Clover. I go by Clover now."

Greta purses her non-existent lips. "Well," she says, "I've called you Clodagh since you were a babe. I don't think I'll remember to call you anything else."

I stare at her until she fidgets. "Is my mother home?" I ask.

"I assume so," she mumbles, looking down. "Don't know where else she'd be."

"Thanks."

I head to my childhood home, trying to school my face so it doesn't reflect the sinking feeling in my stomach.

Aunt Mathilda answers my knock. For a moment she just stares at me as though she's seen a ghost. "Clodagh, your hair!"

I guess I can't blame her. When I lived in the Fringe, I wore my hair long like the girls. Cutting it was the first thing I did when I left; it felt like letting go of an anchor. Now my hair, ginger threaded with gold, barely reaches my chin.

"Clover," I say.

"Yes, Clover, of course, sorry," she says. She steps aside. "Come in, come in! Your mother is waiting."

My mother is in the sitting room, staring out the window. Her cane rests on the couch beside her. She turns when I enter, a smile lighting her face.

She says nothing of my shorn hair or flattened chest. Instead, she opens her arms wide.

I tuck myself inside, soothed as I'd been when a child, though her grip is so much more delicate now.

"Clover!" she says in that melodious voice. "I missed you, sweetheart."

"I missed you too, Ma," I murmur into her hair, the same color as my own. There is much alike between my mother and me: the bright blue of our eyes, the dimples in our cheeks, the magic in our blood. At last, I pull away, duty weighing heavy on my shoulders. "What's happened to Caitlyn?"

Caitlyn is my cousin and the acting Warden, dedicated to protecting the Fringe from the strangeness that occasionally emerges from the woods. I came home because she's missing.

"She never came back from her patrol," my mother says, as I sit beside her. "We searched, but there was no trace. We think she's come to harm in the Wood Beyond."

My stomach sinks. That's my worst fear and the reason I came straight away. Time passes differently in the Wood Beyond, and few can tread its ground safely. My mother would go if her illness hadn't rendered her frail. So, the task is left to me.

"I should go," I say, rising.

"Don't you want dinner first?" asks Aunt Matilda, poking her head into the room. My heart is tender at her offer—her only child is missing, and still, she offers hospitality.

I shake my head. "I should move as fast as possible."

"Aren't you tired? You drove a long way."

My mother and I exchange a look. It's true that I'm tired, but once I set foot in the Wood Beyond, it will matter less and less. Aunt Matilda, having neither witch blood nor second sight, wouldn't understand, thinking only in mortal terms.

"I'll take some jerky," I say, knowing every Fringe household has some on-hand. "For the journey. But I'm leaving tonight."

"Thank you," says Aunt Matilda, and disappears from the door frame.

My room is exactly as I left it. I can't decide if this irks or endears me. I didn't take much upon my exodus—some clothes and a few books I couldn't bear to part with. I wanted a clean break. I was lying to myself. A clean break was never possible, not with my family.

The trunk is at the end of my bed, resembling a hope chest but for the carved runes. I kneel before it, the atmosphere suddenly momentous. I run my fingers along the wood, the grain smoothed by generations of Warden hands.

The interior is surprisingly dull for all the ceremony: a surcoat of forest green, protective spells woven into the fabric and spun into the stitching; an old lantern; a sheathed short sword; and a bandolier and belt, each lined with small pouches. I take the items one by one, then close the lid.

Muscle memory is a strange thing. It's been two years, but my fingers follow the practiced motions of donning the bandolier, buckling the belt. The sword I hang on my right hip for an easy draw and the lantern I hang on my left, to light my way.

There's only one thing remaining. Well, technically, two things.

I never kept my bow and quiver in the trunk because while the other equipment belongs to the Wardens and will be passed down, the bow and quiver belong to me. Some Wardens value a firearm—the speed and accuracy can't be argued, and a lead bullet is as good as any cold iron. But arrows are quiet, and they can be gathered or made when supplies run low. And I may be partial to my bow, a gift from my father on my twelfth birthday, when I was officially named the Warden Heir.

When I step into the hall, Aunt Matilda is waiting for me. "Sorry," she says. She doesn't explain for what. Instead, she opens her hands in offering. Cradled in her palms is a talisman of woven grass—a luck charm, simple magics the Fringe children make for a good exam mark or football win. "Caitlyn taught me," she says. Her voice wobbles. "I thought, maybe it'll help—"

I lay my hands on either side of hers, our eyes meeting. "Thank you," I say. "I'll bring her back, Auntie. I swear it."

She nods, so many unsaid words like a lump in her throat. "Of course you will," she says. "Of course you will."

I take the talisman and carefully pack it into one of my pouches. Such spells are only superstition, but where I'm going, superstition has power.

My mother stands by the front door. The cane takes nothing away from her regal air, nor the power that radiates like heat from the sun. She wraps one arm around me as I embrace her.

"Take care, child of mine," she murmurs into my hair. I pull away, my eyes shining.

"I will," I say, and my voice sounds only a little rough.

Aunt Matilda comes to the door as I leave, and the two of them watch through the open frame as I head toward the wood.

They're not the only ones. People have come out of their houses. No one says anything, but they don't have to. They let their thoughts be known when I left. Now, it's easy to guess from their expressions.

Caitlyn is beloved. She has her father's healing touch and giving heart. After his death, the people of the Fringe came to her to soothe fevers and set bones. She is a kind, gentle soul, compassionate to a fault. She was never meant to take on this mantle.

But I... I was born to this. I learned the tongue of Mab at age ten, spilt blood in a monstrous hunt at fifteen. And, of course, I am my father's child. This was always meant to be my path.

Until I abandoned it.

I can't resent their anger. After all, it's justified. Caitlyn is a powerful magic worker, but she didn't study the intricacies of this role until two years ago. Whatever happened to her, it's my fault. And I'm the only one who can bring her back.

The doorway to the Wood Beyond doesn't look much different from the other trees. Not with mortal sight, anyway. The lantern at my side could easily reveal its true nature, and other Wardens have used it for such. But to my eye, the doorway is as clear as the moon crossing the sun.

There's a great hole in the tree, like the roots peeled back to create an archway. It's enough room to enter if you crouch.

As I pass through the living doorway, there's an audible exhale. I've never figured out if it's the tree, or the wood, or the doorway, or the Wood Beyond, but it's always there. A sigh of relief. I find it comforting.

The doorway turns into a tunnel the further you go. For a moment, it's pitch black, and then there's light. When I emerge from the tree, through what appears to be the same doorway, I'm in a wood, but it's not the one I left.

The Wood Beyond is more vibrantly alive than any mortal forest. The trees sway and bend without breeze, and the birds watch visitors with too-keen eyes. The light is brighter, the sky a more intense blue, the air more fragrant. My breath catches in my throat and tears prick at my eyes.

I've missed this place. I hadn't realized because I hadn't let myself think about it for two years, but I missed it. Missed it like a phantom limb, like an unheard mother tongue. It takes a few deep breaths to force the emotion back, but I have things to do.

When I set off, the speed of my surroundings doesn't match my stride. Everything moves more quickly here, and you can't take your eyes off the world for a second. It's disorienting to mortals, and it takes me a moment to adjust, like getting my sea legs. But then it's just the pace of the world, like the mortal mind discarding the turn of the earth.

It takes no time at all to reach the familiar clearing. The trees weave a protective latticework of boughs, casting dappled shadows over the grass. Off to one side lays a long, low stone, perfect for resting. I sit down, enjoying the atmosphere for a moment before taking out the panpipes.

Small as my palm, they look fragile, each pipe decorated with intricate scrollwork and the binding fashioned into ornate, flowering vines, but like everything from the Wood Beyond, their appearance is deceiving. Wetting my lips, I raise the pipes and let loose a trill, my hands playing the old tune by instinct. Notes, clear and sharp as birdsong, break through the foliage, holding just a heartbeat too long to be made by mortal instruments, the effect eerie and breathtaking at the same time.

I wait in the silence, my eyes scanning the trees, for all the good it'll do me. I fight the urge to play again—I've never had to. When he first gave me the pipes, he promised he'd come with the first call. And as everyone knows, the fey cannot lie.

Just as I raise the pipes to my lips again, a shiver goes through the trees. I look around, but see nothing. A doe-skin shoe taps my shoulder and I look up to find a man perched in the tree above me.

"What have I told you about looking up more often?" he says.

He doesn't look a day over thirty, his black hair thick and blue eyes twinkling. Yet I know for a fact he's several hundred years old, the spawn of the faerie queen's handmaid and an unlucky, handsome mortal lured into the Wood Beyond. The fair folk call him An File Fánaíochta, The Wandering Bard, who can tame the wildest beast with his songs and soften the hardest heart with sweet words.

I smile. "Hello, Da."

He smiles back. "Hello, my child, my lovely Clover."

I open my arms and then he's in them, his own wrapping me in a warm embrace.

Missing my father has been the hardest thing about leaving the Fringe. The worst thing is, he encouraged me to leave, if that was what I needed. Having mortal blood among the fair folk, he knows what it's like to not belong. He's managed to carve his own space, but it wasn't easy.

After a moment, he pulls back and looks me over. Residents of the Fringe think I'm the spitting image of my mother, but that's because they've never met my father. We have the same high cheekbones, the same pointed chin, the same long, slender fingers. These features aren't uncommon in the village—the Treaty's only been in place a few hundred years—so I suppose they've grown accustomed to the sight.

"How are you, love?" he asks, tucking my hair behind my ear.

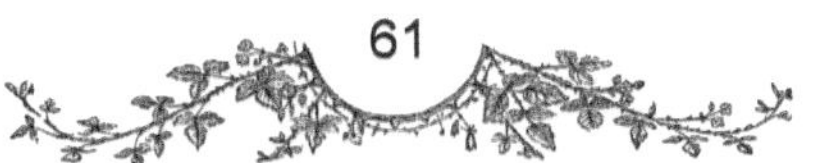

I open my mouth, then realize I don't know what to say. I haven't given much thought to my own mental state. I can't afford to lose focus, not when Caitlyn's life depends on it.

"Determined," I say.

"Good."

He turns away for a moment, singing a sweet song. The branch above us dips as apples swell along its length, full and red and ripe. The scent makes my mouth water. My father plucks two, extending one to me. I take it, my stomach already rumbling.

As one of the Blood, I technically have the right to partake of the Wood Beyond's bounty with none of the repercussions mortals endure. But since I'm here in the role of Warden, a distinctly mortal position, I always wait to be invited. Manners go a long way in the Wood Beyond.

"How's your mother?"

This would be a sore subject between us, if such a thing were possible. When my mother realized she had a progressive illness, my father made her a promise: that once she was able to set aside the mantle of Warden, he would bring her to the Wood Beyond, where the fruits could ease her pain and extend her life, so long as she remained within its bounds. By all accounts, she should be here already. She would be, if I hadn't left.

"The same," I say. "In pain. Resolute."

He nods. "She was never one to complain."

"I wish she would. She makes the rest of us look bad."

My father laughs and bites into his apple. I follow suit. Sweet juice floods my mouth, a taste more subtle, more satisfying than any you can find in the mortal world. I stifle a moan, embarrassed, and focus on eating my fill. The sustenance of the Wood Beyond flows through me, strengthening limb and sparking my heart. I've missed this too, though it isn't something to talk about to those at home.

When I reach the apple core, I break it, scattering the pieces onto the forest floor where they might take root. My father does the same, and for a moment we sit in silence. At last, knowing that time is of the essence, I ask, "Do you know what happened to Caitlyn?"

My father shakes his head. "I don't, little one. I've had my ear to the ground, but I've got nary a rumor. But I know someone who might."

He turns to me, his expression more serious than I've ever seen. "Neith, the web-spinner, catches secrets in her gossamer. If there's anyone in the Wood who would know what became of your cousin, it's she."

My heart sinks. "She'll never tell what she knows. She has no love for mortals, especially a Warden."

"Maybe not, but she can never turn down a deal. Which is why you'll give her this."

My father reaches into his inner coat pocket and pulls out a small, round jewel, no larger than a cherry pit, its opalescent gleam shifting like light upon water.

"Da!" I wrap both my hands around his, shielding the jewel—a Boon, a physical manifestation of debt, which the fair folk give sparingly and guard jealously. "You can't! You don't know what she'll ask of you!"

"Clover, my love," he says, his eyes set and his expression unfamiliar in its solemnness. "Your instinct to protect warms my heart, but you have no right to dictate what I can and cannot do. Caitlyn is my niece—your mother's brother's daughter, your only blood relative on that side. What I give, I give as a member of this family. This Boon is given in love, and I ask that you accept it in the same spirit."

Tears flow down my cheeks as I slowly pull my hands away, cupping them instead. My father places the Boon in my hands and closes my fingers over it before kissing my forehead.

"I don't mean to rush you, love," he says softly. "But Caitlyn needs you. You should head out as soon as you can."

"I will," I say. I tuck the Boon into one of my pouches, then throw my arms around him. "Thank you. I love you. I've missed you."

"I know." He hugs me back, his arms as strong and sure as when I was small. "There will be plenty of time to catch up after."

Knowing he's right, I take a breath and let go. He gives a smile and a wink, and he's gone, leaving me alone in the clearing.

Neith isn't a fan of company; as a result, she's built her home in one of the most unwelcoming parts of the Wood Beyond: the Shardsbreadth Caverns.

This is one of the oldest places in the Wood Beyond. Time and tragedy have left their mark: the mountain is twisted, broken into strange angles and difficult for even the more rugged creatures to traverse.

The entrance to the Caverns is a deep hole. I stand outside, listening for movement. From the darkness, I hear nothing, but the woods behind me rustle.

I free my blade, swinging around just as the creature lunges at me. I'm not fast enough to attack, but I get my free arm up as a shield and the creature's teeth sink into it instead of my throat. The wolf's head growls, eyes wide with battle lust, and its spider legs scuttle, trying to get on top of me to pin me down. Beyond the malformed creature, two more emerge from the brush. They're twisted, stunted and jagged, like everything here, but their teeth are sharp and their legs are spry.

I sink my blade into the creature's flank, unsure if the point will find any vital organs in this nightmare anatomy, but that doesn't matter. All that matters is the iron.

The creature wails and immediately releases my arm, limping backward and whimpering, blood gushing from its side. The skin around the wound blackens, poisoned by the touch of cold iron. I exhibit the stained blade to the creatures, hoping they'll recognize its make.

Fortunately, they're not stupid. They may not know who I am, but they understand the threat. All three back off, the injured one slow and shambling; it probably won't live long.

I clean my weapon and dress my arm before continuing. The bite is deep, but it didn't sever any tendons or nick an artery. So long as I'm not in mortal danger, injuries don't bother me here. Any injury received within the Wood Beyond vanishes upon leaving, like the echoes of a dream.

Before entering the darkness, I light my lantern. The circle of light seems paltry against the blackness, but there's nothing to be done about it. With a deep breath, I step inside.

It's colder than it should be. Gooseflesh rises along my arms and my teeth chatter. I fight to keep my voice even as I call out, not wanting to catch my host unaware, "Neith, are you home? It's the Warden, come to speak with you!"

There's no answer, but I continue to call as I walk, following a winding tunnel barely wider than I am. Behind me, the warm sunlight disappears around a bend.

It's impossible to tell how long I walk, though my aching legs hint that it's been a while. I still call out to Neith, but my voice is hoarse and the intervals are further and further apart.

"Neith?" I call, my voice cracking. "Are you home? It's the Warden, come to speak with you."

My light goes out.

For a moment, I stand stunned in the darkness. It's only the sounds that stir me to action, the skittering of dexterous legs and the clicking of sizable mandibles. I fumble with a pouch as the sounds grow louder, surrounding me, and in my panic I burn my fingers as I light the match, but it doesn't matter. The lantern jumps to life as I set the flame to its core.

A spider the size of a car looms over me, its eight black, glossy eyes considering me. I'm no longer in the tunnel, but an enormous cavern covered from stalactite to stalagmite with fine, gossamer webs.

"Hm," says Neith, her voice chittering over the syllable. "You're far from home, little mortal."

I steel myself, falling into a comfortable stance of authority. "You are right, Neith. I've come further than you know. I seek knowledge, and I believe you can give it."

She moves, eight legs graceful as a dancer's despite her body's bulk, following her webs across the ceiling to consider me from all angles. At last, she says, "I've not seen a mortal such as you before. Are you a man or a woman?"

"I am neither," I say, a little too sharply. It irks me that I should have to explain myself even here.

"Hm." She moves back to her original space and offers, "I have much knowledge, caught in my webs like so many flies. But I prefer to keep them. After all, I hunger like anyone else. Why should I answer simply because you ask?"

"I don't intend to cheat you, Neith. I'm willing to provide something of value in exchange."

"Ah." Her eyes grow larger, rounder. I imagine them bursting like ripe grapes. "And what, pray tell, could you offer me?"

I nearly hesitate, but remember the wish my father made and solemnly pull his Boon from its pouch. Neith's eyes grow even wider.

"A Boon?" she says, leaning closer. I hold it up for inspection, knowing that decorum keeps her from touching until it's officially bequeathed. At length, she settles back, and though it's difficult to see human expression in a spider, I know she's pleased. "An File Fánaíochta is an astute and generous man. Alright." Neith clicks her mandibles, what would be a grin on a human face. "I will answer your question. Ask it, mortal."

"What happened to the previous Warden, called Caitlyn?"

"Oh yes," says Neith, tilting her head. "That was quite an uproar. I don't think we've had a Warden abducted in our history. Murdered, yes, but rarely stolen."

"Stolen?" I lean forward unconsciously. "By who?"

"The Wild Hunt."

My stomach drops. The Wood Beyond is chaotic, but there are rules in place—decorum to keep this place from devouring itself. The Wild Hunt, however, is the oldest and most feral of the Wood's inhabitants, its dark heart. The rules that govern the rest of the Wood Beyond don't always apply.

"Where can I find the Wild Hunt?" I ask.

Neith's eyes gleam. "Where indeed?" she asks, circling me. "I have answered your question, little mortal, generously. To answer another, I need further payment."

My mouth goes dry. "I don't have anything else to give."

"That's not true. Mortals always have something valuable. A year of your life, perhaps."

I shake my head. "My life is not mine to give. Too many people rely on me."

"Perhaps something that is yours, then." She clicks her mandibles thoughtfully. "How about your name?"

I open my mouth to refuse, then pause. My name. It's a very fey thing to ask for. The names of the fair folk are tied to their beings and can't be shed so easily. But I, on the other hand...

"What would you do with my name?" I ask, carefully schooling my features.

"Keep it with my other secret treasures. Take it out from time to time, to see how it glitters."

"And what would happen to me once you take it?"

"It will no longer be yours," she says. "You'll remember giving it, but not what it was, and neither will anyone else. It will be a hole you cannot fill, a dream you cannot remember, a history you cannot tell."

"Done," I say. I spread my hands. "How do I give it to you?"

Neith seems a bit taken aback by my confidence, but she recovers quickly. "Simply speak it," she says, "and I will take."

I take a deep breath. It feels momentous, knowing this is the last time I will hear my birth name, the last time I will ever speak it. "Clodagh," I say, trying to encompass all the complex emotions, good and bad, that are entangled with those syllables.

Neith excretes a small bit of gossamer and weaves a net, which she then wraps into a ball. This she tucks into a corner of the web, where it's soon lost among the other gleaming threads.

"It is done," she says.

Curious, I reach for the space where my birth name used to be, hovering at the back of my mind, and find nothing. It's like a droning buzz, tolerated for so long, has vanished.

"It is done," I say. "Now. Where can I find the Wild Hunt?"

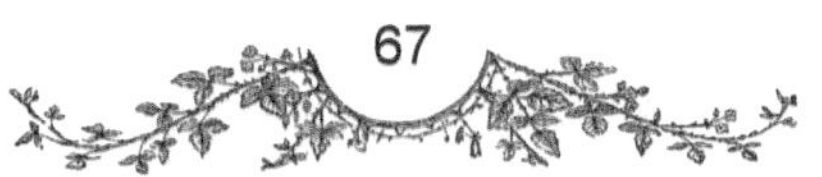

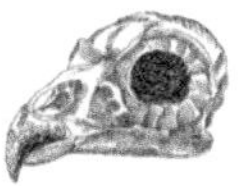

The Dusk Vale is a fickle place. It requires a spell to find, because it can be anywhere from moment to moment. It's difficult to say if its chaotic nature is because it houses the Wild Hunt, or if the Wild Hunt is so incorrigible because it resides there. Like so much in the Wood Beyond, the Dusk Vale is a riddle inside a riddle.

Still, I have to admit it's beautiful. The sky is painted lavender, burnt orange and crimson, with a dusting of midnight blue and strange configurations of stars beyond. A horned moon hangs above the horizon like a sentinel. The grass, driven to whispers by a cool evening breeze, rises above my waist. Cicada song accompanies the shushing, and the dim glow of fireflies light the path to the throne.

It's old—older than anything I've ever seen, even within the Wood Beyond—stone carved so long ago that eons have worn away the intricate etchings and the edges have crumbled away. The raised dais on which it sits has seen better days, cracked and worn smooth where so many feet have stepped.

But the throne and dais are nowhere near as old as the being who sits upon them.

The Horned King is tall. Taller than my father, taller than any of the fair folk I've ever met. He's clad in worn armor, buckles rusted, cape moth-eaten at the edges. His shoulder pauldrons curve to points and the armored gloves have spikes at the knuckles. On his head sits a great helm, crafted from iron—something I would declare impossible if I wasn't looking at it—with curves and spikes in the shape of a crown. Through two slits in the helm, a pair of stag's antlers rise, larger, more intricate, and sharper than any animal could ever grow. Though the front of the helm is open, there is no face—only darkness, with a pair of glowing eyes peering out.

Beside the Horned King, sitting demurely on a velvet cushion, is Caitlyn.

She's still wearing her bandolier, though her weapons and lantern are nowhere to be seen. She looks so small beside him, her dark curls catching in the errant wind. Her eyes are distant, her body too still. She looks more like a doll than a person.

What has he done to her?

"Hail, King of the Wild Hunt," I say, stopping to stand before his dais. I don't bow. As the Warden, none here are my sovereign. "I have business with you."

The glowing eyes fix on me. The voice that answers is hollow and echoing, and doesn't seem to come from the helm, but from all around me.

"Warden," it says, rusted and blood-flecked as an old sword. "Welcome to my realm. What business do you bring?"

"It's not what I bring, but what you've taken." I don't let my eyes flick to Caitlyn, though the urge is strong. "You have my kin in your possession. I ask that you return her."

"This little one?" The Horned King reaches out an iron hand and gently pats Caitlyn's head. She doesn't stir. "She was in the Wood on Midsummer's. It was well within my rights to take her."

"The fair folk and the Fringe have an agreement." I don't quite manage to keep the anger out of my voice. "There's to be no harm to or abduction of mortals. To do so is to forfeit the Wood Beyond's protection and be cast out."

"Abduction? This was no such thing. She came of her own free will." He turns to her. "Didn't you, love?"

Caitlyn nods slowly, looking at neither him nor me. My heart sinks. She must have caught sight of the Wild Hunt, and the chaos magic overwhelmed her, trapping her in a dream. Even I, with my fae blood, would not chance such a thing.

"Still," I say, putting as much steel into my voice as possible. "I am her kin, and I demand that you return her to her rightful home."

The Horned King considers me. I'm not afraid of him lashing out, as even he knows of my father and the powerful connections he wields. But I'm not so foolish as to think he will surrender Caitlyn without a fight. At last he says, "I have taken this child as my ward. I cannot release her from my protection so easily."

I let out a breath I didn't know I was holding. "Then what can I do to convince you? Do you seek payment? Favors?"

The Horned King's eyes narrow. "What good do I, exiled to the Dusk Vale, have for favors? No, I will only release the child if you can prove you are my equal. Then, I might relinquish her without forfeiting my honor."

"And what do I have to do?" I press. "To prove I'm your equal."

"You must best me." Electricity fills the air like a storm is approaching. "I am Lord of the Hunt. Prove to me, Warden: are you a hunter, or are you prey?"

Trees spring up around the dais, giants stretching skyward. In seconds, I stand at the center of a massive forest. From behind the dais, wolfhounds emerge, baring their teeth as they stalk toward me.

I slide my sword free and keep my other hand at the ready, my fingers itching for the pouches on my bandolier. My eyes twitch as I try to count my opponents.

There's no howl, no growl, no warning but the pounding of paws and panting jaws behind me. My body reacts instinctively, spinning around and thrusting the sword forward.

The point pierces the wolfhound's chest, spilling red across white fur, but the lethal wound doesn't stop the beast. As it slides down the blade, it lunges for me, digging its fangs into the meat of my shoulder. I scream and shove at it, trying to force it off my blade. To my fortune, the wound finally affects the beast, its jaws loosening before it tumbles to the ground.

Blood pours from my wound, my surcoat growing heavy with blood. It's my dominant arm, too. The hunt has hardly begun and I'm already at a disadvantage.

Around me, the other wolves circle closer, undiscouraged by their fallen comrade. Trapped, I search for escape...then look up.

Well, I am my father's child.

Hastily sheathing my bloody sword, I launch myself at the nearest tree and start to climb, my shoulder screaming in protest. The hounds lunge for me, but catch only air.

I don't look back until I'm deep in the boughs, camouflaged by foliage. The hounds growl and circle below, snapping in my direction. I take a moment to bandage my shoulder. It's awkward with only one hand and my range of motion is limited, but it'll have to do.

Taking out my bow feels a little cowardly, but I'm not fae. Dying for honor has never appealed to me. Drawing back the bowstring is agony, my arms shaking with the effort, making it impossible to aim true, but I do my best.

The first arrow takes a wolfhound in the neck, crimson spilling onto the white fur as it howls in pain, but doesn't cease its attack. It takes two more arrows to bring it down, and another hound just takes its place.

This isn't going to work. My legs already ache from crouching and the effort has jostled my wound, the blood now seeping through the bandage. I'm going to run out of arrows before the pack runs out of hounds. I need to find an advantage, and I can't do that penned up in a tree.

Shouldering my bow, I stand and whistle softly. The boughs reach out, bending and twisting into a sturdy bridge. I clamber across, continuing to whistle the song my father taught me, the dream stuff of the Dusk Vale even more pliable than most of the Wood Beyond. The hounds, catching the scent of my blood, track me, baying as they race along the forest floor.

Through the trees, I see the moon glinting, larger than she'd ever be in the Fringe, her silver light catching on the fae hounds' snowy fur.

From my bandolier, I grasp a handful of salt and throw it down. The hounds whine as it hits them, fur smoldering where the crystals touch, giving me a few moments to get ahead.

I flee for what seems like hours, running along the boughs to gain some distance, then resting, trying desperately to stay ahead of the pack. If I can just make it until morning, the Wild Hunt will fade away into the dawn mists.

Battered, bloody, and exhausted, I look to the sky, searching for the telltale light that heralds the sunrise.

The moon hangs in the same place, an empty smile.

Realization dawns on me, churning my stomach: there is no time in

the Dusk Vale. It is always the twilight hour, the strange half-step between waking and sleeping. This isn't a game of endurance, but a test of wills.

I'm a fucking idiot.

All this time I've been fighting the hounds, but they aren't in charge here. They may be a manifestation of the Hunt, but they aren't its master.

So then: how does one kill a Hunter?

I look for the dais and find it gone. Perhaps the Horned King is biding his time, waiting for the pack to do his dirty work. If that's true, only one thing can make him reveal himself.

I sigh as I start unbuckling my bandolier.

The hounds howl in triumph, fighting to be the first to sink their teeth into their trophy. The scent of blood is heavy on the air.

The Horned King steps out from behind a tree, his glowing eyes trained on the wild pack. He snaps his fingers and they pause, heads turned toward him, ears alert.

There's no spoken command—the connection between Hunter and Pack is so strong, there's no need for words. A single hound, catch in its mouth, approaches the Horned King and lays the item at his feet. It's impossible to gauge the Horned King's thoughts as he picks up the shredded surcoat, bloodstain blooming across the shoulder.

"A ruse," he murmurs, so softly it's nearly impossible to hear.

Behind him, a branch snaps.

The Horned King whirls around, yellow eyes searching for the sound's source. They narrow as they light upon two figures struggling through the trees: me, leading a zombie-like Caitlyn.

With a snarl, the Horned King points his iron gauntlet. The hounds rush past him like water rapids toward where I stand in horror.

The pack falls upon me, teeth sinking into tender flesh, hot blood pouring into panting mouths as I scream.

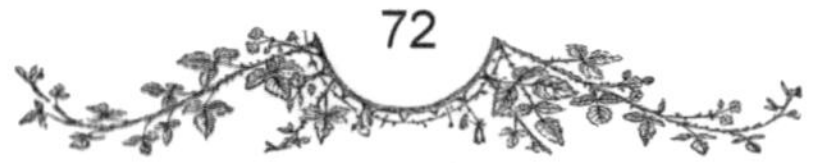

The Horned King chuckles and strides forward, eager to lord over my gutted corpse. His second step halts abruptly, his foot hanging in the air. He looks down in confusion to find a line of salt, surreptitiously laid while he was distracted.

The rustle of leaves is the only warning before I leap from the trees above, landing on his back. I grit my teeth as several spikes puncture my legs and abdomen; the wounds are superficial but they fucking hurt. Clutching a large spike to steady myself, I plunge my sword into the sliver where helm and armor meet. The metal cuts through flesh—or whatever he's made of—like butter, notching into the space between two vertebrae and severing his spine. The Horned King falls beneath me as I clamber to the ground.

The hounds turn to us, confused now that the illusion—another lesson from my father—has disappeared, my concentration broken. Before the pack can make a decision, I move around to the fallen king and grasp his helm, pulling it back to expose his throat. Arm trembling with the effort, I raise my sword and slit his throat, hot, acrid blood splashing against my hand before I let his body go.

The Horned King's body sags forward, barely touching the ground before the hounds are on it. The wet rending of flesh fills the air, the scent of iron so heavy I can taste it. The hounds' white muzzles are stained red, blood and saliva dripping from their jaws.

In what feels like the blink of an eye and yet an eternity, the hounds pull back, sated. Where the Horned King once lay, there's nothing but a crimson stain.

Slow clapping fills the air and I jump, whirling around and holding my sword at the ready. The Horned King sits upon his dais, untouched, applauding my efforts.

"You are a worthy opponent, Warden," he says, laying his hands to rest on the arms of his throne. Out of breath and aching, I can only nod. "Well," he says, and it may be my imagination, but his voice seems a little sad. "I have given my word and I am bound by it. Child."

He stands and reaches out a hand to Caitlyn. Like a sleepwalker, she takes it and stands. He walks her to the edge of the dais and I, belatedly realizing what's expected of me, climb the stone steps, waiting to accept her.

The Horned King pauses just before the steps. He brushes a stray stand of hair behind Caitlyn's ear, his touch surprisingly gentle for such fearsome gauntlets. "Take care, child," he says. "The world outside is cruel and hungry. I hope you do not fall prey to it."

I fight the urge to roll my eyes as he passes Caitlyn to me. I lead her gently down the steps, hardly able to believe it's over. She still moves like a sleepwalker, but I assume that will fade. If not, my father will know how to remedy it.

As we turn to leave, the Horned King holds up his hand in farewell. "Until we meet again, Warden," he says.

Suddenly, Caitlyn and I are in the middle of a brightly lit wood, birds chirping and butterfly-sized fey fluttering among the wildflowers, leaving trails of sparkling dust. There's no trace of the Dusk Vale.

Beside me, Caitlyn groans and rubs her eyes as though waking from a long sleep. She blinks at me, brow furrowing as her eyes focus. "Clover? What are you doing here?" Her eyes widen. "What the hell happened to your shoulder?"

Relief flooding through me, I wrap my arms around her and hold her so close it hurts. After a moment of shock, she returns my embrace, considerately not commenting on the sobs I'm trying and failing to stifle.

"Something bad happened, didn't it?" she says into my hair.

"Yeah," I say. I'm relieved she doesn't seem to remember, though it stokes my anger with the Horned King. Who knows how long he would've kept Caitlyn like that, subject to his whim. "But it's okay now."

For a long time, we simply hold each other in the cheerful sunlight of the Wood Beyond. At last, when there are no more tears to shed, I pull away. "Come on," I say, grateful to speak the words. "Let's go home."

Caitlyn was understandably disoriented when we arrived at the Fringe. She'd been gone for more than a month and remembered nothing from her time with the Horned King. It's probably for the best, as while I have no doubt she was safe as his ward, the Wild Hunt isn't kind or beautiful. What she saw would change her utterly, and even without the memories, she's a little fragile. For now, Caitlyn is convalescing under the care of her mother and mine, and she becomes more like her old, bright-eyed self every day.

I'm still acting as Warden, though there's been little to do besides delivering messages between my father and mother. I don't dislike it. They've missed each other, and I hope to see them together and happy soon.

In the few weeks since Caitlyn's return, I've had my own developments, though I've kept them to myself. Most of my wounds vanished upon re-entering the Fringe, as expected. The bite from the Wild Hunt, however, did not.

Instead, it scarred, leaving jagged teeth marks across my shoulder. I asked my father if I should be worried, but he considered it a sign of respect.

"It signifies your triumph over the Wild Hunt and your title as a Hunter on par with the Horned King himself," he said, with pride. "Anyone who recognizes those teeth marks will think twice about tangling with you."

Anyone in the Wood Beyond, at least. Here in the Fringe, they make up their own stories. I'm not really that averse to it, when I think about it.

Even without them truly understanding, things are different. There's respect in my neighbors' faces on the few occasions I've been out and about. Not respect for the Warden—there's always been that—but respect for me. Clover. The odd part-fey, part-witch who never quite fit into the outlines they drew for me.

Before, it made me apart. Now, well, I'm still apart, but also elevated? It's hard to explain.

And it certainly hasn't miraculously fixed everything that drove me away in the first place, but it's starting to feel like there's a place here for me. One I'll have to carve out myself, one I'll have to fight to define on my own terms, but the possibility is there.

A week into Caitlyn's convalescence, I decide to make a call. There's no reception in the Fringe—I have to go all the way to Ashbourne.

I move as quietly as possible through the house, careful not to wake Caitlyn, who has been sleeping late, and Aunt Mathilda, who hasn't left her side. I'm almost to the front door when I hear a soft voice from the den, "Going somewhere, love?"

My mother sits by the window, a steaming cup of tea in her hands. I walk into the doorway and lean against the polished wood. "Just need to make a call," I say.

She smiles like she has a secret. "Do you want me to tell Caitlyn? Or would you rather do it?"

I tap my keys against my thigh. Of course my mother knows what I'm thinking. She always has. "I'll do it. I'd rather wait a bit. Until I have everything settled. Back in the city."

"Of course." She takes a sip of her tea. "Drive safe, dear."

"I will."

Despite the early hour, the Fringe is already bustling. I return nods of greeting as I head to my car, hoping no one will stop me for a chat.

No such luck.

"Good morning!"

I look up to find Greta waving at me from her front garden. Sighing internally, I muster a smile and say, "Good morning, Greta."

"Going somewhere?"

"Just running a few errands," I say. "You know how it is."

"Of course," she says, though I know she doesn't, as she's never owned a car.

I see the struggle on her face as she debates whether or not to ask about what happened in the Wood. Everyone is wondering, but she's the only one nosy enough to ask.

Before she can cross the line, I say, "Well, I better get going. Have a good day."

"Oh, of course. Have a good day—" Her brow furrows. "Oh. Oh, dear. I must be getting old."

Despite already turning away, I pause. "Are you alright?"

"I'm fine," she says, fretting with her petunias. "I suppose it's just a senior's moment. Just think, I've known you since you were a babe, and yet for the life of me, I can't remember your name!"

I blink, then smile. "It's Clover."

"Right. Clover." Greta tries to put on a smile, but she's still confused. "Well, good day, Clover."

"You, too, Greta."

I grin to myself on the way to my car. I wish I could thank Neith for her greed, but I doubt she'd understand, no matter how wide her tangled webs reach.

With a cheerful heart, I get in my car and head toward Ashbourne.

I've got some moving arrangements to make.

A Girl Called Winter

By S.O. Green

The new skin fit tight. A squeeze to keep all of itself inside. The girl with the basket had smelled of herbs and mead. Tavern wench, maybe. She'd tasted like rabbit. Delicious.

Now her soft lips hid its pointed teeth and her delicate toes pushed what had once been her bones into the mud beneath the bridge until they looked like nothing but white rocks. It smoothed out its new frock, its dirty travelling cloak, and wondered if this one was pretty enough to lure others to the bridge. Maybe, if it smiled at them in just the right way, and whispered the right things in her voice.

The rain had come while it fed, like the gods of Avalon wept at the way it snapped the girl's neck and pulled her inside-out. It didn't care for the gods. It only wanted to be free of the fairy land. It wanted a sturdy bridge to hide under and a good supply of fresh meat.

It sat down to wait for the storm to pass. The lashing of the rain above masked the sound of the stranger sliding down the embankment to the edge of the swollen stream until they ducked into the shelter of the stone

archway and threw back their hood.

"Fuck me, it's raining," the woman gasped, wringing out her cape.

It said nothing. It looked the stranger over, from her fancy leather boots to her tangle of copper curls, and felt the groan of hunger in its belly.

Seconds? Yes. It thought it would.

The woman looked over, saw what she must have assumed was a pretty, young girl, and smiled. Her expression changed subtly when she mistook the gluttony in its eyes for lust, and she winked.

It assumed this was what humans called 'flirting'.

"Hello, beautiful. What are you doing down here in the middle of the pissing rain?"

"I was picking flowers for my mother."

It gestured to the wicker basket, fallen in the mud. Its impression of the tavern girl pleased it. It wasn't an easy thing, to mimic a voice you'd only ever heard screaming in fear and agony.

"What a sweet thing you are. Still, it's dangerous to be out here on your own. Especially down under a bridge. We've had word there's trolls in the area."

"Trolls?"

"Well, *a* troll. Some people from the village have gone missing. And a couple of goats. Apparently, they like goats too."

Yes, they certainly did like goats.

"I'm not on my own anymore," it said.

The woman smiled some more and came closer. The groaning in its stomach intensified. The newcomer was strong and well-fed. Perhaps from the capital. A fine meal, and her skin might carry more authority, but that would mean keeping it all intact.

Maybe it would just keep the tavern girl and enjoy wringing this lady out like a damp cloth, catching all the blood on its long, grey tongue.

"Aren't *you* travelling alone?" it asked. It had to be sure there weren't more on the bridge that might hear her screaming. "Aren't you afraid of the troll?"

"I'm not afraid. I've got an enchanted sword, so I'll keep us safe."

She twitched her cloak aside, exposing the ornate pommel jutting from her belt. It studied the sword, hoping the interest would come off as wide-eyed enthusiasm rather than predatory focus.

To its delight, the woman drew the blade and held it out, inviting inspection. It took the weapon and lay it across its knees. A sharp-toothed smile formed, so wide it began to tear the corners of its dainty, new mouth.

"This sword isn't enchanted," it hissed.

"It isn't?"

"Not at all. It's just a heavy, sharp piece of metal. You'd have to be *very* lucky and *very* smart to kill a troll with it. And you aren't either."

It rose to the skin's full height and then kept rising. It tore at the knees, at the elbows, at the shoulders. Its pointed toes and razor fingers split and curled out, gnarled, grey skin ripping from soft, pink flesh. It twisted the girl's face into a savage rictus. At its full size, the sword was like a dagger in its massive hand.

But the woman was still a fine meal.

"Okay, I lied," she said, without appropriate terror. "I don't have a magic sword. I was just trying to impress you so that I could get under your skirt. The truth is, *I'm* the one that's magic."

It laughed, because humans weren't magic. Oh, they could carve runes on mundane objects to imbue them if they knew how—magic sticks and magic armor and magic swords—but they could never *be* magic. Only fae were magic.

And there were no fae in Avalon. Only delicious humans. A full larder of them.

"It's the strangest thing," the woman said. "All my life, I've had this ability to make creatures from the fairy land do what I tell them. Like if I say: 'Stop'..."

Something happened. Its muscles went rigid and its joints locked out all at once. It tried to move. Nothing happened. Its eyes swiveled behind its twisted mask and its teeth gnashed but it was frozen.

Stopped.

"Or if I say: 'Cut your own arm off'..."

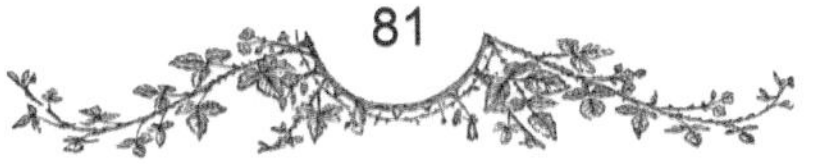

It lifted the sword, splayed its fingers. Every fiber trembled but the power of those words sang in its blood. It shook its head in denial, even as it complied. It sawed through skin and muscle and bone, shrieking with the pain, until its twitching hand dropped into the crimson mud with a splat.

"Getting cruel now, aren't I?" the woman considered. "It's a character flaw. We're all works in progress."

"Who are you?" it snarled.

It meant to ask *what* she was. After all, humans weren't magic.

She said, "Me? I'm Rena, Princess of Avalon. And you were going to stick that sword in your eye for me because I asked nicely."

It resisted with every fiber of its being but the cold compulsion could not be denied. It took Princess Rena's heavy, sharp piece of metal and pierced eyeball, skull and brain. The last thing it felt was the point of the blade scoring a groove down the inside of its cranium.

Rena wiped her sword on the troll's cloak and sheathed it. She touched the pale cheek of the face it was wearing and blew out a sigh.

"Sorry, love. I should have come sooner."

You can't fix all the realm's problems, her father said, which in his mind was a good enough reason not to fix any of them.

Too busy making war with the neighbors to drive out the bloody fairies. If only humans would listen to her the way they did. Then she could oust the old tyrant, make examples of his rich friends before they bled the wealth out of the nation, and establish real law and order.

She'd start with the fairies from the Winter Court, sneaking through the veil to eat all the pretty girls. So many in the last few months. She'd lobotomized a dozen trolls just like this one all by herself, and that wasn't including the withered dryad colony she'd used as kindling, or the nest of pixies she'd put to the torch. Fire was too good for those little bastards.

She'd watched them strip a man to bones in seconds.

The rain had let up by the time she climbed the slope to the bridge-head. She stuck her fingers in her mouth and whistled. Seconds later, Tiny came crashing out of the woods, leaving the timbers quaking in his wake. He skidded to a stop in front of her, panting, steam rising off his furry flanks.

"Who's a good boy?" she asked, raking her fingernails through his pelt. She'd need to buy all the room in a decent-sized stable so she could comb all the knots out.

Who knew keeping a dire wolf as a mount was such hard work?

"Told you I'd kill that nasty troll. You thought I was going to bite off more than I could chew."

Tiny huffed. Actually, he'd seemed more concerned that the troll was going to bite something off.

Rena sighed. "There has to be a better way to fix all this than just running to put out one fire after another," she grunted, swinging up onto his back. "Or start them. I mean, what am I supposed to do? Order other people to do everything for me? How can I trust them to actually *do* it? Or do it right? How do people even rule nations anyway?"

Tiny, being a giant wolf, didn't have much insight into the politics of royalty. The closest he'd come to being a courtier was the time Rena had snuck him into the kitchen as a pup to nurse him back to health. Poor baby was the runt of the litter. You could tell because he was only as big as a shire horse.

He padded on, sturdy and dependable, through the mud and drizzle and the fog rising off the road. As they rode, Rena wondered if she should go after the other troll rumored to be hiding in the north, or the satyr that had left an entire village a smoking hole of fatal carnality.

She was still wondering when they came to the fork in the road. The path to the left was signposted 'Tollhaven'. The other had no sign, but Rena knew where it led.

They were deep in the Witchwood. Along that track of worn dirt were the standing stones that marked the boundaries of the fairy land, the source of the sickness seeping into Avalon's soil. She'd tried posting guards at those sites, to see off the witches and stop the fairies from crossing over. Her father would never leave them there long before pulling them back. Needed at the front, he always said.

Asshole.

Very rarely in life were you presented with a choice as clear cut as this. A literal fork. It was important to think carefully and make the right decision.

"Fuck it," she grunted, and steered Tiny towards the stones.

And what might have been the biggest mistake of her life.

The stones were in sight when Tiny reared with a growl and a yip and refused to go any further. He paced at the treeline but wouldn't enter the clearing. Rena sighed and dismounted. Difficult to blame him, considering the reputation of places like these and the dried blood still staining the altar.

"It's fine," she said, patting him on the snout. "I'll go alone. Ride back to the city. If they see you in the trees, they'll know not to come looking for me."

She took a step. Tiny caught her hood between his teeth and jerked her back.

"Dad's made it clear that, if I want to fix this problem, I have to do it myself. I can't just ride around hoping the answer's going to fall into my lap. I need to go to the source. You understand, don't you? These people are my subjects too. I have to do *something*."

Funny, but if it had been anyone else, she wouldn't have felt the need to explain herself. She'd have just told them to fuck off.

There was something that she *couldn't* explain though, and that was the song of the stones. They called to her, like nothing she'd ever felt before. A voice, a whisper, a tender shiver on her skin. Beautiful and haunting and oddly familiar.

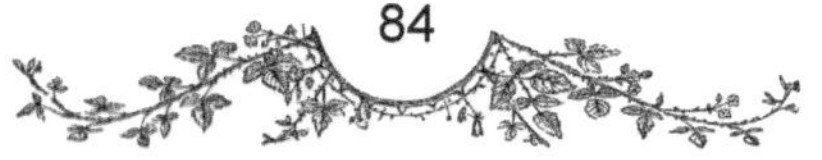

"I *have* to go," she said, and started walking. Tiny released her cape with a whine and she stepped past the altar, past the blood, and through the towering archway into...

On the face of things, the forest didn't change. The trees ringed the clearing as thick as ever, green canopy above and a carpet of fallen leaves below. Only the fog had lifted and the sun filtered through, dappling the ground. Sparks danced in the air and color rippled in their wake.

Behind her, through the arch, was a different forest. Foggy and forlorn, grim Avalon under its shroud of mist and misery. Tiny watched her with sad eyes, then turned and padded away. Because, like the fairies, and unlike mostly everyone in her life, he actually listened.

"Good boy," she muttered, checked her sword and forged on.

This was the fairy land. Now the real danger began.

Danger, in Avalon, was a knife in an alleyway or a cutthroat on the road. It was a soldier's blade or a bear's claws.

Here, in this place, it was dainty figures with glass wings that could tear off all your flesh, or the sound of panpipes that made you dance and dance and dance until your body shudderingly gave out. Or it was the sound of trickling water and beautiful song.

"Ignore it," Rena warned, already straying towards the stream. "Ignore it, idiot."

She couldn't. Whatever cord in her the gateway had plucked, this voice—magnificent and rich—seized it like a fishing line and reeled her in. It would loop around her neck and string her up and she'd smile all the while.

The compulsion was so strong she almost walked right into the water. She skidded to a halt at the bank, stones slipping away under her boots and plinking into the crystal pool. The surface rippled. Then someone rose from the water. The ripples, the moment, the world centered on them.

Her hair was warm sunlight, her skin the ripest peach. Her lips were rose petals and her eyes were the deepest, darkest, most haunted places of the forest. Glorious and naked, she swept out her hair and smiled at Rena in a way that almost made her topple into the pond.

"A visitor?" she asked, and Rena realized she hadn't been the one singing. The song just seemed to follow her, filling the air like the scent of honeysuckle and rosehip. "How unexpected. Join me, won't you?"

Rena's knees quivered. The woman watched her in breathless anticipation.

She opened her mouth to speak and the words jammed in her throat. She shook her head instead.

"I only just got dry," she managed.

The magnificent smile widened. "You're refusing me? Any other mortal would have disrobed and plunged into these waters at the very sight of me. And here you are, standing resolute where I cannot reach. How is that?"

"I'm here on a mission," Rena said.

Yes! The mission! Focus on that and not on her—

"Fairy creatures from the Winter Court are coming into my realm and harming my people. I want to stop them."

"Is that right?"

The woman wasn't moving, but it definitely seemed like she was getting closer.

"You are looking for the Winter Queen then. You leave me heartbroken. Alas, summer is my domain, so you have not come searching for me."

In her haste to take in every inch of the stranger, Rena had missed the details. The threads of light under her skin, making her glow. The horns growing from her hairline that formed a golden ridge in the shape of a crown.

"Are you...Titania?"

"You have heard of me. Delightful."

"You're the bloody Summer Queen."

"Sometimes, when the mood takes me," she said, "though mostly I am *just* the Summer Queen."

She rose out of the pool then. She didn't climb, or even stand. She simply floated up until she was standing on the water's glassy surface and stepped onto the bank. Rena gulped and stared up at her. Up and up and up, because the Summer Queen was taller than any humanoid she'd ever met.

"And what do you intend with the Queen of Winter? Should I be jealous?"

"C-could you put some clothes on before I answer?"

"Is my magnificence intimidating you?"

"Maybe just a little."

Honestly, it was difficult not to be intimidated by that much pristine skin. And, if Titania wasn't going to be embarrassed herself, Rena would just have to be embarrassed for them both.

She reached out a graceful hand and curled her long, slender fingers around the shafts of light falling through the canopy. They snared her wrist like the tail of a snake and began to slither down her arm, twisting into a thickening glow. Before long, the light had bound itself into something resembling fabric and fit to her body in a loose robe.

Mostly, it was just a different type of provocative.

"You didn't answer my question, dear."

"I suppose I'll just ask her to stop?"

"And you think she will listen?"

"Usually, when I ask fairies to do things, they listen."

Actually, a lot of them did those things even when they didn't want to. And, at first, she'd asked them to please leave and never come back. After the first troll she'd encountered had just moved to another village, she'd decided it was time to stop asking nicely.

"Yes, you certainly have a will about you," Titania said. "I feel it myself, brushing against my mind, trying to force itself inside of me. A cold, hard thing you wield almost like a sword. I have never felt quite so compromised. It almost makes me want to obey you. But, you see, I have a will of my own. Perhaps you have felt it. Warmer and sweeter than yours."

Rena nodded. But the Summer Queen's will wasn't any less dangerous.

"Perhaps we can help each other," she said, and cupped Rena's face in her hands like she was thinking of drinking from her mouth. "Would you like that?"

"What can I do to help you?" Rena managed, despite the complete lack of moisture in her mouth.

"If you know of me, you know that the Winter Queen and I are bitter enemies. I will tell you how to reach the Winter Palace and, in return, you will slay her for me and bring me her silver crown."

Rena flicked a glance at Titania's golden horns. Would the Winter Queen's crown be similarly attached? Messy.

"Aren't you eternal enemies though? What makes you think I can kill her if you haven't managed it in thousands of years?"

"You seem a resourceful and motivated woman." She lay her hands on Rena's shoulders and smiled down at her. "Just think of all that you will win. Peace for your realm. My undying gratitude. Once the deed is done, we can discuss how I might repay you further."

Rena, who'd been fighting a losing battle against her libido from the moment she'd seen Titania rise out of the water, took a step back. Everything about her, from her glossy, lustrous hair to her silky skin to her rich, warm voice made her head swim. She couldn't focus on anything other than the Summer Queen, and the words 'undying gratitude', which were playing out in various positions in her head.

She needed to stop the fairies from the Winter Court anyway. If this was the only way to do it, it was fine if she took a little something for herself along the way.

A tiny part of Rena, consigned to a dark and dusty corner, started screaming that this was a new, all-time biggest mistake of her life when she let Titania's hand engulf hers and lead her away into the forest.

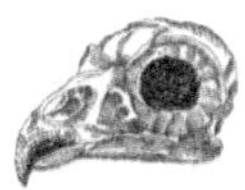

"Where's the Winter Court?" Rena asked.

She'd asked that question already. It was hard to focus. The mission kept slipping out of her grasp, like it didn't matter anymore, and she'd find herself wandering the forest, holding hands with the Summer Queen, smiling like an idiot.

"Are you so eager to stain your hands with blood? Humans are such violent creatures."

"I saw a troll wearing a girl's skin today. I don't think that's a great testament to fairy-kind's peaceful nature."

"Perhaps you are right. But we hide our wickedness so well, do we not?"

She smiled. Rena bit the inside of her cheek until she tasted blood. *Focus!*

"The Winter Court. Where is it?"

Titania's smile flickered. "Will you force me to show you?"

"If I have to."

"I am almost eager to see you try."

A spark flickered in the giant woman's eye. Too much warmth could cause a fire eventually. Then they would all burn. That was why they needed winter.

"Here," Titania said, and gestured to a cave mouth that might have been there the whole time, but the Summer Queen was eminently distracting. "You will enter her domain through this tunnel. Find her palace, slay her and bring me her crown. Then you will have your reward."

Rena stood in the cave mouth. A chill wind blew from below, but she could see light ahead. Unlike the gentle sunlight falling through the canopy of summer, this was cold and oddly colored. Rena wondered where it was coming from.

"My only regret is that I cannot watch you work. I think it would be exciting, watching you indulge your bloodlust. I wonder what kind of mood we might both be in once you finish."

Titania's fingers glided through Rena's hair, but there was an eager tension in her hands, like she might pull hard on it at any moment. Life with her would be a constant parade of distraction.

What kind of ruler did a woman like this make anyway?

"I'll do what I need to do to save my realm," she said, stepping out of Titania's reach before she could decide not to let go.

"I'm sure you will, my dear. And I'm sure you will learn a great deal about yourself in the process."

Rena scowled at her. It was also difficult to figure out when the Summer Queen was mocking you. Maybe that was just the way she spoke and Rena was being paranoid.

"I take it you're going to wait here."

"I cannot enter the Winter Court unless I am invited. My rival is most inhospitable."

"Yeah, winter's like that."

"But you will be sure not to keep me waiting long, won't you? I yearn for you already."

Rena took another step away. Titania's laughter followed her into the depths of the cave. It echoed off the walls and in her ears and chimed like silver bells until the cold took hold and her breath misted in the air and she realized she wasn't in summer anymore.

The tunnel opened into a snow-swept cavern, where a bitter wind blew through a crevasse high in the ceiling, carrying with it a dusting of frost. Spears of ice hung above, like pointed teeth.

The damp of Avalon's rain still clung to her clothes. She shivered and pressed on, wondering why she hadn't taken Titania up on her offer to wash her back.

"The things I do for my people," she muttered.

Through fissures in the ceiling, she saw only night. The light came from seams of crystal in the wall, casting auroras of pale, colorful light across the caverns and tunnels. Like Titania's domain, it was beautiful, but unsettling.

The weeping didn't help. The deeper she pushed, the louder it became, until she stepped into an immense chamber with a deep, frozen basin at its center. Judging by all the withered roots jutting from the walls, there must have been a forest just beyond that cave.

The sound of sobbing from a dozen throats echoed around the chamber, maddening. Rena found the cut on the inside of her cheek again, reopened it, trying to keep her focus.

Sculptures rose from the surface of the pond. Delicate female forms, stretched out into balletic poses, shimmering in the light of the crystals. It was magnificent, until Rena made the mistake of stepping closer and saw the looks of horror stretched across their faces, realized that they weren't dancing but clambering over one another in their desperation to escape the pool.

"What have we here?"

The voice came from behind her. What she'd taken to be a snowdrift turned out to be an ancient-looking woman in a white cloak. She stood, snow shaking loose from her bony shoulders, and smiled at Rena from under her hood.

"Another intruder from the Summer Court, is it?" she asked, leaning on a stick that was about as gnarled as she was.

"I'm a human from Avalon," Rena insisted. "I want to speak to the Winter Queen."

That was true. She'd start with diplomacy. The sword would come later.

"Well, you're fleshy enough that could be true. I doubt you'll look anywhere near as pretty as the nymphs when you're frozen. Still, I'm always happy for another decoration."

Rena wanted to tell her it didn't have to come to that, that she'd be on her way. Instead, the old woman breathed deep and exhaled a blizzard. Rena scrambled behind a jutting rock as the blast of ice rushed by her, and almost throttled herself when the end of her cape froze to the ground. She shrugged it off and unsheathed her blade.

"Oh, don't try to talk, human. Your lungs will freeze in your chest if you open your mouth. I'd like you to stay alive, at least at first."

That's fine. I was done talking anyway.

The crone—a cailleach, Rena assumed—tapped her stick as she

walked. The cavern echoed, but Rena thought she could pinpoint the thing's exact location by that noise. The only question was, what was she going to do about it?

She hacked off the frozen part of her cloak and pulled the rest to her. Stones on the floor. Twinkling icicles frozen to the ceiling. A plan was starting to form.

She wrapped one of the stones in the strip of material that had once been her cape and spun it around in one hand. She stepped back so she had a clear view of the ceiling, making sure the cailleach couldn't see her.

This had better work.

She loosed the stone. It shattered ice to pieces, cleaving through the roots of the great spikes above. One fell, then another, bringing down a portion of the frozen ceiling. Jaws snapping shut. Frost bite.

The cailleach screamed, and then the screaming stopped abruptly. When Rena dared to look, she saw a mess of shattered ice, streaked red, and a few tatters of cloak.

"You should have let me speak," she said.

Her eyes flicked to the weeping ice sculptures. Nymphs. Intruders from the Summer Court. Fairies, definitely. They weren't her business. Not her responsibility. She needed to find the Winter Queen, stop the attacks, then she could...

She never had been able to ignore a crying girl before.

"Just a second," Rena said, and started hacking at the roots in the cave wall. "I'll get you out."

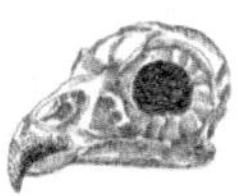

She built the fire by the pool and warmed her hands and feet while she waited. The nymphs' weeping turned to tears of gratitude as they slowly returned to their original state. By the time the pool had thawed, they were little more than a curved hip or slender leg flashing on the water's surface.

Rena tried to keep in mind that nymphs tempted people to drowning.

Why did everyone want her to come swimming today?

"Are you sure you won't join us?" the leader asked. She'd introduced herself as Aquaria, as soon as her lips could move again, and she'd poured thanks until Rena was soaking with it. "We can take away all your cares."

"Humans can't breathe underwater," she pointed out. "And not caring doesn't make the problem go away."

"Such a pity," Aquaria said. "Why did our savior have to be so boring?"

"I'd have gone with 'air-dependent' myself. Look, I know fairies don't have a great appreciation of death, but dying's our equivalent of being frozen for all eternity. Does that make sense?"

Aquaria rippled. "Yes, I suppose it does."

"So, you came from the Summer Court?"

"Yes. We are refugees from the queen's cruelty. We only wished to play, but she planned to give us orders. She would have sent us into the mortal world and we didn't want to. So we fled."

"Wait, she'd have sent you into the *mortal* world? Why?"

"To sow chaos and discord. To spread panic. To tempt humans into the fairy land so that they could entertain her with folly." Aquaria considered. "The usual reasons."

"Why did you come here? Isn't the Winter Queen your enemy?"

"She isn't *our* enemy. And rumor has it that she's weak. She has no will of her own. She couldn't give us orders, even if she wanted to. We just wish it wasn't so cold."

Something didn't add up. The Summer Queen was sending fairies into the mortal world. The Winter Queen had no control over her realm. Why was Rena even on this quest?

We hide our wickedness so well...

"Do you know these underground lakes?" Rena asked.

"We chased each other in the waters, far and wide, before the cailleach came."

"Do you know how to reach the Winter Palace from here?"

Aquaria hesitated, but she couldn't refuse to answer. That was Rena's power. It looked like the nymph was only just realizing she was being compelled.

"Yes. We can show you the way."

"Good. After that, I'm going to order you to return to the Summer Court."

"Please, no…"

"Find the standing stones that form the gateway to the mortal world and go to Avalon. Then find a stream or a pool, far away from anywhere, and live out your lives."

Aquaria nodded slowly, realization dawning. Then she smiled and touched Rena's hand. Water dripped down her fingers.

"Thank you."

"It comes with a condition. If you, or any of your sisters, allow harm to come to any other living creature, climb out onto a rock and let the sun claim you. Is that clear?"

"As clear as water," Aquaria said. "But we aren't sisters."

"Oh?"

Rena glanced past the nymph's shoulder, saw the others kissing and twining fingers and flowing over and into one another with sensuous grace. She flushed.

"Oh."

"Are you sure you don't want to swim with us?"

"Yeah, I'm fine. I'm more of a 'one at a time' kind of girl."

"Your loss."

Aquaria plunged back into the pool, and Rena made a note to let Avalon's scholars know that the correct collective noun was an orgy of nymphs.

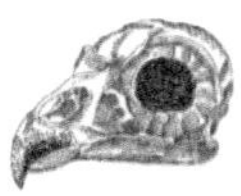

The orgy showed her a passage that connected the caverns to the palace. Rough-hewn stone speckled with frost at first, slowly transforming into shaped ice and flawless, white marble.

Rena ran a hand down the palace's outer wall. The way the caves abruptly ended, it looked like the palace had been driven into the heart of the Winter Court like a dagger, cleaving every artery, vein, muscle and tendon, before striking bone. She wondered what it looked like above ground. Majestic? Or terrifying?

"Thanks, girls," she said, and waved the nymphs off. They surged up through the caverns on their way to Avalon, giggling and frolicking as they went, and Rena hoped she hadn't made a terrible mistake.

She placed her hand on the wall again, felt a shiver pass through her. But the shiver passed through the palace too, and when she stepped forward, the wall didn't resist her. She walked through cold and darkness and emerged into...

An empty antechamber of the same ice and marble as on the outside. The same crystalline light glittered on the bare walls and floor, only here the crystals had been mined and refined into orbs and sconces that glowed with gentle luminescence.

Silent as a tomb, no servants, no chatter of courtiers, no arguments from a ruling council. Gods, if only her own palace sounded like this.

She carried her sword unsheathed, but there was nothing to slay. She'd expected to have to cleave her way through half the Winter Court to get to their queen, but nothing. If the place cared that she was there for murder, it kept its silence.

Cold passages and silent chambers gave way to a grand hall, where the icicles had been gathered into a shimmering chandelier, and the walls had been shaped by magic. She expected to see foolish mortals and unruly fairies imprisoned in the walls. Wasn't that how the fae queens rolled?

She took the sweeping staircase to a door that could only open onto a throne room. She'd stopped shivering and the pinch of cold in her cheeks had abated. She wondered what that meant.

She'd always found it more useful to kill without the throb of adrenaline, to be cool and detached. This felt like the same thing, like winter had gotten inside her.

The sooner she was done here, the better.

She kicked the door open. The magnificent, obsidian throne was empty. No naked women rising from pools in winter.

She checked the corners as she crossed the room—she *definitely* checked the corners—so she was doubly surprised when a blast of cold air howled in from her flank. She leapt aside, tucking into a roll, and came up in stance, facing off against the Winter Queen.

The hooded shape loosed another crackling ball of frost from a glowing staff. Rena remembered the cailleach, but there were no dangling murder spikes waiting for a rock to smash them here. She doubted Winter would have been quite so careless.

"Stop!" she ordered, throwing her hand out like that was how will-power worked.

The Winter Queen responded by shooting at her again. Rena scrambled out of the way.

She'd expected it wouldn't have been that easy, but even Titania had felt *something*. And Aquaria had told her that the queen *had* no will.

And why the fuck was she using a staff?

"Alright, what's going on here exactly?"

She circled, waiting for her moment. She saw the queen coiling, preparing another blast, and lunged. She dropped, skidding along the icy floor, watching a coruscating ball of frozen death pass over her head, scraping up crystals of ice with her boot. Then she hacked the staff clean in half.

"No!" cried the woman under the hood, a second before Rena hooked her on the jaw and knocked her on her ass.

The hood fell back. Rena stared at the Winter Queen for a long, hard moment, then grabbed her under the arm and wrenched her to her feet.

"Who the fuck are you?"

The woman didn't answer. Her eyes were wide, terrified. She looked like she was going to faint. The fact that Rena couldn't stop shaking her probably didn't help.

"Seriously, who the *fuck* are you? What's going on here? *Why do you look like me?*"

"No," the other girl gasped. "*You* look like *me.*"

Both were true. They had the same fire-red hair, the same pale, cold-pinched skin. The only difference was the color of their eyes—icy blue for

Rena, leaf-green for the queen.

"Explain," Rena ordered, because she was the one with the sword.

"I'm Rena, Princess of Avalon. Years ago, the Winter Queen took me from my bed and left a changeling in my place. She brought me to her court to use me against her enemies in Summer. Who better to teach her how to be brutal, how to win a war, than the child of a notorious tyrant?"

Rena hesitated. She thought she could see the not-so-complex twist in this tale.

"But you were only a child, so you couldn't teach her anything."

"Apparently, fairies don't age like humans, and they inherit their natures exclusively from their parents when they're formed. I suppose it was an easy mistake for her to make."

"So, you grew up here?"

The queen scoffed. "Yes. A non-magical girl with no power of will in a world of fairies. I've learned to adapt."

"Yeah, I can see that."

Rena kicked the sundered staff away. She let the queen go, since suddenly she didn't feel like shaking her anymore.

"How did you become queen?"

"I didn't. Mother dearest vanished one night while I slept. I took up the mantle because the reputation was the only thing that could keep me safe. Only reputation is a diminishing currency when you have nothing to back it up, isn't it?"

"You've got the crown," Rena said, pointing at the silver horns on the other girl's head.

"Oh, you like the crown? Here, take it."

The queen decoronated herself and shoved what turned out to be a daintily-carved wooden decoration covered in silver leaf into her hands. Rena stared at it with a sense of soured triumph.

The crown of the Winter Queen, just like Titania had asked.

"This is all fucked up."

"We haven't even talked about how you're actually a fairy yet."

"Honestly, I was trying not to think about it."

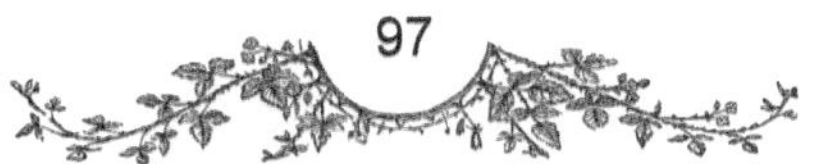

Mainly because the puzzle pieces were slotting together, one after another, making it clear that everything the 'Winter Queen' said was true.

Humans weren't magic...

She has no will of her own...

All my life, I've had this ability to make creatures from the fairy land do what I tell them...

The Winter Queen took me from my bed and left a changeling in my place...

"Gods damn it, I'm a fucking fairy."

"There's no sense in being angry about it. Do you know how many times I wished I wasn't human? The truth is, you are what you are. Live your best life."

"And how am I supposed to do that?"

"You were created by the Winter Queen. You have her will." Real-Rena tapped the silver adornment in Fairy-Rena's hand. "And her crown."

"So, you want me to become the Winter Queen? What about you?"

"I'm the rightful heir of Avalon, remember? I have a crown of my own waiting for me."

"You think you can survive in our father's court?"

Real-Rena's face lit up in a devious smile. "Probably better than you have. I've been watching you for a long time, and you never did learn the finer points of diplomacy. Why don't you leave the old man to me? And I'll leave the fairies to you?"

"I suppose that seems fair."

A human queen who'd learned trickery from the fae. A fairy queen who'd learned brutality from humans. Maybe, between the two of them, they could turn their respective worlds around.

Plus, she was pretty sure it would piss the Summer Queen off tremendously that her plan to rid herself of winter had borne a different, more delicious fruit.

"If you cross me, I'll ruin you," Fairy-Rena said.

"Spoken like a true queen of winter. Don't worry. You can keep watch over me, just like I did to you. That's just one of the secrets of the fae queens."

"Anything else I should know?"

"Yeah, don't trust Titania." Real-Rena's face screwed into a scowl. "She's a bitch."

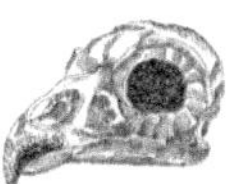

"Froza, maybe? Icerella? Snowanna? What kind of name should the Winter Queen have?"

One thing was for sure, she wasn't Rena. Since taking the throne and perching that little, wooden crown on her head, she'd ceased to be a changeling, ceased to be a copy of a human princess. Her hair had turned black like the midnight sky above, her skin white as fresh snow. The only thing that hadn't changed were those wintry eyes, but at least now they matched the rest.

"Maybe I'll just go by Winter."

She'd found the orb, a black glass eye that let her look through the veil into the human world. She missed Avalon—its trees, its valleys, its gentle rains, its people—but there were some advantages to being the Queen of Winter, like being able to clear a room with a simple, "Get out".

They listened to her here, in a way her father and his war-mongering cronies never had.

It looked like everyone was listening to Rena now too. The king had fallen ill—people whispered, very quietly, that he'd been poisoned—and his daughter had risen to the challenge of his vacant crown. She smiled so pleasantly in the throne room, but there was an edge to her benevolence, and Winter watched the drama unfold with barely-contained delight.

She really had been born to rule Avalon.

"You go, girl," she muttered, and let her focus slip away from the eye.

She retired to chambers fit for a queen, bare feet gliding over the icy floor. She didn't feel cold anymore. Or, it was more accurate to say, she *preferred* the cold. She'd spun herself robes of office from midnight and trimmed them with frost and her sword—she still preferred to carry one—was a peerless blade of unthawing ice.

She was about to call it a day, because she hadn't quite shaken the diurnal cycle of life in Avalon, when she realized there was someone in her bed.

"What the fuck are you doing here?"

Titania smiled and patted the mattress beside her. The black satin sheet was draped artfully over her hip, exposing a length of golden leg, and she was wearing a severely cut-down version of the sunlit dress she'd worn in the forest, what felt like a lifetime ago.

"I am here to congratulate you, dear. You brought me the Winter Queen's crown, just as I asked."

"I *am* the fucking Winter Queen."

"Yes, isn't it wonderful?"

"I thought you said you could only come here if you were invited."

"You invited me, dear. With the lust in your heart. How could I possibly refuse you? And, like any good lover, I will celebrate your coronation with you."

A coronation. She'd watched Rena's through the orb. It had been a long-winded, over-formal affair and she'd been very glad it hadn't been her ass in that chair for five hours. What did a fairy coronation look like?

Titania plucked the facsimile crown out of her hair. It turned to ash in her fingers and she blew it away with a smile and a laugh.

"That was mine!"

"You don't need it. You already have the crown of the Winter Court, infused into your spirit. You only needed to claim it."

The words were a riddle. A riddle that was answered a second later by a piercing agony in Winter's temples. She screamed and recoiled, one hand reaching for her head, the other for her sword. But there was no enemy to fight. The attack was coming from within.

She touched blood on her forehead, felt something hard curling out of her skin, like she was sprouting horns. They twisted and contorted, fusing together over her head, grinding against one another until her teeth ached and her eyeballs throbbed and she just wanted it to end. She'd have given *anything* for it to end.

Her hands slithered to the floor, keeping her from keeling over. She breathed hard, fighting to push away the enduring agony. Slowly, she clenched fists. Master of the pain. Master of herself.

She looked up, caught her reflection in the ice, and saw the silver coronet nestled in her hair.

"Poor Rena wasn't the only one watching you, my love. When I saw the kind of woman you were becoming, I knew I had to have you for myself. The old queen had become boring. She wasn't even trying anymore. All I needed was a compelling reason to bring you home. As you can see, my plan worked perfectly."

"Fuck you!"

"Would you like to? I am quite eager to know how your passion tastes."

Titania seized her by her crown and wrenched her to her feet. She studied her face, studied the blood trickling down her cheek like a crimson tear. She stole a drop of red away with her tongue and a rapturous heat bloomed in Winter's skin.

Then she shoved the Summer Queen back and leveled her sword.

"Get your fucking hands off the Queen of Winter."

Titania seemed surprised for a moment. She recovered herself quickly, touched the blood staining her lips.

"My... Still so willful. I see that you are going to be a great deal of fun."

"Why don't you come over here and I'll show you what fun looks like?"

Titania arched an eyebrow. Honestly, she looked like she was considering it. Instead, she chuckled.

"You cannot resist me forever, my love."

"No? Fucking watch me."

"Oh, I will. In every waking moment, I will be watching. And, when the time comes, I will come to claim you for my own. Until then, at least *try* to entertain me."

Winter crossed the distance between them in a surging heartbeat. She slashed the air and her blade turned to steaming water. Titania favored her with a glorious smile that recalled hips and lips in a sun-dappled forest pool.

Then she was gone, leaving Winter alone to her rule.

But, she realized, never truly alone.

In every waking moment, I will be watching...

The Voynich Puzzle

By Donna J. W. Munro

Loan spent his off-hours in the back of the camper writing about his wishes. There was magic in words. Bindings. Loan knew all about being bound.

"Get your ass over here, monster," Dan said, though the meanness of it softened when the man burped the word out.

"Fuck you," Loan said, grabbing a couple of brews out of the mini-fridge.

He tossed one at Dan, who plucked it out of the air and popped it with a deft flick of his hoof. He yawned before he took a swig, flashing his sharp, yellow teeth and split tongue as he did. Fat Dan, the Minotaur Man. The circus folks loved him. They assumed he'd tattooed his skin blue and body-modded the tongue, the teeth, the huge, curving horns that sprouted out of his forehead. He'd fit right in with the sword-swallowers and flame-eaters.

"Watch some shows? Breaking Bad? New Girl?" Dan asked.

His voice, usually booming and hard, became soft whenever they were alone in the camper together. Delicate and musical, with notes that made Loan's heart beat that quicker with every utterance. It was what he'd had fallen in love with about Dan in the first place, back when Loan had been made of rainbows and feathers, and ran as fast as song and flew as high as the ruby dunes of Sargosen.

He was tempted to plop down next to Dan and lay his head against his strong shoulder, let him run the edges of his hooves against the soft skin of his inner arm. He shook his head. The work. He had so much to do.

"Later? I have to—"

"I know." Dan shifted forward, rolling his belly up before him like a ball. He'd been hard muscle once. Sleek and terrifying. But the love they had and this place had made him soft. Maybe it was the lack of predators of the dark who'd hunted him in the passages, or the heroes trying to cut off his head for his ivory and a trophy. Or maybe it was just because he liked donuts and Big Macs. Who could say? "Why do you bother though? No one will understand the stories but us."

Loan nodded. "You worry about me? That I'll slide into madness or disappear?"

It was a joke, but the way Dan looked at him... He was sorry he'd reminded him what could happen.

"Do you want to go back? Please don't make me. I can't go back, Loan. No matter how bad it is here. I just—"

"Don't worry, Dan. I'd never do that to you. I love you more than I loved my feathers and the wind."

Dan's features warmed with happiness and Loan knew he'd said the right words, even if every one was a lie.

Nothing was better than the wind.

He kissed Dan between the horns and then on the lips. A good kiss that cemented what he'd said about love. "See you in bed."

Dan nodded and turned back to surfing through canceled shows and reruns, just a Minotaur Man winding down from a long day of work.

How appropriate.

He and Dan were canceled shows themselves.

The carnival midway no longer used freaks to thrill the patrons. It wasn't done in this age of enlightened entertainments. The old freakshows closed, but many of the performers stuck around. There weren't many places for them where they'd be truly accepted. The strong men and the geeks ran the rides. The conjoined twin girls, Noni and Roni, ran the cotton candy stand. Dan fed the horses and the dogs that worked in the show. He spread hay and carried tall piles of crates, but didn't interact with the townies anymore. Loan worked the ticket booth, and sometimes he ran messages between the main tent and the trailers.

He could still run.

The bitter taste of disappointment washed away the lingering sweetness of Dan's kiss. No matter how hard he ran in this lanky, bald body, it never thrilled him like it had before. The push of the breeze against his cheeks felt like nothing compared to the memory of blasting whirlwind wakes he made during real runs across the desert passes. Running here was nothing like flight along the shifting, orange sand of home.

He moved through the narrow trailer, back into the bedroom they shared. It was just a bed, a little closet, and a tiny desk with a sheet of parchment rolled out and held by smooth, iridescent rocks lit from within by a spark of home. Precious stones he'd once kept inside his stomach to help grind off the armor of beezel bugs and carnot thistles. In this body and in this place, they'd just been rocks he'd expelled in his afterbirth on this world.

He picked up a soft quill out of the desk drawer, the only of his scarlet feathers that had made the passage with them.

Why had he lost his body when Dan got to keep his? The old resentment flared up, consuming the love he'd nursed.

There was magic in words. Bindings.

He was counting on that.

Loan dipped his quill in amber ink and began to scratch their story onto the parchment, using letters that only those of his world would know. He poured this story onto the paper again, this time explaining the herbs used to trap him and Dan in the labyrinth. How Dan's starvation made him hunt anything that moved, and only Loan's wings and fleet feet kept him alive long enough to hear Dan sing.

Every night, after the killing ended, Dan retreated to the middle of his maze. Loan followed, slipping up over the walls, perching there, watching with his sharp eyes and tilting, sleek head.

Dan would warble and sob, then his mouth would open and the sweetest tones of mournful music flowed from his gore-streaked lips. How Dan hated himself then. His songs had no words, since none had been taught to him, but any creature with a soul would have felt the desperation in the notes, the loathing and loneliness that wound through Dan's melodies.

Loan fell in love and sang back.

Loan's scratching quill paused as he remembered those weeks of chasing, singing, and making love. No one had ever loved Dan. They'd feared him. Hidden him. Used him. And Loan's own people hadn't known how to save him from the nets that had caught him. They'd blamed him for being slow as they abandoned him to his fate. Two rejects in hell.

Wasn't until the masters of the maze had thrown a wise man into the depths that the gentled Dan and Loan learned how to escape.

"Bright lovers," the man had said, "I've been to another world. One not as beautiful as this, but safer. Peaceful. You might find the sun there, together."

Dan's eyes had lit like lamps. He'd never seen the sun in his whole life.

"There's a price to be paid, my friends," he said. "If I send you through, you'll never see these red hills, purple sunsets—"

"I've never seen those," Dan said, sadness a tone he couldn't shake.

"And you, my bright bird. You will never run with the wind again."

"But we will be together?" Loan had asked, blinded by his love and longing for an escape. A happy ending for them both where, for so long, there'd only been darkness, hunger, and mourning to punctuate their time together.

"Yes. I've been there. I found that the bright pain of this world is better than that one. That I wanted the cannibal plants and the drowning goddesses that pull you to your own watery death more than I wanted peace. I had been trapped for years, but I wrote about the plants and the goddesses, over and over. I spilled all I knew with a clumsy hand onto the pages to get the doors to open. To come back home. I wrote because words have magic. The right words bind and loose and remake the world."

The elder picked up a stick and wrote some words, and the wall swirled like a pool of bright stars in the night sky. Dan pulled Loan's hand into the crook of his arm and smiled at him. It couldn't be that bad in another place, could it? Not as long as they were together. Loan had many fears, but the thought of them being together kept him moving forward.

Through the portal the elder made for them.

Through the portal into the muddy, blue skies littered with grey clouds. The customs of towns and cities with belching smoke and brown rivers snaking through them. People. Only people who spoke. Birds that lived in cages. Animals behind bars. The transition was...hard.

For Dan, the first thirty or forty years were bliss. They'd found the carnival, and people accepted them, mostly. They'd traded one prison for another, though they had each other and the sun.

This sun? This weak, yellow thing that washed the world in a cheery brightness that never really warmed Loan's quick-beating blood? Dan had never felt the triple sun, the deep thrumming heat that lasted all day. He'd never preened and perched in the setting of the three, their light exploding in vivid beauty against the sandy hills, rising again before they ever went completely away.

For Dan, the dark of the night was normal. His maze had been lit only by false stars and fire torches.

For Loan, dark was death come to visit every night.

He scratched these thoughts in the ancient writing, letters perfect and squared, on the page.

The old man had told them he'd gotten home by spilling all the words on the pages. All the memories and everything he knew. Writing every detail and remembering. Every night, that's what Loan did.

And he'd also tracked down the old man's book.

Called the Voynich Manuscript, it was a crude thing made six hundred years before. The humans who studied it thought it was a witch's book or a madman's ramble. Some thought it to be ancient wisdom. They took pictures of the pages and put them on their internet. Loan read them for what they were. Wishes to go home.

"Loan, come to bed," Dan said, suddenly on the bed.

Loan shook off the depth of his wishing and dropped the quill, then turned to his lover.

Dan's hands, breath and kisses enfolded Loan in almost enough heat, almost enough wind, to keep him from wishing. Almost.

Afterward, when Dan's breath whistled through his wide nostrils and his eyes twitched with dreams of his own, Loan returned to his writing. As much as he'd wanted their great love to be enough, it wasn't. Not when his skin itched from the lack of feathers. Not when he'd never fly again.

He picked up the quill and scratched away at the parchment, filling it up with his memories, pictures and power.

The old man had made over three hundred of these pages, leaving his lover to find them when he'd disappeared one night without a kind word or a kiss goodbye. The endnotes, written by the abandoned lover, told Loan that the split between them had torn at the abandoned one's heart for many years, but that he'd understood finally. Perhaps he'd always known that the old man's soul didn't belong to this dull place.

Loan hoped Dan would eventually find peace when Loan's own words bound a magic doorway.

Once, Dan had said, "What if you did go back? Do you think you'd have your feathers and wings if you went back there? Do you think just because you returned...?"

He'd trailed off and turned away, probably because the words were so hurtful.

The universe couldn't be so cruel, could it?

There was always a consolation, even if there was a terrible price.

Loan kept writing, because there was magic in words.

And he still knew how to fly.

FAERIE FIRES
BY FRANK SAWIELIJEW

Brianna's horse refused to go into the forest. It bucked and brayed and she felt its thick muscles tremble between her thighs. She steered it toward the nearby river and dismounted. She gently stroked its flank and whispered calming words into its ear. With the dreaded forest out of sight, the horse relaxed and lowered its head to drink.

Brianna tied its reins to a young tree and said, "I don't want to go either, old boy, but I have no choice."

She ran a hand through her short-cropped hair and took a deep breath. It was drenched with sweat. Wet strands stuck to her forehead. The Faewood exuded an atmosphere of dread that set her warrior's instincts on edge. Only few slivers of moonlight managed to penetrate the dense canopy and illumined the treacherous underbrush with its tangled roots, thorny bushes and slippery moss. Every fiber in Brianna's body urged her not to enter.

With her fingers wrapped tight around her sword's hilt, she crossed the threshold into the Faewood. A gust of wind rustled the leaves, and their stirring sounded almost like a hoarse chuckle. As she went deeper, the sky vanished completely behind the tangled ceiling of branches and leaves. Swarms of fireflies bathed the forest in an otherworldly glow, the only source of light in this dark labyrinth of trees and thorns.

One swarm gathered around her, buzzing to and fro before her eyes, a mass of fluttering lights against the dark canvas of the wood. As she swung her hand to swat them away, they moved forward, forming a beacon in front of her. When she resumed her march, the fireflies went ahead, showing her the way.

Brianna decided to follow their lead, as she had nothing else to guide her. They led her across rough terrain, where thick, gnarled roots and jagged moss-covered rocks caused her to stumble and stagger. In the dim light of the firefly swarm, she could barely see the ground underfoot. And as if the lack of visibility was not enough, the roots seemed to be alive, writhing and wriggling as she stepped on them. When she tripped over and fell to her knees, the rustling leaves snickered at her mishap.

The journey was long and tiring. The fireflies led Brianna on a winding path that made her lose all sense of direction. Finally, after what felt like hours, a portal appeared out of nowhere. Between two tall oaks rose an arch of twisted branches, flowering with red, blue and purple blossoms, petals glowing with mystical light—the gate to the realm of faerie. Her guiding fireflies gathered around the portal and landed among the luminous blossoms.

Brianna approached it cautiously. Soft whispers reached her ears, but whether it was the wind or something else, she could not tell. Behind the arch, a man stood leaning on a gnarled, flint-tipped spear. His skin was grey as ash, his hair and beard black as coal. Two long, twisted horns protruded from his forehead and his eyes were pools of blackness, darker even than the benighted forest.

He pointed his spear at Brianna and said, "Halt, mortal! Beyond this portal lies the realm of fae. It is not meant to be seen by mortal eyes." He raised his spear to her face, its jagged, flint tip hovering dangerously close to her eyes. "Are you a wanderer who lost her way, or do you come with purpose?"

Her fingers wrapped tight around the grip of her sword. The spear was so close she felt a tingle at the bridge of her nose.

"I come with purpose," she said.

He lowered his spear and some of the tension left Brianna's muscles, but her heart still beat fast in her chest.

"And what purpose might that be?"

"I come to ask for help... And I'm willing to offer something in return."

A mischievous grin formed on the fae's lips, revealing a set of sharp, yellowed teeth. "How delightful! It is always such a joy to strike a deal with mortals. Go and meet our queen so she may hear your proposal!"

Brianna took a deep breath and mouthed a silent thank you. She knew she would come to regret this, but she had no other choice. It was their last resort; a final desperate attempt to prevail against impossible odds. Only the dark magic of fae could save the lord she served.

And the lady she loved.

She stepped through the portal, but felt the sharp flint against her chest and froze in place.

"Wait!" said the guard, pointing at the sword on her belt. "You carry iron. That vile metal is not permitted within our lands. The winged ones will dispose of it, and then you may continue on your way."

Whispers carried by the wind again reached Brianna's ears. There was playful laughter in those voices, and they seemed to come from the bushes and trees. Their leaves rustled with commotion.

Suddenly, small winged women emerged from the foliage, wielding little blades of silver in their tiny hands. They had rosy, human-like skin and flitted through the air on bright butterfly wings. Their eyes were little beads of purple light, glimmering with mischief. They circled around Brianna and tugged at her clothes. One wrapped its arms around the sheath of her sword and pulled at it.

"There's the iron! Vile iron!"

"Take it! Take it! Throw it away and turn it to dust!"

One of the little women hovered before her face and wagged an accusing finger at her. "Iron is nasty and cold! You should not have brought it to these lands so bold!"

"Take it! Throw it away!"

A sharp, silver blade sliced through her belt and one of the little faeries took it away, vanishing into the bushes.

Brianna would have to face the queen of fae unarmed. She swallowed the lump in her throat and asked, "May I proceed now?"

"No! No! Your clothes! How can you wear such dreadful things?"

"She is covered from head to toe! How rough the fabric is, and ugly!"

"She cannot face our queen like this! Hideous!"

"Take it off her! Take it off!"

The little faeries cut into her tunic with their silver knives, ripping out large chunks of cloth and tossing them into the air. Shreds of red fabric sailed down like falling autumn leaves. Brianna tried to shoo them off, twisting and turning, but the faeries laughed and cheered, thinking her movements to be a dance. They flew around her in circles, cutting and tearing at her tunic, her trousers, even her leather boots until they were all reduced to shreds.

"Much better!" said one of the faeries when she beheld Brianna's naked form. "Look at her beauty!"

"And how she can dance!"

"Our queen will love her!"

"Go! Go to our queen! She wants to see you, lovely mortal!"

"Yes! Go! Our queen awaits you!"

The winged faeries vanished back into the foliage, giggling with excitement. Their voices receded as they went away, turning into a barely audible whisper on the wind again.

"Follow the path and you will find her throne," said the guard and pointed his spear at a path of smooth flagstones leading deeper into the realm of fae. "She will hear your offer now."

"Thank you," said Brianna, and set out on the path, naked and unarmed.

She knew the fae were mischievous tricksters who loved to toy with mortals. What was a tragedy to men was joyful comedy to the fae. Had there been any other way to save her lord and her beloved, she would never have come here.

But it was the only chance they had left.

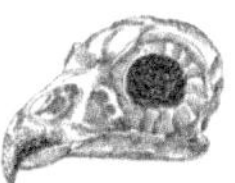

The heart of the faerie realm was not dark like the outer Faewood. It was a large clearing in the middle of the gloomy forest, illumined by thousands of little lights floating through the air like glowing specks of dust. They gleamed in countless, vibrant shades of blue, green and purple, bathing the landscape in a kaleidoscopic dance of colors.

The way to the faerie queen's throne led past a shimmering lake, alive with the midnight song of frogs and crickets. Glittering dragonflies the size of rabbits hovered over the still, calm water. This place had a supernatural beauty to it, and had she not known any better, Brianna would have found it inviting.

But she could still hear the laughter of the winged faeries on the wind, and the oppressive gloom of the surrounding forest was felt even here, despite the illusion of peaceful calm.

Her bare feet followed the path of cool, smooth stone until she reached the throne of the faerie queen. It stood in the center of a large mushroom circle and was grown from living roots, moving and twisting even as the queen sat on it. Large balls of orange light circled above the throne, illuminating its surroundings with a warm, inviting glow like that of candles. Armed guards flanked the throne on either side, clad in armor made of thick bark and bearing flint spears.

Brianna approached the throne and bowed before the queen of faerie. She sat naked on her throne of roots and beheld her mortal visitor with eyes that shone like a pair of sparkling sapphires. Her skin was a pale purple, and the long hair that cascaded down her body and covered her nakedness was dark maroon, with fresh, green leaves and brightly colored blossoms woven into it. The nails on her fingers and toes were black and sharp as claws.

"Queen of faerie, I seek your aid," said Brianna.

"Most mortals avoid these lands, yet you seek me out." The queen's

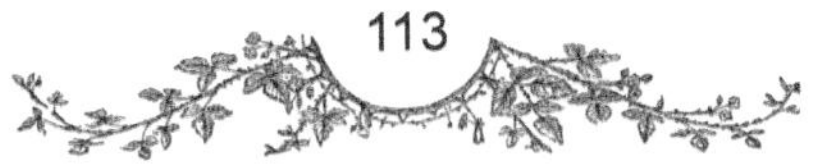

sapphire eyes gleamed with curiosity. "What is it that brings you here?"

"I serve Duke Niall of Gavendir. His castle is under siege by a conquering army, vast in number and known for their brutality. If they prevail, my lord and his family will be enslaved, his lands devastated, his servants slain. Our attempts to repel the besiegers were of no success. The dark magic of fae is our last hope."

"You brave the Faewood to save your lord. Such loyalty and devotion! How delightful!" The queen rose from her throne and took a step towards her mortal supplicant. "I will gladly make a deal with you, brave mortal. State your request and what you are willing to give in return, and I will consider it."

"I want you to prevent the enemy from taking my lord's castle." Brianna paused. Despite the cool breeze and her lack of clothing, her entire body was covered in sweat. Everything within her screamed at her not to say it, to run away and abandon this mad endeavor, but she forced the words out. They emerged in a shaking whisper. "And I am willing to give you anything in return. Anything you wish."

The faerie queen laughed with great mirth, and the giggles of the winged faeries joined her on the wind. "Anything for your lord! He is lucky to have such a devoted servant. Are you aware what you are offering?"

Brianna closed her eyes and took a deep breath. It seemed like the world stood still for a moment. She was well aware of the wicked nature of fae, but there was much at stake.

She had no other choice.

She nodded.

The queen of faerie pointed a finger at Brianna's bare chest and whispered a word of magic. Her claw-like nail grew long and stabbed into Brianna's flesh, penetrating all the way to her nervously pounding heart.

Brianna let out a pained gasp, but after just a moment the claw retracted again, leaving not a single mark on her skin. But on the faerie queen's fingertip sat a single drop of blood, taken straight from Brianna's heart.

The queen lapped up the drop of heartblood with her tongue. Within the innermost secrets of Brianna's heart, the faerie queen sought an appropriate reciprocation for her aid. Her sapphire eyes glimmered with inner light as she dug through Brianna's brightest hopes and darkest fears.

"Oh, what a delicious secret I discovered," the queen said after a while, her voice sweet with delight. "You and the duchess are lovers, and your lord knows not of it! A secret affair full of passion and longing..."

Brianna swallowed the lump that built in her throat. Beloved Muireann. She treasured her more than anything else in life.

"Yes," she managed weakly. "I love the duchess."

"There is great power in love," said the queen. She paused, savoring the growing look of despair in Brianna's eyes. "There is even greater power in death."

Brianna did not respond, but she knew what the faerie queen was going to ask.

"Give me the life of your beloved, and I will make it so your lord's castle will never be taken by any foe."

The offer hung in the air, ready for Brianna to grasp. The magic of fae was powerful enough to change reality at a whim. It was the only way to save the lord she served, but the price was unbearable. The mere thought of taking sweet Muireann's life sent cold shivers down her spine and painful aches through her heart.

The otherworldly beauty of the faerie queen's face was slashed with a sharp-toothed smile of pure mischief. Her offer had given Brianna no way out, and she knew it. To accept would mean the death of her beloved at her own hands, but to reject would mean her enslavement at the hands of the enemy. Whichever choice she made, it would haunt her for years to come.

Brianna's voice was shaky when she replied, "I accept. Her life for your aid."

She could hear laughter on the wind again, dozens of mirthful voices giggling and whispering.

What was tragedy to men was comedy to fae.

"Then my aid you shall have. Take this knife and use it to cut out your lover's heart." The queen gestured towards a bush, and a winged faerie emerged bearing a silver blade as long as she was tall. The little faerie giggled joyfully as she placed the knife in Brianna's outstretched palms.

"You must kill her while you embrace her with a lover's kiss," the queen demanded. "There is power in love; there is power in death. Give me her life while it radiates with love, and I promise that the power of my magic will be equally great."

Brianna looked at the knife in her hands. It was an elegant weapon, hilt decorated with floral designs and blade curved like the crescent moon. It was so sharp that a single touch drew blood.

"Yes," said Brianna. "I will do as you ask."

Even if it cost Muireann's life, it would guarantee the freedom of her husband and son, the continuation of her bloodline and legacy. Brianna knew it would break her heart beyond repair, but it was the lesser of two evils.

The faerie queen clapped her hands and shouted, "A deal has been struck! The mortal is to be considered a friend of fae and shall be treated as such! Bring her gifts and garments worthy of an honored guest!"

Winged faeries swarmed from the bushes and trees. Three of them carried a green garment which they pulled over Brianna's head, a knee-length dress of soft fabric, adorned with colorful, floral patterns. Two of them carried leather sandals which they strapped onto her feet. Another fastened a belt around Brianna's waist, with a sheath for the silver dagger. The last of the little faeries sat down on Brianna's head and combed her fingers through her short-cropped hair. It grew longer under her touch, laying itself over her ears, descending down past her shoulders.

Brianna tried to shoo the faerie away with her hands. "Leave my hair alone! It's long enough as it is!"

The faerie jumped off her head with a giggle, but kept pulling at her hair until it reached all the way down to her waist.

"You should not reject the gifts of fae, mortal," said the queen. "There is great magic in them, and you will be thankful for it when the time comes."

The other winged faeries started to weave flowers into Brianna's new hair, colorful blossoms of red, blue, yellow and violet. When they were done they vanished back into the bushes, but their laughter remained in the air.

The queen of faerie approached her mortal guest and offered her a pouch. "Before you go, take this gift as proof of our friendship. In this pouch you will find a handful of faerie dust. Use it when the situation is dire and it will lead you to safety."

Brianna accepted the gift wordlessly and turned around. She tied the pouch to her belt and headed back towards the portal through which she had entered the world of fae. The colorful lights that had seemed so inviting on her way in now seemed to mock her with their joyful radiance. The faerie queen's magic was hers, but the cost was more than she could bear. She quickened her pace and broke into a run, wanting to get out of this accursed place. The laughter of the faeries, amused at her plight, followed her all the way to the portal.

As soon as she passed through the gate, she was back at the bank of the river where she had left her horse. The dark Faewood was behind her, and even though her journey had taken hours, the moon and stars were in the same position as before and no sun showed on the eastern horizon. It was as if she had awakened from a bad dream.

But it had been no dream. Her hair was now long and decorated with flowers, and her muscular body was clad in the elegant dress of fae. The sword at her belt was gone, replaced with a silver knife intended for her beloved's heart.

She knelt down at the riverbank and rinsed her face with the cool, clear water. It streamed down her cheeks like tears, but she did not allow any tears to come. She had to be strong—for Niall, her lord, and for Muireann, her love.

She mounted her horse and set out for castle Gavendir. Her lord and lady awaited her return, and she bore news that the queen of faerie had accepted the deal.

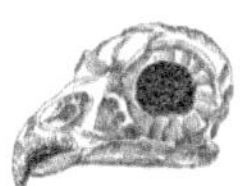

The sun rose in the east, peeking out above the forested hills and coloring the clouds a deep orange. The besiegers stirred in their camp, getting ready for another day of soldierly routine. Cooking fires sent pillars of smoke into the sky as the cooks prepared breakfast for a ravenous army. They had robbed the granaries of Gavendir's villages, leaving their peasants to starve while they feasted on fresh bread, salted beef and mutton.

Brianna kept her distance, careful to avoid the eyes of their sentries. The castle stood atop a hill, mighty stone walls reaching up to the sky. A hidden door at the foot of the hill, obscured by dense shrubbery, led into the secret tunnel that had allowed her to slip out unseen. It was located at the other side of the castle, where the hill was steepest. The camp of the besiegers, with its improvised wooden barricades and watchtowers, was erected near the castle's front gate to block any attempted sally of the defenders. They paid little attention to the opposite side, where the hill was too steep to climb and the massive stone wall unbroken by gate or passage.

Brianna circled around the camp of the besiegers and made for the secret passage on the steep side of the hill. As she approached the castle wall, visions of her beloved Muireann and the grim task that was before her invaded her thoughts, images of blood on her hands and an unfathomable guilt on her conscience.

So distracted was she by these thoughts, the patrolling soldiers managed to catch her by complete surprise. She felt the tip of a pike pressing into her thigh and her battle-trained horse kicked out at the assailers.

Brianna reached for her sword but found it missing. She glanced at her belt in confusion and remembered. All the faerie queen had given her was the silver dagger, much too short for fighting on horseback.

But then her fingers found the pouch, and she recalled the queen's words. If ever she found herself in trouble, the faerie dust would lead her to safety.

She reached into the pouch and drew out some of the dust, which she tossed at her attackers. They shielded their eyes, blinded by its sparkling radiance, and her horse broke into a sudden gallop. Enchanted by the faerie dust, its hooves trod the air as if it were solid ground. Brianna felt like she was riding on the wings of a bird as her steed took to the sky.

The defenders manning the wall stared at the horse in awe as it sailed over their heads and touched down in the courtyard.

Brianna dismounted and examined the wound in her thigh. It was bleeding, but it hadn't cut very deep. Compared to the searing pain in her heart, she barely felt it.

Muireann...

"Halt! Who—? Lady Brianna?" The guard who approached her with sword drawn froze, surprised by her appearance. "I didn't recognize you. Your hair—"

Brianna offered a smile. "I met with the queen of faerie. Please – tell me where I can find Duke Niall and his wife. I must speak with them immediately."

"The queen of... Of course! They are taking their breakfast in the dining hall." His eyes lit up with newfound hope. "Does this mean the faeries agreed to help us?"

Brianna turned away and headed to the dining hall without answering his question. Her flower-adorned hair billowed behind her as she quickened her pace, eager to see her beloved duchess again. To look deep into her eyes, hear her sweet voice, feel the warmth of her touch one last time before...

She couldn't finish the thought. It pained her too much.

She barged into the dining hall and announced her presence. "My Lord, I return from the realm of faerie."

Duke Niall was seated at the long dining table next to his wife, Muireann, and their son, Donall. Brianna had intruded upon their simple breakfast of oats, cheese and cured ham, and they stared at her with incredulous eyes.

When recognition dawned on him, Niall rose from his chair to welcome his most faithful knight. "Brianna! Your clothes, your hair... Did the fae strike a deal with you? Are they willing to help?"

Brianna closed her eyes and took a deep breath. A voice deep within her told her to say no—that there was no deal, that they had to survive this siege on their own. But when she opened her eyes again and saw the hopeful look on her lord's face, she knew there was no other choice. One life would pay for the freedom and prosperity of not only Niall and his heir, but the entire duchy of Gavendir.

"Yes, my Lord. They have agreed to protect the castle from the ruthless conquerors. Their magic will keep us safe."

Niall sighed with relief, all the tension built up through weeks of uncertainty gone in a single breath. "That is wonderful news, Brianna. I didn't even dare to hope, but..." He left the rest unsaid. The look in his face said enough; a great burden had been lifted from his shoulders, and he could finally breathe easy again.

"I knew you could do it," said Muireann, her beautiful voice sweet as honey to Brianna's ears. "I always believed in you."

"What did the fae ask in return?" asked Donall. At sixteen years of age he was still young and his thin, blond beard had not spread to his cheeks yet, but he was a clever boy who knew much of the world and its workings.

"I gave them something dear to my heart," Brianna answered, without meeting his gaze. She stared at the wall between Donall's and Muireann's shoulders, unable to look either in the eye.

"How do you know they'll keep their end of the deal?" the boy asked. "The fae love to toy with mortals. What if they took your offering and gave only false hope in return?"

Brianna shook her head. "They gave me gifts as proof of their friendship... And the queen seemed sincere when she offered me her aid. They'll keep their end."

As long as I keep mine, she thought.

Niall put a hand on his son's shoulder and chuckled. "Always the skeptic, my good son. But I understand his doubts. I can hardly believe it myself. You met the queen of faerie herself? What did she tell you? When is she going to send help?"

"Their magic must be invoked with a ritual," Brianna said. She needed an excuse to be with Muireann alone, so they could embrace each other as lovers. One last time. "May I speak to milady Muireann in private? The magic of fae requires...feminine energies. We must work it alone."

"Of course." Niall looked at his wife and showed her an encouraging smile. "Go with Brianna, my dear. I trust her to keep you safe through this invocation."

"I trust her too, my love," said Muireann. "I know she will protect me with her life."

She left the dinner table and led Brianna upstairs into her bedchamber. They had met here many times before, two secret lovers whose affair was unknown to all but themselves.

Today, they would meet here for the very last time.

As soon as Muireann had closed the door behind her, Brianna fell upon her with a tight embrace and allowed her tears to fall freely onto her lover's shoulders.

"I love you, Muireann. I love you more than anything in the world."

Muireann wrapped her arms around the sobbing Brianna and stroked a hand through her long hair.

"Shh, be calm. All is well now. You're here in my arms. There is nothing to fear." She stood in silence for a while, offering Brianna a steady frame to hold onto. When Brianna's breathing had steadied again, she said, "I saw it in your eyes when you entered the dining hall. Something is wrong."

She removed herself from Brianna's embrace and took a step back. Her hand touched Brianna's chin and tilted it upward until their eyes met.

"I like your new hair," she said, with a warm smile, "but what else have they changed?"

Brianna wiped the tears from her cheeks and shook her head. "They didn't change me; they just... Oh, Muireann, please hold me! The faerie queen asked a heavy price in exchange for her aid. She asked for my heart."

"Your heart?" Muireann put a hand on Brianna's breast and felt the rapid beat beneath. "She will take your life?"

"Not my life, but my love." She looked Muireann in the eyes, those deep blue eyes in which she could lose herself for hours. It hurt to lie to her, but she couldn't tell her the truth. "The love between us will be gone after the ritual. That is the price she demanded."

"Oh, Brianna. There is no magic in this world that could ever extinguish my love for you."

She embraced Brianna again and placed a kiss on her lips. Those soft, loving lips melted all sorrows away from Brianna's weary mind and released the tension from her stiff muscles. They pressed their bodies close to each other and bathed in each other's warmth.

This was the Muireann she loved—passionate, loving, full of life and happiness. But visions of her in chains intruded into Brianna's mind. Disgusting men at a faraway slave market, haggling over her beloved like peasants haggled over cows. Niall and Donall carried elsewhere, all separated from each other, never to meet again. Gavendir in ruins, its walls reduced to rubble and its people dispersed to the four corners of the Earth.

The vision strengthened Brianna's resolve. To die in a moment of happiness was a better fate than to live as a slave, separated from one's land and family.

"Summoning the might of the fae involves a ritual of love," she whispered into Muireann's ear. "For there is great power in love."

Muireann understood. They sat down on the bed and kissed again, a passionate kiss filled with mutual desire. Their tongues fenced with each other in a playful duel while their hands went underneath their garments and explored each other's bodies.

Their lovemaking was a passionate dance of skillful fingers on soft, sensitive skin. Brianna allowed herself to drown in the warmth of her beloved until she felt as if their bodies were not two separate beings but one. Her heart sang in joy as their two souls danced in unison to the rhythm of their pulse.

At the height of their passion, she pulled the dagger from her belt and drove it into Muireann's chest. The silver blade slid effortlessly through her flesh. A red rivulet sprang from the wound, running between Muireann's breasts like a river between two hills. Streams of tears emerged from Brianna's eyes and fell down like waterfalls, mingling with Muireann's blood.

Brianna inserted her hands into the wound and broke away the ribs to lay bare her beloved's heart. Shock and terror stared through Muireann's eyes into Brianna's, and each cry of pain felt like a needle's stab into her own heart. But when her fingers closed around the heart, she thought she could see understanding dawn in Muireann's face. Her beloved's lips twitched upward in a final smile, as if she accepted her sacrifice with peace of mind.

With the silver blade in her right hand, Brianna severed the arteries, and with her left she lifted her beloved Muireann's still-beating heart out of her ravaged chest.

"Here is her heart, accursed fae!" she screamed. "I kept my part of the deal. Now come and fulfill yours!"

A stiff breeze came through the window and she heard the faerie queen's mirthful laughter on the wind. The flowers in her hair untangled themselves from her tresses and sped into the air on butterfly wings, turning into little, winged faeries before Brianna's eyes. The floral patterns on her dress jumped out of the fabric and mingled in the air, dancing around each other until they turned into a prancing satyr whose goat-like hooves clattered loudly on the wooden floor. The straps of her sandals unlaced themselves and grew into winged serpents with sharp teeth and flaming breath.

Brianna stared at the spectacle with wide-open eyes.

"You... You've come to protect the castle," she said. "The faerie queen kept her word."

The satyr gave a bleating snicker. "Yes, yes, we've come. We will make it so your castle will never be taken by any foe, no matter how fierce. Go on, little ones! Do your work!"

The serpents sailed up on their leathery wings, ascending to the ceiling high above. They cast their fiery breath upon the heavy wooden beams until they were aflame. The winged faeries flitted from place to place and cast strange magics upon the masonry, stones breaking apart and crumbling into sand under their touch.

Brianna sat helplessly and watched as the creatures of fae laid waste to the room.

"But...we had a deal!" she yelled hoarsely. "You said you would aid us! You promised!"

The deep wound in Muireann's chest moved like a pair of lips, and Brianna almost fell from the bed in shock when she heard it talk. It spoke with the voice of the faerie queen.

I said I would prevent your enemy from taking the castle, and so it is being done. Once your castle is reduced to smoldering ruin, no foe will ever deign to conquer it. The besiegers will break camp and move on without setting a single foot inside these walls.

Of course. They had tricked her, and now they laughed at her fate.

What was tragedy to men was comedy to fae.

Brianna sat motionless on the bed, the lifeless body of her beloved beside her, as her world burned. Searing flames consumed the castle's woodwork and she heard walls collapse in the distance as the faeries went from room to room, turning solid stone into fleeting grains. The desperate screams of men and the mischievous laughter of fae echoed through the collapsing halls of Castle Gavendir. Brianna sat and waited for the roof to collapse and bury her; there was nothing left to fight for. To share a grave with Muireann was the last solace she had left.

But then, screams from a familiar voice reached her ears and returned life to her. Niall. Donall. They were still alive. They could still be saved.

Brianna jumped from the bed and ran towards the source of the shouting. Her bare feet slapped against the cold stone as she sped down the stairs. When she reached the dining hall, she emerged into an inferno of raging flames. Niall and Donall were somewhere in there, but she could barely see through the thick, black smoke that filled the hall.

"Niall! Donall! Where are you? I can't see!"

"Brianna! Over here!"

It was Donall's voice, hoarse from the smoke he had inhaled. She climbed over a collapsed wooden pillar, still alive with writhing flames, and a pile of rubble that cut into her bare soles with its jagged shards of stone.

Donall was lying on the floor, right leg pinned under a wooden beam that had fallen from the ceiling.

"Donall! Thank the gods, you're still alive! Where's your father?"

Donall pointed to his right, and Brianna felt another stab through her heart when she spotted her lord's mangled corpse. The same beam that pinned Donall's leg had smashed his father's head, contorting his face into a grotesque grimace.

"Where's mother?" Donall asked. He saw the blood on Brianna's hands, red up to the wrists. "Did she make it?"

Brianna did not answer. Could not answer. Even thinking about what had happened to Muireann made her nauseous and brought her to the edge of unconsciousness, and she had to stay focused.

She tried to lift the beam from Donall's leg, but it was too heavy even for her strong arms. Again and again, she strained her muscles against it, but it did not move an inch. With each breath, smoke filled her air-hungry lungs, and with each attempt at lifting the heavy beam, her arms grew weaker.

Donall said, "Leave me. Go and save yourself."

"No," Brianna replied, under heavy coughs. "I can't."

It was her fault. All of this was her fault. Saving Donall was her only chance at redemption, and she would rather die in the attempt than give up. But her strength was waning and her arms alone could not free the young man's leg. If only she had a tool...

Brianna touched her belt and found the pouch of fairy dust dangling at her hip. She tore it away and poured its entire contents on the heavy wood. The magic dust caused the heavy beam to float up like a weightless cloud, and she pulled Donall to his feet before it fell back down.

He couldn't walk on his crushed leg, so she had to carry him outside. The courtyard was filled with screaming men and women, guards and servants alike running in panic, the fire-spitting serpents chasing them, setting their clothes and hair on fire. The granary, the armory, the servants' quarters, the main hall—not one building of the castle was spared by the flames. Roaring flames devoured everything they touched with ravenous hunger. Brianna ignored the screaming around her and headed towards the secret passage that led out of the castle. All that mattered was bringing Donall to safety.

She cursed when she found the passage blocked, a pile of crumbled bricks and stones covering the entrance.

"It's alright," said Donall. The weariness in his voice made him sound much older than his years. "A duke should go down with his castle."

Brianna shook her head. "I'll get you out of here. I have to."

She looked to and fro, searching for another way out of the burning castle. To her right, she spotted a section of wall that had partially collapsed. The breach was wide enough to allow a man to pass.

"Over there. The hole in the wall. Come on."

She got to her knees and climbed through the breach, and Donall followed. Brianna offered him a helping hand but he refused, too proud to let himself be dragged. He pulled himself up with his hands, supported himself with his good leg while his wounded leg dangled uselessly below. They pushed themselves through the narrow gap in the stonework and reached the other side, atop the steepest side of the hill where the castle was built.

"We have to slide down the hill. Your leg..."

"I'll manage."

Donall went first, grinding his elbows into the soil to slow his descent. He caught the impact with his good leg, but still grunted in pain. Brianna followed and landed next to him.

They sat at the foot of the hill for a while, catching their breath. Neither of them spoke a word.

Until Donall broke the silence.

"Why?"

Because I was a fool, Brianna thought. But she said, "The faerie queen tricked us. Her fires were supposed to chase away our foe, but instead..."

She left the thought unfinished. She didn't want to think about this mess anymore. Every muscle in her body ached with exhaustion, but her heart most of all.

Muireann. Beloved Muireann.

"Can you walk?" she asked her beloved's only son.

"If you support me."

Brianna helped him up and put an arm around his shoulder. Together, they walked away into the rising sun, leaving their burning home behind.

"What happened up there?" Donall asked, after a while. The hand Brianna had on his shoulder stained his tunic with blood. "To mother? To you?"

"I'm sorry, Donall." A tear rolled down her cheek, washing away the stains of blood and smoke on her face. "I'm so sorry."

Donall turned his face towards the warrioress, trying to find an answer in her mournful green eyes.

Brianna didn't look back at him. She was too ashamed, too wracked with guilt. She couldn't look him in the eyes, not after what she had done.

She wouldn't be able to for a long, long time.

Under the Rainbow

By K.B. Elijah

"Doughnuts," Brook mused, with an aching wistfulness as if it had been years since they'd had the chance to taste the deep-fried dough instead of just a week. "I miss doughnuts the most. And chocolate. And vanilla milkshakes."

I snorted. "Anything that isn't food?"

Brook shrugged their shoulders, conceding the point with a grin that was as infectious as it was wide. "Are you telling me you actually enjoyed any of that leafy shit they've been serving us?"

"Brook," Sandra said tightly from the other side of the room, where she was meticulously refolding every item of clothing Brook had carelessly shoved into her suitcase. "What did I tell you?"

Brook rolled their eyes at me, but fell silent. We both remembered the lecture our boss had delivered before we'd stepped through the Gate.

"Say what you want in the privacy of your own homes when we get back," Sandra had warned us, "but for fuck's sake, don't even *think* anything impolite of our hosts while we're in Faerie. There's no knowing if or how they'll be monitoring us, and I don't need to tell you that the Fae don't work like humans." Her eyes had flashed then, with the type of steel that was rarely directed our way. "Be on your best behavior and don't make any presumptions that could jeopardize our work."

Our work. Sandra was good that way, always referring to us as a team as if we were equals, when really we were only here because of her. She'd offered me a translator job straight out of university, a chance none of my peers had, and I could judge by them where I'd be if she hadn't. Flipping burgers or scanning groceries.

And Brook... Well. The career opportunities for an unqualified, non-binary Scandinavian whose working visa was best described as 'creative ingenuity', and at worst as an utter forgery, were limited, to put it nicely. We both knew we owed Sandra everything, and as much as Brook liked to push her buttons—because, as they put it, what else were personal assistants for?—we also knew when to toe the line.

"The meals have been delicious," I said clearly and carefully, just in case any pointy ears were turned in the direction of our suite. "And understandably vegetarian. Just because your fat ass lives on pizza and burgers, B, doesn't mean we all have your low standards."

Brook shot me a grimace that attempted to be threatening but was filled with resigned fondness. *Kiss-ass,* they mouthed.

Offering a wink in reply, I scratched around for a topic of conversation our fearless leader would appreciate. "There might be things from Earth we're looking forward to returning to, but I for one know I'm going to miss how clean the air is in Faerie."

Sandra's lips twitched in amusement, and I could imagine what she'd be saying to me if she believed us alone. *I'll make a diplomat out of you yet, Cai Bennett.* It was a sweet nothing she often sent my way, like how a parent might ruffle their kid's hair or pin their painting up on the fridge: frequent praise and encouragement that meant a grand total of shit, as we both knew how useless at it I really was. My emotions got the better of me far too easily to follow in Sandra's footsteps.

"Indeed," she agreed, so readily and enthusiastically that one could easily imagine they had been the words she'd longed to speak herself. It was a tactic she often used while working, pretending she and whomever she was working her charms on were operating at exactly the same wavelength. "And the ability to see the stars at night."

"Their world is very pretty," I added, and even Brook shrugged in half-hearted agreement at that one.

"There's a type of peace here," Sandra said, dropping the pair of socks she was holding and leaning back into her chair.

We'd worked together long enough for me to fill in the gaps the diplomat left unsaid: *Even if the rest of it is fucking terrifying.*

We'd heard of the Fae's seemingly mindless cruelty before we'd even arrived—Sandra's warning to us hadn't come from nowhere, even if Earth had only recently had First Contact with the world of Faerie—but had been lucky enough to only witness two counts of it during our stay here in the Summer Court.

Once, at breakfast on the second day, when a young sprite serving tea tripped over her own feet and sent cups crashing to the floor, one of the Summer Court's own princesses had torn into her, verbally *and* physically. Sandra had ushered us from the hall with a polite smile, and a hiss into our ears not to say a freaking word. The second we hadn't seen happen, but I could still taste bile when I thought of the winged Fae corpse with the rope around its neck, swinging in the wind as we returned from a tour of the local lands. A corpse that certainly hadn't been hanging from the gates when we'd left.

"Brook," Sandra now coaxed, resting her chin on her hand. "I'm sure there's something you enjoy about Faerie?"

Bless them, Brook looked anywhere but at Sandra as they clearly attempted to find a response that wasn't a blatant lie. "Er, yeah, there is?" It came out as a question. "There's...no bugs here!" they said brightly after a moment, but I shook my head.

"Sorry B, I saw a cockroach in the east wing just last night," I said. "Although I haven't spotted any spiders yet, thank fuck."

Brook pretended to gag. "A cockroach? Urgh. Tell me you squished it?"

"Of course," I said. "I just hope none have got into our luggage. I've kept my apartment back home cockroach-free for six years, and I certainly don't intend to allow any magical Faerie types in."

"What were you doing in the east wing, Cai?" Sandra asked quietly, and I froze as I realized I'd fucked up.

"Just coming back from the dinner," I said, as airily as I could manage, trying to banish the overwhelming sensation of *blue* from my mind. "Hey Brook, did you see that dance they were—?"

"You said you would return directly to our suite," Sandra accused with narrowed eyes, clearly not letting go. "That was the only reason I consented to leave you alone to finish your wine. If you—"

"You were tired," I countered. "There was no reason for you or Brook to stay. I left the dinner as soon as I finished my drink, just like I promised."

And I had. Technically, he'd found me in the corridor on my way back. And when he'd guided me to his rooms with his hands in my hair and his mouth on mine, I'd neither noticed nor cared in my drunken, turned-on state that it was the opposite wing of the palace to where I was supposed to be.

"Cai probably just got lost," Brook chimed in, placating her. "You know he has an absolutely atrocious sense of direction."

Their eyes sparkled with a look that told me I'd be sharing the full story with them before the day was out. And as long as it never got back to Sandra, I was fine with that, although it could get a little judgy and majorly awkward if they ever asked the Fae's name, seeing as I didn't have a single fucking clue.

But hey, how many blue-haired Fae could there be around here? Most of the Summer Court had the same silvery-blonde locks, and I'd been sober enough to notice his frigging wings, so I knew he had to be one of them.

"We should—" Sandra began, but then the door to our suite burst open and a Fae strode in, chin high and eyes cold.

My heart skipped a beat as I thought I saw *him* in the Fae's sharp cheekbones and thin lips, and then it promptly restarted as I realized that my mind was just filling in the gaps between memory and sense. This Fae's hair was pink, not blue—a sweet, happy shade that reminded me of cotton candy—and it draped down over his shoulders in a soft flow of color. He was wearing a formal, button-up coat in the grey and gold of the Queen's colors, and his gossamer dragonfly wings buzzed behind him. Another of the Summer Court, then.

"Prince Archon," Sandra said, wheeling her chair around so she could face him.

She bowed her head, and he returned the gesture, folding at the waist in a precise movement. I cleared my throat, stepping forward and translating the title into Faerie, more as protocol than anything, since names were the same across all languages. I always liked that about them.

"Ambassador MacFarlane," the Fae greeted her, his voice soft and melodic, and too fucking familiar for my liking. He turned to Brook and then me, repeating the bow he'd given Sandra. "Mx. Larsen. Mr. Bennett."

Fuck yes, I'd heard that voice before. As a whisper in my ear, at my throat, as a moan around my—

"Cai?" Sandra prompted, and I shook myself before repeating his words in English.

"Do we have an update on the time for our departure, Your Highness? I'm sure you can appreciate we're keen to return home, as pleasant as our stay here has been. Your mother has been most generous with her home and her time."

I stared at the Fae as I passed on Sandra's enquiry. At Archon, at the hair I could have sworn had been blue last night. Sure, it had almost looked black by the time I'd dragged myself from his bed and back to our suite, but I'd blamed that on the darkness and the beginnings of my hangover, that surprisingly enough, had disappeared with a couple of hours of sleep. Whatever magic was in that Fae wine, I wanted it for the cheap-ass vodka I usually drank at home.

"I'm afraid I have poor news to report, Ambassador." Archon's glances in my direction gave no hint that he recognized me, and my relief at that vied with my disappointment. "Prince Maximus was murdered this morning."

Sandra's fingers flew to her mouth in horror as I relayed the gruesome message, and Brook sucked in a breath.

"Murdered?" they asked. "But...how? By whom?"

Sandra was more eloquent, even as she fought to shut down the fleeting expressions of shock and frustration that darted across her normally composed face. "Our condolences on the loss of your brother, Prince Archon," she murmured, looking every inch as sympathetic as she sounded. "I hope you are able to discover what happened. Can we be of any assistance?"

The Fae's eyes flickered between each of us in turn, holding our gazes just long enough to make us uncomfortable when he failed to blink. "I have questioned each of the other Courts currently visiting Summer. And now I come to speak to your delegation, humans."

"Of course."

Sandra was all brisk efficiency, wheeling herself back to the table and pulling a pad and pen from a pocket in her suitcase. Her voice was soft, placating. "I assure you none of us had anything to do with such a horrendous act, but I appreciate you need to be thorough. I will write down where each of us were last night so you may eliminate us as suspects. How did it happen?"

"He was..." Archon's eyes fluttered closed, and it was the most emotion I'd seen on the Fae's face since he walked into the room. He lifted a hand and uncurled his pale fingers, showing us a small, wooden box resting on his palm that was about the size of a matchbox. "Destroyed. There was barely anything of him left."

"Good Lord."

I'd never seen my boss cross herself before, yet she did it twice now, with almost fervent vigor.

I felt like joining her. The Fae had been eviscerated so thoroughly that his remains fitted into a fucking matchbox? What kind of monster or weapon could have done that?

Sandra had gone pale, but she held onto her usual business-like efficiency with sheer willpower. "Do you know the approximate time? We've been here in our suite all morning since we were advised about the delay to the Gate, and haven't left since about 11pm last night when Brook and I left the dinn—"

Sandra faltered, looking up at me, and I knew what she was thinking. *When Brook and I left Cai all alone.*

It wasn't that she suspected me. We'd known each other for too long to let a little thing like a murder get between us. But she knew that it weakened my alibi, putting me at risk in a foreign world where we were barely starting to understand the rules. That's what this trip had been about, after all: send an ambassador to establish relations, give the Fae and humans the chance to learn about each other before attempting to integrate the worlds more thoroughly.

"...when we left the dinner," I finished in Faerie, including myself in that statement. If the prick truly didn't recognize the man he'd been pinning on his bed only a handful of hours earlier, then that was entirely his fault.

But Archon cocked his head, eyes narrowing at me. "*You* were not here all morning," he accused, with a glint in his gaze.

"Nice of you to finally acknowledge me, asshole," I shot back at him in his language, and then grimaced.

How many times had Sandra told me not to ad-lib when translating? I may have been excellent at learning new and dead languages in a matter of days, but my inability to stick to the script was what had gotten me into trouble—and nearly unemployment—more times than I could count.

"Cai?" Sandra asked, and I plastered a smile on my face as I turned to her.

"Just clarifying that I left only a few minutes after you," I lied.

"Don't say a word that I haven't," she instructed. "Let me get us through this, please. It's my job."

I nodded, ignoring the sympathetic look Brook shot me, and relayed Sandra and Archon's conversation as he asked if we had seen anything of relevance. Both parties grew frustrated as the questions continued without any particular result, and I got the sneaking suspicion that this wasn't just a formality. The Fae suspected us of this murder for some reason, and the prince didn't like what he was hearing.

I kept my voice neutral as possible, wanting to avoid relaying any impression or sentiment Sandra hadn't intended, but after the fourth time Archon asked if she was sure—like we could accidentally murder a prince of the Fae and have forgotten about it before breakfast—and Sandra came up with a new, but equally diplomatic, way of saying 'yes, we're fucking sure', he fixed me with a glare that bored down into my bones.

"Is she telling the truth?"

"Is she—?" I began, but Archon shook his head, pink hair coming untucked from behind his ears.

"Do not translate that. Just tell me."

"I..."

I faltered. Of course she was, but she'd also specifically told me not to say a word of my own. She was right to imagine that, left unchecked, I would flounder and could end up saying exactly the wrong thing. Like that time with the ambassador of Belgium. There had been some serious apologizing to do after that one.

Archon cocked his head, studying me, and then tucked the box containing his brother's remains into a pocket of his coat. "You will accompany me outside. Walk with me."

I turned to Sandra and Brook, but the prince stopped me.

"Just you. You are useless in her presence, and I wish you to speak to me without influence."

"Cai?"

It was Brook this time, picking up on my discomfort as they always did. We'd only been friends for the few years since Brook started working for Sandra, but it hadn't taken much time to realize how well we fit together. Our humor, our movie preferences, our love for inane reality TV. Really, the only thing that separated us was our distinct taste in food. And by that, I meant they ate nothing but crap.

"What's he saying?"

"He...wants me to go with him," I said.

"Absolutely not," Sandra shot back instantly, although her smile remained fixed in place where the Fae could see. "We stay together, particularly now there's an alleged murderer on the loose."

"Is there a problem?" Archon was already halfway through the door, lifting an eyebrow at the three of us.

I shrugged. "My boss says she'd prefer I stay with them."

"Ah." Archon's lips twitched into a cruel smirk. "Then I shall make it no longer a choice."

His wings fluttered behind his back as he strode forward, lending him speed, and it seemed as though his boots only touched the carpet twice before he was at my side, sharp fingers closing around my bicep.

"Prince Archon!" Sandra protested, all pretense gone from her expression as she leaned forward in her chair as if to hold him back. But her body was inoperative from the waist down and Brook was too far away. Neither of them could stop him.

And nor could I. I tried to pull my arm from his grip, but it was immovable as the walls surrounding us, and I could do nothing but mumble baseless assurances to Sandra and Brook as the Fae dragged me from the room with as much care as one might haul a garbage bag. Archon's boot kicked the door closed behind us, and then my breath left my body as he strode down the corridor with supernatural speed, wings quivering behind us, my feet scrabbling for purchase on the long rugs that lined the palace hallways as he dragged me along. My weight and clumsiness didn't seem to faze the Fae at all, and he was mostly carrying me by the time we reached the ground floor of the palace.

A set of huge double doors drew close, but Archon didn't slow as we approached them. Two guards reached forward to open the doors just in time to let us pass through.

"Get off me," I hissed, not appreciating the manhandling, but we were several hundred meters into the grounds before the prince complied, letting go of my arm as abruptly as he had seized it.

I rolled my shoulder, knowing his bony fingers would leave bruises. I should have been terrified at how easily he'd been able to drag me away, but in truth, I was mostly irritated that this was happening at all. Damn it, we were meant to be home by now, where I could watch TV and trawl garage sales for old comics.

Where we weren't being accused of murder.

"Do you really believe one of us could have killed your brother?" I asked, when it became clear the Fae was not going to speak first. He was watching me closely, gaze intense and cold like he thought if he stared hard enough, he could read all of my secrets.

"Perhaps," he said.

"Sandra can't leave her chair."

"We are well aware of your mistress' frailty."

"She's not my 'mistress'. She's my boss. And *yes*, those two things are entirely different on Earth," I added, as Archon opened his mouth to respond. "But she's not frail. If you'd spent more than two minutes in a room with her, you would know that."

"I admire the human's tenacity," he admitted. "But a Fae without the use of her legs would not last long in Faerie. Nor would Mx. Larsen."

I scowled. I hadn't noticed any queer-bashing in this world in the week I'd been here, but I knew it would only be a matter of time before someone said something insensitive about Brook.

Archon sighed at my expression and turned his face to the sky, closing his eyes as he bathed in the sunlight. He looked so vulnerable like that, utterly defenseless and surprisingly young, and my thoughts turned into delicious mush as I watched him. At how the prince's ears tapered into a gentle point, far more subtle than those of the Tolkien or fairytale elves. How the rose-tinted strands of his hair brushed over his cheekbones, softening their edges, as if the wind were trying to show me a different side of him. The side I thought I'd glimpsed last night.

And then the Fae opened his eyes and caught my gaze. My cheeks flamed as he caught me blatantly eye-fucking him.

"Like what you see?" he asked, in a low and dangerous voice that sent flutters of heat through me.

"Why pink?" was all I could think to say, and Archon lifted an elegant brow.

"I beg your pardon?"

"Your hair. Why did you dye it pink today?"

Archon snagged a lock of his hair from over his shoulder and lifted it to his face, examining it as if he'd never seen it before.

"Dye it?"

"Yeah, it was blue yesterday," I pointed out. "Why'd you change it?"

"Blue." The Fae gave a dismissive snort. "Only humans would attempt to capture such an infinite range of hues with such a simple word."

I let out an impatient breath. "Fine. Aqua, azure...what do you want to call it?"

"A shallow pond reflecting the sun at noon, after a storm has cleared the sky," the prince mused, twisting his hair around his finger. He began to walk deeper into the gardens and I trailed at his side. "Today it seems to favor the base of a tulip petal relishing its first breath in the Spring Court."

I resisted the urge to tell him it was fucking pink.

"*Seems* to favor?" I asked instead.

"Oh, yes." Archon let go of his hair as if it burned him, tossing it back over his shoulder once more. "I do not 'dye' my hair, human. It chooses its own color."

"That's..." *Kind of cool.* "Kind of disturbing."

The Fae did not seem perturbed by my words. "My father is of the Autumn Court."

I frowned, trying to remember which Court bore which type of Faerie.

Winter were the shadow nymphs. Summer, the winged creatures like the one who stood before me. Spring was full of the smaller beings that made up much of Earth's folklore: brownies, sprites, pixies and such. And the Autumn Court was...

"The shape-shifters?"

Archon inclined his head. "And while the Queen's Summer genes bore out," he said, gesturing at his wings, "and I cannot transform into animals and insects like some of my siblings, my hair did not get the message."

I let out an impressed breath and the Fae gave me a half-smile. The dappled sunlight through the trees danced at our feet, the smell of warm grass soothing my nerves.

Archon stepped up next to me, and I glanced to my right as one of his wings caught in my peripheral vision, no longer buzzing but held still in the summer haze of the blaring sun. It looked so soft, like the thinnest strands of silk.

I knew I was being a fucking idiot, but I couldn't help it. Call me a lovesick fool, but I wasn't adjusting well to the guy I'd spent a glorious night with turning up to interrogate me the morning after.

I reached out and ran a finger along the delicate edge of his wing, opening my mouth to ask him what it was made of. It was as soft as I imagined, and gently quivered under my touch.

Without warning, Archon twisted around and shoved me against the nearest tree, the breath leaving my body with an involuntary gasp. The Faerie rested his forearm against my neck and dropped his other hand to my jeans, roughly cupping his fingers around my cock and balls through the denim.

"What?" I spluttered.

"Oh, I assumed you were initiating something," Archon said, with a playful lilt to his voice, as he squeezed tighter and I gasped. "That is the only reason to touch a Faerie's wings. Rather like this," Archon added, glancing downwards with a meaningful look, and I cursed as I realized how badly I'd messed up Sandra's rules not to make assumptions about other cultures.

"I didn't know—"

"Clearly," Archon said, releasing me so suddenly that I half-slid down the tree before I regained my feet. Then he leaned in and kissed me, a sudden, unexpected pleasure that was over by the time I realized what was happening.

The ghostly touch of his lips lingered on mine, even as the man himself moved to put distance between us. "Archon..."

"The delegates of the other Courts did not kill Maximus," Archon said. Fuck, we were back to murder talk again. "And nor did Summer."

I scowled at the abrupt change of subject. "And why do you believe them and not us?"

The Fae's eyes narrowed. "Because they told me they did not."

"So did I!"

Archon reached out and trailed a pale finger down my cheek. "Ah, but Fae cannot lie. Unlike humans, which makes you the only variable that cannot be accounted for, Cai Bennett."

I smacked his hand away. I was sick of the confusion he was creating in me. Was he interested, or did he believe I was responsible for the death of his brother? He couldn't be both. That would just be fucked up.

"I told you, we didn't kill him," I snarled. "Go find someone else to play with."

I turned on my heel, not really sure where I could go but still intending to make a point *damn it*, only he grabbed my arm in that vice-like grip of his, stopping me.

"We are not done here." Archon's voice was cold again as he hissed the words in my ear.

"Oh, we're done. You have no proof that we were involved, and I will not stand here and listen to you say otherwise. Take me back to Sandra and Brook!"

I suddenly missed the calm presence of my boss, the way she always knew how to defuse such situations. I felt like control was slipping from me with every word, every emotion the Fae before me seemed to cycle through as if we had been out here for weeks, not minutes. How could one being be so...complicated?

The prince cocked his head, suddenly all smiles once more, but his words did not match his expression. "Not until you tell me what I want to know."

I sneered at him and turned my head away, but there was an audible snap and blinding pain shattered my vision. I cried out, wrenching my gaze back to the wrist Archon held. The wrist he'd just broken with a mere twist of his fingers.

"You fucking psycho!" I hissed, clawing at the Fae with my other hand, but Archon took the scratches without flinching.

"If you will not speak, I must move onto harsher methods," Archon said mildly, as if we were discussing the weather. "I assure you that I am well-trained in escalating pain until the subject breaks, Cai."

"Done it often, have you?" I accused, but my intended snarl came out as more of a whimper.

"Indeed. As Fae can't lie, our only defense against the truth is to hold our tongues. And I have significant experience in loosening those for the protection of both my Court and Queen."

So that was why he was investigating his brother's murder, rather than any of the other thousand Fae we'd seen around the palace in our week here. But of course, out of said-thousands, I had hooked up with the Fae's head torturer.

Wasn't that the story of my fucking life, attracting pain from whomever I started dating? I couldn't say it had ever been quite this literal.

"Speak, human, or I will be forced to continue, and my attentions will turn rather more painful."

"You're crazy!"

I bucked against him, but the prince was as immovable as rock, although he was decidedly warmer and smelled much nicer. And perhaps in another situation I wouldn't have minded being pressed against him like this, if my wrist wasn't fucking shattered.

"Very well," Archon said quietly into my ear. "Escalation it is."

"Wait!"

To my surprise, the Fae did, stilling as he allowed me to speak.

"Torture is a waste of time," I said desperately.

"Not in my experience. It's just a matter of knowing the right questions to ask."

I wet my lips. "You might break Fae that way, but with humans... Well, we'll just say anything to make the pain stop. We can lie, remember?"

Archon stiffened and loosened his hold. "I had not considered that."

He cocked his head and watched me, not an ounce of fucking regret on that perfect face. Just thoughtfulness, as if he was pondering philosophy.

"Then I shall have to adjust my methods of interrogation to account for the innate dishonesty of your kind."

"Innate dishonesty?" I repeated, cradling my broken wrist to my chest, and then I let out a surprised sound as Archon passed his hand over it and the pain eased, the bones snapping back into place as if it had never happened. But I'd be damned if I would thank him for healing the injury *he'd* caused. "You make it sound like everything we say is a lie!"

"No?" Archon rocked back on his heels, an amused spark in his eyes. Was the prick laughing at me? "Then tell me, Cai Bennett, how many lies have you uttered in your twenty-four years of life?"

I faltered. "How do you know my age?"

"We vetted you all before you arrived. Answer the question."

"I don't know," I snapped.

Archon tipped his head. "Because there are too many."

"Not all lies are bad lies."

"I fail to see how your skewed ideas of morality feature into the concept of dishonesty. Is it not, by its definition, bad?"

Grinding my teeth together, I shook my head. "Sometimes lies can protect people we care about."

"Those are still lies."

"Oh, for fuck's sake," I swore, using English because the expletive just felt so much more satisfying than in Faerie. Then I switched back, so the Fae would understand me. "You're so hot and cold! Trying to kiss me one minute and torturing me the next!"

"Would you prefer I attempted both at once?" Archon asked, lips twisting into a smirk.

"I would prefer you to settle on one fucking position! Be consistent!"

"Consistent." The Fae mused on that for a moment. "Like the evenness of stitching on a coat? Or the steadiness of a gentle breeze?"

"Sure," I said. "But I'm talking about *you*."

"I do not think the word *consistent* has ever been applied to a Fae before. You are a funny little human."

"It's not hard," I said through gritted teeth. "It just requires someone to not change their mind three times a second."

"You can stop your mind from changing? What mental discipline you must have!" Archon said curiously, his tone amazed, and I sighed.

"No wonder none of you having fucking personalities. You just flit between things as if it doesn't even matter, don't you?"

"Fae live in the moment," he agreed. "How can you do anything but, when the moment is all you have?"

"Eternity has a shit ton of moments. Aren't you guys immortal? Would it kill you to slow down?"

"Slow down?" he repeated, blinking at me.

"Yeah. You were happy a minute ago, when you kissed me. Just be happy a little longer, yeah?"

Archon frowned. "If we act based on an emotion we previously felt, or in response to an act that has already been completed, then we are dragging out the past. I was happy *then*. I have nothing to be happy about *now*. And it would be sheer foolishness to live for the future, when you don't know what it will bring, or if it will come at all."

"Look at those bird things," I said desperately, pointing up into a tree at some balls of chirping blue feathers. "They're all cute and fluffy, and animals seem to cheer you Fae up. Doesn't that make you happy?"

"It does," the prince said, his wings fluttering slightly as he beamed at the birds.

"See! It's not that hard."

But when Archon looked back at me, his face was stoic again. "I do not understand," he said. "You expect me to retain happiness even after its cause is gone?"

I stared at him.

Were the Fae's fickle and mutable emotions why this interrogation was so sporadic, as his mind flitted in and out of thoughts of his brother's death?

Archon looked back up at the birds, his face once again alight with inexplicable joy.

He unexpectedly slipped his fingers into mine and tugged me upstream with a laugh, past the willows and towards a steep embankment, where the water dribbled down in a small waterfall. He wrapped an arm around my waist without warning and we were suddenly airborne, the Fae's wings fluttering as they carried us to the top of the cliff.

My heart jumped into my mouth at the unexpected change in direction, and I gripped his back a little tighter than I would have liked, considering the smart thing to do would have been to put some much-needed distance between us after he'd gone all psychopath on me and snapped my wrist.

Archon's childish glee had already disappeared from his face by the time his boots touched gracefully on the grass at the top of the cliff, and I slithered out of his arms with decidedly less finesse.

"How long will we have to wait until the Queen of Faerie Gates us back to Earth?" I asked.

"My mother will not make a Gate for potential Fae-killers to flee her realm."

I scowled at the ground and nudged a tuft of grass with my toe. "So we're stuck here?"

Archon frowned at me and shook his head, and then his wings. "If the murderer confesses..."

"How many fucking times do I have to say it? We did not kill your brother!"

"Come," Archon said brusquely, and strode back towards the palace.

We weren't far from the edge of it, although it was a different side of the building to where we'd departed, and Archon led me to a heavy steel door guarded by two Summer Court Fae. As one of them pushed open the door for their prince, the stench hit me at the same time as the heat.

"What—?"

But the prince had resumed his favorite hold on my arm, the one that told me he wasn't fucking around, and dragged me through the doorway before I could fully articulate my protest. My guts heaved and threatened to make me vomit.

I waited impatiently for my eyes to adjust, and when they did, wished immediately that they hadn't.

A wingless Fae was hanging by her wrists from iron chains dangling from the ceiling, blue blood dripping down her naked form evident even in the gloom. She was sobbing and pleading in Faerie.

Another Fae was stretched out on a rack before us, limbs spread to gruesome angles, and I was surprised at the lack of screams before I realized his chest wasn't moving, and what I'd first assumed to be clothing was his gaping and bloodied rib cage.

On the wall there was an eagle, stuffed into a cage barely wide enough to accommodate it, eyes cut out and wings torn. The bird was shrieking and writhing, and I swore as I realized it was a Fae in its shifted form.

I caught sight of other shapes deeper in the room and resolutely drew my eyes down to my shoes. My head swam as I stared at grubby, grey canvas and laces, backdropped against a bloodstained floor.

"Cai," Archon said, and his voice sounded almost gentle. "Do you understand this is what could happen to all three of you humans if one does not confess?"

"Who are they?" I managed to get out, before clamping a hand over my nose and mouth to block the smell of piss and vomit and death.

"Members of the Autumn Court delegation who attended the diplomatic meetings this last week," he said, and I realized that if I looked at any of their faces, I would probably recognize them. "They were among the first I questioned after my brother's murder came to light."

"I thought you said all of the Fae had denied involvement in his death?"

I was choking on the heat, the smell, the gruesome images that still flashed before my eyes despite keeping them stubbornly facing downward.

"They did," Archon confirmed. "But in their interrogation I discovered they had plotted to steal from the palace under the guise of diplomacy. An unforgivable offense."

Unable to hold it in any longer, I leant forward and vomited over the already filthy floor. Archon's boots stepped neatly backwards, but he didn't say anything as I heaved my guts out. Once I was done, he guided me back outside, away from the door guards, and handed me a silk handkerchief to wipe my mouth.

He had ordered that. The torture and death of his father's people for simple thievery.

I could feel his presence beside me, the Fae with the prettiest pink hair, as if he wasn't as much of a monster as any beast with fangs and claws. More so.

"Do you not see how gentle I have been with you and your companions in comparison?" Archon pulled me upright by the collar of my shirt, and I met his gaze reluctantly. I could see no beauty in his emerald eyes anymore.

"Cai," he continued. "If the Queen is not delivered her son's killer soon, she will order you all to be put to my mercies."

I swallowed back more bile. *Fuck.*

"Just so I'm clear," I said through ragged breaths, "you're saying that to spare the other two, one of us has to confess to the murder of a Fae."

Archon inclined his head, but I didn't miss the way his eyes darted around us, as if afraid we might be overheard.

"You know this is bullshit," I snarled. "A false confession is as good as none at all."

"No," the prince murmured, clamping a hand over my mouth. "It will satisfy the Queen. She lives in the moment even more than I, little human. Once she has closure, she will move on, and I believe I can persuade her to Gate the remaining two of you back to Earth. And she will not have my head."

Oh, it all made sense now. Archon's desperation to find the killer, even a fake one, was for nothing more than self-preservation. Whether he was being blamed for failing to resolve the investigation quickly enough, or for his lack of judgment in sleeping with one of the potential murderers, I didn't know, but it all boiled down to him getting back into his mother's good graces.

I peeled his hand from my mouth, and surprisingly, he let me.

"You would ask one of us to willingly endure such torture," I hissed, knowing he meant it to be me. Why else would he have separated me from the others?

But Archon shook his head. "A confession will result in a quick death," he murmured. "Those Fae were only being hurt because they attempted to hide their crimes from me. As you *all* will be assumed to have done if the killer is not found soon."

"And what about the lack of evidence? Won't it come out in the trial?"

The prince gave me an incredulous look. "Are you working with human notions again?"

"Things like truth, justice and fairness?" I shot back. "Yeah, apparently I am."

"There will be no trial. Just a confession, followed by an execution."

My heart sped up. Fuck, could I do this? *No!* my entire body screamed at me, but if I didn't... It was stupid, it was insane, it was unthinkable...but if I didn't do it, Sandra and Brook would be...

Scratch that, all *three* of us would be strung up in that horrific room of heat and death, and I couldn't even think about it without feeling nauseous, let alone endure it.

Would it be Archon holding the knife, the lever, whatever other fucked-up implements of torture had been in that room?

He wouldn't care. He had flirted one moment, and hurt me the next. It seemed Fae had no concept of trust or loyalty. Hell, even the Queen's own enforcer and son was looking to betray her with a false declaration of justice.

It came down to two options, one choice. Stick to the truth, and all three of us—brave, fierce Sandra, and funny, loyal Brook—would live and die in agony. Or buy into Archon's little scheme and take a quick death, one which bought the lives and freedom of my friends.

Oh fuck.

"I understand," I said quietly. "You'll have your confession."

Archon's face lit up, and he pressed a kiss to my forehead. "Thank you, Cai," he said. "You do us all a great service."

And then he took my limp, sweaty fingers and led me around the walls of the palace until we found another door, and I let him guide me through a maze of corridors and stairs of the palace proper.

"Mx. Larsen did not tell you about their condition, did they?" Archon commented abruptly, and Brook's name drew me from my stupor.

"What condition?"

"The reason I told you they would not survive in Faerie for long," he said. "The problems with their heart."

"Heart?" I knew I was just repeating Archon's words, but I couldn't get my mind to function properly. "What? Why do you think—?"

Archon pressed a fingertip to his pointed ear. "I can hear it. The stutter, the struggles. The organ is under pressure, and it is growing worse. They do not have long left."

"How long is 'not long'?"

But we'd rounded a corner before he answered, and I barely registered the shock of blonde hair of my best friend before I was scooped up into a bear hug.

"Cai. I'm glad you're okay," Sandra said crisply, but she betrayed her attempt at professionalism by holding out a quaking hand to me. I took it, seeking solace in her cool touch even as I clutched Brook closer.

"What did that prick do to you?" Brook snarled, and Sandra's expression of relief soured when they laid eyes on the Fae at my side, one of the few times I'd ever seen my boss lose her diplomatic smile.

"Please kindly tell Prince Archon I consider his kidnapping of you to be a severe insult that demands redress."

"We have bigger problems," I said.

As much as I usually enjoyed watching her take assholes down, this one was too unpredictable. Dangerous. I didn't want her near him.

Sandra smoothed her expression back to one of cautious neutrality as she gave me a sharp nod. "We were escorted from our suite to wait here under guard," she said meaningfully, and I followed her glance to the two armored Fae standing at the far wall, watching us. "But not one of them speaks a word of English, and seeing as my translator was missing..."

I looked up at Archon. His hair was now less pink than it was white, although I was sure he would have called it moonlight dappled in blossom, or some shit.

"Why did you have them brought here?" I asked him in Faerie, and his lip curled as he watched Brook press their face into my shoulder.

"You know why," he said. "This is the antechamber to the Queen's throne room." He lifted his chin and spoke to the guards. "Please inform Her Majesty that we have a confession to the murder of Prince Maximus, to be delivered by the linguist Cai Bennett." They both nodded, and one slipped through a side door.

I swallowed, and peeled Brook off me. "We're going to see the Queen," I told them and Sandra. "And there's going to be a lot of talking and I'm not going to be able to translate it all, but I need you both to trust me, okay?"

Brook looked at me closely, and then nodded, but Sandra wasn't so easily convinced.

"Cai, I need to know what's happening. Let me talk to them. That's an order," she added, and her eyes flashed with steel. Normally, I'd have given in—my boss was scary as hell when she was riled up, and I'd seen her reduce fully grown men to tears—but this was a matter of life and death, and sure, we'd met with the Taliban that one time where the same could have been said if I'd gotten my Pashto mixed up, but mostly our diplomatic missions were peaceful and boring as fuck.

This was something else. Something Sandra couldn't help us with.

I took a deep breath, my legs suddenly like jelly. It was real, so damn real; in a matter of moments, I'd be speaking the words that signed my death warrant.

"How will I die?" I asked Archon, and it was suddenly the most important question in the world.

Would I lose my head? My breath? My blood? What would I leave behind on the floor of the throne room, as Sandra and Brook were forced to watch?

Archon let out a sudden hiss of breath and strode forward, knocking Brook out of the way and ignoring Sandra's protests as he took my face in his hands. I flinched and tried to pull away but he held firm, brushing my lips with his thumb. "You stupid, stupid boy," he snarled. "You did not listen to a word I said."

"Prince Archon!" Sandra yelled.

"I listened!" I said indignantly. "One of us to save the others!"

"But not you!" the Fae growled, yet his voice was low. He was keeping his plan from the remaining guard. "What part of 'Mx. Larsen has a fatal heart condition' did you not understand?"

I froze. "No. Not... Not Brook."

"Cai?" Brook asked, evidently recognizing their name, even if the remainder of what I'd said had been in Faerie. "What's going on?"

I had to know. "Do you...? B, is there something wrong with your heart?"

Brook paled, glancing down at Sandra. "It's nothing to worry about," they said, in typical Brook understatement. "The doctors said there's an irregularity, so I'm getting it checked out in a couple of weeks."

"Why didn't you tell us?"

Sandra started fussing over them, even as Archon whispered in my ear that my friend would be dead by then. And Fae didn't lie.

"They have days, at most," the prince said. "There is nothing that can be done for them. But they can do plenty for you."

"I'm not selling Brook out!" I hissed, shoving him away from me.

But the idea had taken root like a festering wound, creeping across my brain until it was all I could think about. I watched Brook rub at their chest, shrugging as they explained to Sandra they hadn't thought it a big deal.

It's big enough that a Fae can hear your death coming, I thought.

Would that make my sacrifice less, saving someone who would almost certainly die a few days later? My own heart twisted at the idea of sweet and cheerful Brook no longer gracing this world.

But this world was Faerie, the land of wings and teeth. Of beauty hiding the rot underneath, the sheer cruelty that all its people seemed to possess, even the laughing, rainbow-haired man who had whisked me off to his bed in a haze of wine and promises. The same man who had broken my wrist not twenty minutes ago, and threatened to do much worse if one of us didn't agree to lie for him.

It would take more than sweetness for us to escape this place.

Sandra would survive, no matter what. It wasn't even an option to name her the killer, even if my broken heart would have allowed me to consider such a horrendous act. No one would believe she could kill a Fae when she was bound to her wheelchair. But who would walk through the Gate with her? Me, or Brook?

I whirled on Archon. "Why do you care if it's me or them?"

The Fae set his jaw and pulled himself to his full height, staring over my head. "I do not care. I just thought it might make the choice easier for you."

Bullshit. I had been asking about the method of my own execution; there was no need for the prince to have gotten in my face about my choice of victim. But the idea that he didn't want it to be me made no sense at all. He hadn't shown the slightest indication that he gave me any thought, other than the occasional moment of flirtation, and was seemingly ambivalent about causing me pain. This place was so fucked up.

I pressed my fingers to my temples, feeling the beginnings of a headache starting to bloom behind my eyes.

A cool hand pressed to my forehead, and I smelled Brook, the scent of toothpaste and cigarettes so familiar to me that I didn't need to raise my head to check.

"Cai," they said gently. They didn't know what was happening, but they'd always been able to pick up on my mood.

Fuck, fuck, fuck.

Brook pulled me close, pressing our foreheads together. "You and me, Cai," they swore, repeating the mantra we'd always use whenever we got ourselves into trouble, and that just fucking broke me.

It was clear which of us Archon wanted me to choose, but I still didn't know myself.

If I gave Brook's confession to the Queen on their behalf, pretending to translate their words with no one any the wiser about what had been said on either side? It would be quick, Archon had promised, and painless.

He would know. He'd probably be the one ordered to do it.

Sandra would protest, of course, when Brook was dragged from our arms, but I could feign ignorance, pretend to pass on her words even as I listened to their sentence. We would cry together. It would hurt, it would fucking hurt, but we'd be alive.

My own death, or that of my friend. It was an easy choice before I knew of B's fatal condition, and I almost wished Fae could lie, so that I could bask in the certainty of uncertainty. Of choosing to let Brook live and knowing there was a chance they would.

But they couldn't lie, only omit the truth. And there was nothing ambiguous about what Archon had told me about Brook's condition and their impending end.

No, there had to be something, some loophole or third option I hadn't considered...

"Her Majesty, Queen Ariadne of the Fae and its Four Courts, bids you enter," called a voice in Faerie, and we all looked around to the doors at the back end of the hall which had opened without our notice. My heart raced at the realization I'd run out of time.

Archon took my arm as if escorting me to a dance, yanking me from Brook's grasp with a sneer. He guided me past the guards, and Brook darted behind Sandra's chair to push her along behind us.

They can only omit the truth.

Oh. How could I have been so stupid not to have *asked*?

I stopped walking, but Archon didn't even pause, dragging me forward with his unnatural strength.

"You personally questioned all the Fae on the palace grounds, didn't you?" I whispered, and Archon tipped his head in assent as we moved along the long room towards the gathered crowd at its end.

"But who," I hissed, "questioned the questioner?"

The prince's lips peeled back to bare his teeth, slightly pointed at their ends. My tongue had felt their sharp edges not so long ago. "Are you accusing me, little human? If so, then ask."

"Did you kill your brother?" I whispered, and Archon scoffed.

"Do be a *little* more specific, Cai. I have nearly a hundred siblings."

"Did you kill Maximus, Archon?"

I expected him to balk, to change the subject, to revert to threats. He did none of that.

"No," the prince said, with utter certainty. "I did not."

Fuck. I was so sure that had been it, the ace in the hole that would have saved us all. Expose Archon as the real killer at the last moment, earn the Queen's favor. Isn't that how it happened in the movies?

Archon's fingers dug deeper into my arm. "While I didn't think it needed to be said, when you present yourself before the Queen, please take note of *who you speak for*, Cai Bennett."

Oh, I was taking note alright. It would be the hardest decision I'd ever had to make.

We reached the dais and its throne far too quickly, and my thoughts were still in a mess as we bowed to its occupant, Sandra ducking her head as much as her paralysis would allow. We'd met the Queen before; she'd been present in each of our meetings over the last week as we'd attempted to forge a long-lasting relationship between humans and the Fae, but she was just as intimidating as the first time we'd been introduced.

How long ago that seemed now, back when my biggest worry was Sandra not having anything to show for the ambassadorial visit when we returned to Earth, of being pestered with questions of whether the newly-discovered Fae were everything they were rumored to be.

"Your Majesty," Archon said, beaming a smile that looked so genuine I started to question everything I knew about him and his intentions to lie to his mother. "You look beautiful today."

The Queen gave a pleased smile and they delved into small talk, which I dutifully translated for the benefit of Brook and Sandra. For fuck's sake, didn't anyone remember that one of her sons had been murdered only this morning?

But I didn't have long to wait before the Fae's fickle moods turned somber.

"You have news of Maximus's end?" the Queen asked, worry suddenly evident in her voice, and Archon nodded.

"I do, Mother. I have a confession from one of the humans. It was hard won, considering their natural propensity to lie."

I seethed at the duality of his insult of my species wrapped up in a self-congratulatory statement, even as I continued to make up inane chatter to translate for the others. Telling them what was really being said wouldn't help anyone. Not now.

"Let us hear it," the Queen declared, and Archon smiled.

"Cai," he coaxed, letting go of my arm. "Please tell the Court and the Queen exactly what Mx. Larsen admitted to you a few minutes ago, and what you dutifully relayed to me. Word for word, please."

All eyes, human and Fae alike, turned to me, even if Brook and Sandra had no idea what was being said. I swallowed, throat dry, and Archon gave me an encouraging nod. I looked away, unable to stand the look of smug fucking comfort in his gaze, as if I was a brave soldier daring to reveal his commander's atrocities rather than a man contemplating who to condemn.

The prince slipped his hand into his pocket to draw out the box of his brother's remains, as if wanting whatever part of him was in there to hear the confession. What an overly-dramatic asshole.

I couldn't throw B to the wolves. I couldn't.

But if I didn't, we would both die.

I could name myself. But was it worth it? Was my sacrifice still honorable and noble if it had only half its intended effect? If Brook died in a hospital in less than a week, joining me in death?

Fuckfuckfuckfuckmeorbrookmeorbrook—

"Brook Larsen killed your son," I blurted, unable to believe it even as the words erupted from my lips. "They admitted it in the presence of myself, my boss, and the prince. They left our room unseen in the early hours of this morning and took Maximus's life."

Fuck you, Cai Bennett. Damn you to hell for this.

I was trembling, and I couldn't stop. Brook's hand fell on my shoulder and they offered me a smile, having no idea what I had done. Perhaps they hadn't even caught their name in the rush of words I'd blurted out.

I'd expected the Queen to at least ask why, but the capriciousness of Fae astounded me once more.

"Kill the perpetrator," she said, turning her beautiful face away as if signaling the end of the discussion.

Was that truly it, the end of the matter? A confession and an execution, just as Archon had said?

"Your Majesty," Archon interjected, and my heart soared as I hoped it was to plead for mercy on Brook's behalf. "I promised Mr. Bennett and Ambassador MacFarlane that you would Gate them home, considering their lack of involvement in the crime."

Oh.

"Are you sure they are blameless?" the Queen asked, and I didn't like the hungry way she eyed me. "Perhaps you should question them more to be certain."

"I am, Mother," Archon said firmly, cutting off any objections with the absolute authority in his tone. I hated that I was grateful to him for it, thankful for him merely following through on his promise to save us, even as he'd manipulated me into betraying my best friend.

My *dying* best friend. It was taking away the pain of their last few days, and buying our lives in the process, that was all.

If I told myself that enough times, would I believe it?

"Very well," the Queen said, disinterested, as if it was of no consequence despite her eagerness a moment earlier to see us tortured.

A moment. A fucking moment. If we had enough moments, perhaps the Fae would forget about the whole thing and all three of us could escape.

But we didn't.

A Gate was forming to our left, a swirling portal of darkness and spitting sparks, and Archon was wrenching Brook away from us as they swung their head around in confusion to ask me what was happening, and Sandra was raising her voice, demanding that Archon let go of her assistant immediately, and I was shaking my head, unable to speak, and the Fae wrapped his hand around Brook's throat and my own hands were on the handles of Sandra's wheelchair, pushing her towards the Gate as she screeched at me to stop, and Brook was clawing desperately at Archon as the Queen watched, her eyes wreathed in black—

"Cai!"

The prince with the rainbow hair and soft smiles gave me an amiable

wink in one moment and snapped Brook's neck in the next, dropping their limp body to the floor. As the Gate swallowed me and Sandra whole, I saw the small box reappear in Archon's hand.

I saw him pry open the lid.

I finally saw its contents, a mess of squished brown carapace and legs.

And as the Gate blacked my vision, I remembered what Archon had said.

While the Queen's Summer genes bore out and I cannot transform into animals and insects like some of my siblings, my hair did not get the message.

Maximus was descended from the Autumn Court, just like his brother, only instead of color-changing hair, he'd had the ability to properly shape-shift. But not into a bear, or an eagle, nor any of the other dozen animals I'd seen in our time here.

No. A cockroach.

My left foot felt as heavy as my guilt as the Gate tugged us back to Earth: me, Sandra, and the lingering, sticky remains of Prince Maximus on the bottom of my shoe.

Hunters and Grinders

By Neen Cohen

The Hunter's heavy feet slapped against fallen autumn leaves, calloused hands pushing through thick foliage. Leaves and rough bark cut the skin of his palms, while branches pulled at his clothes and carved gouges into the flesh beneath.

Above, the sound of bare feet dancing along branches hid beneath Pheon's laughter; a cackle that bounced among the trees.

The Hunter's breath sped. The rush of his blood pumped his heart near capacity. Birds twittered and squawked, as though discussing the plight, while unseen creatures scuttled. Even the wind had its opinion of the chase, whipping the leaves into a shaking frenzy.

"This is nothing compared to the fear she felt."

Pheon dropped from a branch a dozen paces in front of the Hunter. To his credit, he didn't scream. He stopped, a sliver of relief palatable in his eyes as he struggled to catch his breath. He looked like a fit man, a typical Hunter. But the run had pushed him to his limits. The run, and the fear.

"What the gods?"

"No. There are no gods left. You and your kind made sure of that. We are all that remain."

She took six, long-legged steps to reach him. Her hand, as strong as any of the branches surrounding them, wrapped around his throat. Beneath her grip, his Adam's apple struggled.

But she had run out of time. The sun was slipping down beyond the horizon and soon the Witches and Sprites would be out. Technically they were aware of her position as Enforcer of the Woods, one of four. But there was a chasm between knowing and seeing.

Only the Fairies seemed unaffected by the things she left behind. But the fairies, their lands on the other side of the river, were in their own league—true and pure creatures of the forest. Though she didn't know anyone other than fairies who believed that.

Pheon shook her head, focusing on her job. She would have loved to take her time, to have him fear right up to his last breath, just like his latest victim. She knew it hadn't been his first; the cruelty and precision were too well-practiced.

"Grack you, freak. The grinders are here now, and you don't stand a chance." He croaked a laugh, gasping for air as her hand tightened.

"Grack yourself."

Her free hand slammed into the back of his head, while her fingers tightened hard enough to make his eyes bulge. She looked into them and smiled wider.

There you are, true fear.

With a swift movement she snapped the Hunter's neck. The silence around her was absolute. The wind had stopped, no birds twittered, no bugs shuffled beneath brush or leaf. It was always the same. The taking of a life was rending, even the life of one who didn't deserve the gift.

But Pheon would be lying if she said she hadn't grown to like the taste of it, just like the chili her mother used to make before... Well, simply *before*. She could still remember the pain and sting as it danced on her tongue that first time. She remembered the burn of tears that wet her eyes, and her sniff as everything in her head seemed turned to liquid.

Her mother had smacked her upside the head for that sniff. She had never sniffed in front of the Witch again.

Pheon laughed as she dropped the dead Hunter to the forest floor.

Her mother was a strong and powerful Witch, a force in her clan, but she couldn't control her daughter's nature, or her later anger. She had rejected Pheon and the memory still smarted. Nothing but a disappointment to her mother, and more importantly, to her mother's clan.

Pheon's strength and magic came from her father, not that he and his tribe accepted her anymore either.

Pheon shook her head, shook off the memories and pain. They always reared their heads after a catch. She was proud of her job; she loved it—except for those few moments after, when she remembered why she became an Enforcer in the first place—but she had to find a place in the forest somehow. At least she enjoyed protecting the Fae, despite their disdain for her lower status.

With a deep breath, she crouched, before using powerful, sinewy legs to jump into the air. Once she was through the canopy of the trees, the hum of the forest seeped through the roof of leaves. Airborne and alone, she let her head fall back, eyes closed to the pinprick stars starting to wink awake. She let out a low whistle. The skin and shirt on her back tore and released her heavy, black wings.

Her father's gift and curse. She was the corrupted consequence of the night her parents gave into their primal lusts. She was the pointing finger, keeping the memory of their mistake alive.

With slow, steady beats of her wings, she opened her eyes and oriented herself in the darkness. She was one of the few winged willing to push beyond the canopy of the trees. Her Witch blood no doubt, the curiosity of the beyond that they couldn't beat out of her. But if only the Fairies could see the beautiful tapestry of their world from up here, perhaps the old grievances between the races, the pompous arrogance, would seem as insignificant as Pheon believed them to be.

"Grack..." she muttered, as she noted how far she was from her own camp. There was no way of getting back now, not without encountering the Sprites. And her mother's people would be out this close to the full moon.

With a resigned sigh, Pheon pushed herself toward the waterfall that was the beginning of the great river that split the land in two. At least she could make the trip worthwhile, personally and professionally, even if she hadn't yet made her report about the latest Hunter. She couldn't deny the thrill of being near the waterfall so unexpectedly, but the Hunter's words scratched at the back of her thoughts.

When the stars filled the black velvet of the sky, she let herself fall back through into the forest. She was still a short run from the waterfall, but dropping close was a dangerous endeavor. She had done it just the once, the night she met her lover. Her ankle itched at the memory of the burning ice that lashed around her and dragged her down, but then a different type of heat had washed over her. The heat that had begun once Nyami had unwrapped the coil from Pheon's ankle, and the two had spent the first of many nights rolling naked beneath the brush.

A wide smile spread across Pheon's lips as, with pointed toes, she lighted back down to the floor of the forest. Sprite lights created patterns and paths through the trees, and her smile slipped. She knew the way without their guidance, but she enjoyed the dancing lights, whether they wanted her to or not. Even the Sprites looked at her with nothing but fear and disgust.

Though there was one exception.

The run was refreshing, as cold air whipped around her, the cooling evening turning her breath into a dragon's mist. By the time she made it to the edge of the waterfall, sweat slicked her bare arms and legs, her heart thudded in her chest, and rushing blood itched her skin.

"Hello, my half-breed. I hadn't expected to see you, especially on a full moon."

Pheon smiled, taking in the surroundings, shoulders sagging with relief at the silence and stillness. They were alone.

"You know, you really should stop pretending you look better in clothes."

Pheon took her attention away from the surroundings and focused back on the head peeking out of the water, the Sprite's body blending as one with the water. She slipped the tank top over her head and Nyami's eyes turned to sparkling sunlight reflecting on ice.

"Hello, Nyami."

Nyami continued to stare until Pheon looked back, eyebrows raised.

"Oh, come on." Full lips pouted, and sent a flood of heat rushing through Pheon. "You cannot tell me you think that band of elastic feels nice."

The band of elastic and the small tight shorts Pheon wore were a special fabric, cotton and something else, something synthetic that had cost her the money from two jobs to get made.

"You get used to it."

"But this is so much better." Nyami glided up into the air, a waterfall in reverse, until she stood, feet on top of the water, her curvaceous figure one Pheon ached to touch and caress, ached to see fleshed and under her hands once again.

But she had to focus. The Hunter's words, and worse, the thing in his eyes that overtook even his fear until the last moment.

"Indeed it is." The warmth building between Pheon's legs turned into a raging fire. It had been too long. "But when jobs call for me to go into the Hunters' world, I can't exactly blend in with nothing covering me."

"I suppose…" Nyami slid back down into the water. "But what a waste. The visit is business, not pleasure." It wasn't a question.

"Unfortunately," Pheon said, swallowing down the lump in her throat.

It had been *far* too long. When it came to Nyami, Pheon suspected she would feel the same even if she had been gone less than the two weeks her last job had taken to finish.

"What is it, Pheon?"

"Have you heard of 'Grinders'?"

Nyami's mouth quirked up and her eyebrow rose. "*Grinders?*"

"Oh, stop," Pheon insisted, but a smile spread across her face.

"No, I've never heard it in context of Hunters."

"Will you keep an ear out and let me know?"

"Of course, sugar."

"Thanks."

Nyami nodded again and her smile, filled with beauty and mischief returned. "Any other business we need to discuss?"

"None whatsoever."

Pheon's fingers nimbly peeled off her bandolier and shorts, and dumped them on top of her torn tank top.

Standing naked, she watched as Nyami rose again and made her way to the edge of the water. As her feet stepped on to the ground, they began to shift and solidify. Where once Pheon could see through her, she now saw pale flesh and the curves of her lover's body. She pulled in a shuddering breath. It didn't matter how many times she saw her, the sight remained breathtaking.

Pheon trailed her eyes over long legs that rose to wide hips, up a toned torso to large, heavy breasts and square shoulders that had winded Pheon the first day they met. After lashing Pheon's feet immobile with a water whip, Nyami had slammed into her and knocked her to the ground when she landed too close to the waterfall.

When she met those crystal blue eyes, a heat she could barely contain washed over her.

"Hello, my love." Pheon's voice was low and rough.

"Hello, my opposite."

It was a contentious pet name Nyami had given Pheon from their first kiss, but one Pheon was learning to accept, if not love.

One night, after worshipping each other's bodies into sweaty exhaustion she had let slip how the term affected her.

"Do you know about the fifth Sprite?" Nyami had asked, seemingly unconcerned about Pheon's dislike.

"Fifth Sprite?"

Pheon had laughed. There was no fifth sprite. The Sprites came from four ancient lineages. The water, the plant, the earth, and the sky, and none of the Sky Sprites had been seen in the forest for generations.

"There is a story we are told, about the fifth Sprite. The flame."

"The flames come from the Hunters. They are dangerous."

Nyami laughed and slapped Pheon playfully on her bare stomach. "Would you listen?"

Pheon smiled and rolled her eyes. "Of course."

Nyami narrowed her own eyes, but continued.

"As the story goes, the others banished the flame because they could not control her. She left, not wanting to be where she was not wanted. But she told them that when they learned to love their opposites, they would find what love truly means, and they would not be so scared of her own differences. So, we Sprites, we have learned the beauty of finding and loving our opposites."

Pheon was certain Nyami had made it up to say what she wanted to say, without having to actually say it. She looked at her lover now and still wondered if they really were as opposite as Nyami kept insisting. But then again, she had yet to meet a Sprite who didn't speak as though they knew things without hesitation or doubt, and who wasn't aggravatingly vague about details.

"Are you with me, my love?"

The term pulled Pheon back to the present and she smiled. The past fell away to inconsequence.

Their mouths came together, like waves crashing against a rock face. Pheon's heat sizzled as her body merged with the cool perfection of Nyami's.

Hands groping and searching, steam rising around them, Pheon let herself go, her guard and thought dropping away. Stars birthed and died in their ignorance of time as they brought each other to that cliff of pleasure, jumping and pushing the other to flight.

Beneath the blanket of leaves that had fallen over them since they lay, temporarily satiated, Pheon breathed deeply of the smell of home, the only real home she had ever known. And while the words danced on her lips, she still couldn't bring herself to tell Nyami these things. Instead, she contented herself with running strong, calloused finger through the silken, blonde strands of Nyami's hair as her head rested on her shoulder.

"Where are your thoughts, Phe?"

"There are no thoughts; you've gracked them out of me."

Nyami laughed and playfully slapped Pheon on her chest, resting her hand to cup Pheon's breast. The tremble went up her body, and she knew it wouldn't be long before she wanted those hands exploring other areas again.

"Please, tell me?"

"These Grinders worry me. The Hunter was about to die, and he knew it. But still, he spat the word out at me and laughed. He was so sure I was to get my comeuppance."

"He's a Hunter; they are all arrogant shizzes"

"Not at the end."

Pheon sat up, knowing Nyami's falling hand would leave her cold, but not wanting this topic to invade their warmth.

Nyami sat up and rested her chin on Pheon's shoulder. "There has been talk."

"About Grinders? You told me—"

"No." A gentle kiss on her bare skin. "Not about Grinders. But about things changing, shifting. There have been more Hunters in the woods, and..."

"And what? Tell me."

"Fairies have been going missing. My father and the other Sprite leaders met with the Fairy leaders last moon. There were accusations of Sprites luring Fae folk across the river."

"What?"

Pheon jumped up and stalked to her abandoned pile of clothes. Nyami didn't move but watched as Pheon reefed the clothing back over her skin. Pheon's wings had shifted back into hiding, but as she grew more angered, she felt them itch to push their way out again.

"Phe..."

Pheon continued to dress, ignoring Nyami. When she had the tank top back on, ripped at the back but all that she had, Nyami was on her feet.

"Phe!"

"What?"

"There is more."

"More?"

"Apparently, Hunters are bringing their families into the forest as well, and the wind is talking about the Sky Sprites returning."

"Families?"

"At first we thought they were simply grouping up, no longer coming in alone."

"But, they are families?"

Nyami nodded and place a hand on Pheon's shoulder. She gave it a small squeeze before she walked away, heading back to her home. Pheon watched as her lover's body, so strong and real, turned transparent as she drew closer to the water.

This is why I don't tell her. I have nothing to offer, except a job that keeps me leaving.

Pheon took a deep breath.

A leaders meeting, accusations between Fae and Sprites, Hunters bringing families into the forest. And what had Nyami said about Sky Sprites? How was that even relevant?

Still, not even that rested easily on her shoulders, especially with everything else happening together. At least the Witches hadn't been mentioned. A confrontation with one parent was enough for an entire moon cycle or three.

A heat, that had nothing to do with her recent activities with Nyami, spread outward to her limbs. It was time to get this over with.

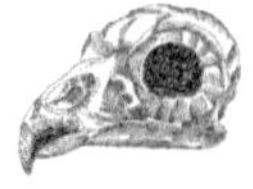

She let her wings out, stretching them as wide as they would go as she soared above the trees, making circles and delaying what she needed to do. On the fifth loop, she forced herself to stay true and crossed over the river.

The light danced around her shadow as she looked down on the deceptive, dark water below.

It had been more moons than she could remember since she last kept space in the Fairies' land. Her father called it the land of the true Fae. His elitism ran deep. No wonder he was unimpressed with his own living off-spring.

Overall, Fairies were nicer to her—all but her father—but that nice-ness was harder to leave, and her job required that too often. It seemed to be all it offered her at times. A chance to not stay still.

The lands below her had many more open spaces. They did not fear the Hunters the way Sprites did. The Sprites were known to the Hunters, and their powers stolen through the removal of their eyes. Or worse, from other body parts, if the Sprites tried to change. Pheon had seen too many dead Sprites, empty eye sockets staring into oblivion, the horror of their death twisting their features, limbs half-transitioned and amputated with-out tourniquet, left to bleed out in agony.

"Pheon?"

The voice came from behind her the moment she stepped down upon the true Fae land. She turned, schooling her face into a serious mask, the mask of the Enforcer.

"Hello, Father. I have come about the feud between you and the Sprites."

"Why?"

"Because Enforcers should be aware of such allegations."

"And you assumed I did not tell anyone. Still so much to learn."

"Did you?"

Pheon swallowed back the bile and tried to dampen the heat inside of herself without shrinking the square of her shoulders. Her father's silence was answer enough.

"You have accused the Sprites of luring true Fae." The term, her father's bigotry, tasted liked ashes on her tongue. "With what proof do you accuse them? For what purposes have you ascertained?"

She had expected him to glow bright, remind her of what she was not, what she failed to be. She had even been prepared for screaming and a backhand, or worse. The reaction she got was far more terrifying.

He pulled in a sharp breath, rubbed hands over his face and nodded. "The Enforcers will be told. I was hoping it would not have to come to that."

"Come to what?"

"Things have changed since the meeting."

"How?"

"Come." He strode off, full confidence she would follow and continue listening to his every word. "It will be easier to show you."

Show me? Show me what?

She didn't bother voicing her question aloud. The moment her wings sprouted black and leather, instead of the soft, white feather of true Fae, he had stopped answering the smallest of her questions. She did follow, soft blades of grass, bright and shimmering in the moonlight brushing against the skin of her feet. Her mouth watered at the memory of the sweet taste of it. Only a river separated the places, but it might as well have been oceans. Everything in the land of Fairies was sweet to her. The tastes, the smells, and even the touches.

She almost ran into the back of her father's wings, always out, muscles bunched across the rest of his bare back. They stood at a small outcrop of trees. Two Fairies, strong and trained, stood at guard. Behind them, the leaves were restless, and the sound stiffened Pheon's spine and raised bumps along her skin.

On the right was Lia, a woman she had been friends with when they were children, before. Everything good about this place was from before. Lia avoided Pheon's eyes and nodded at her father. The other guard was unknown to Pheon. He was strong and fierce. His eyes met hers and he nodded. It was these small moments, when someone simply acknowledged her existence as a person instead of just an Enforcer, that made this side of the river both better and worse.

"She is permitted. One time."

The last two words, though spoken after a pause, twisted inside of

Pheon's chest. The words he didn't speak were all-too clear. Pheon was not to be trusted alone; she was not one of them.

Pheon lifted her head and pushed back her shoulders. This was nothing new, nothing more than an old scar being scratched at.

The line of trees they stepped through was four trunks thick. It wasn't a grove as it appeared, but a clearing with a barrier of several rings of trees. Off to one side was a slab of granite and a girl, covered in blood and curled into a fetal position.

"What happened?"

Pheon rushed forward as she asked, half-expecting someone to stop her. But there were no hands grabbing her back, or calls for her to halt. She dropped beside the girl. No, she was a woman, half-aware of the sting of cold Earth beneath her knees.

Her father's voice rang behind her. "They took her tongue. She cannot name the villain."

Pheon's mind whirled. Were Sprites responsible for this? The thought foreign; it itched uncomfortably against all she had experienced with them. They didn't like her, but they were not cruel or self-serving. That was something she more often attributed to her father's race.

She could smell the metal and fire on the Fairies skin, the calling card of the Hunters.

Why was Pheon here?

Hesitantly, Pheon reached out and laid her hand on the woman's cheek. The woman's eyes flew open, and the pain and fear were raw, so raw. She fell on to her backside, her hand dropping, but a connection had been made, and her eyes held the stranger's.

Can you hear me? The voice pierced into Pheon's mind.

Pheon shuffled back to the woman, fingers trembling, but oh, how her mind spun with intrigue. A spider's web of questions. She dipped her head the slightest amount, hiding what was happening, a habit of old, and laid her hand on the woman's cheek once more.

What happened?

The strength of the voice inside her mind froze Pheon to the spot.

You are in danger. They took my wings, but I wasn't supposed to be hurt, I wasn't part of the deal. But my baby was. Please, you have to save my baby.

Pheon closed her eyes, trying to keep the words together, ensuring her mind didn't fall into the depths of the woman's pain and fear.

Please, show me. But slowly.

And the woman did.

Time had no bearing on what Pheon saw. Though days passed in the exchange of memories, Pheon had no idea how long she was crouched, touching the woman's face. It couldn't have been long, since her legs held no stiffness when she stood back up.

I will find her.

"So, you see? We believe the Sprites have told the Hunters about us, and are now trading their lives for our own."

"That's a rather harsh leap," Pheon all-but growled at her father.

He flinched slightly, eyebrows furrowing for half a beat, but recovered his regal pose quickly enough.

"She was found on the other side of the river. It is not such a leap."

"Perhaps not. Do the Sprites know of this woman?" *Jia, her name is Jia.* "And that she is here?"

"No. But what they did to her tongue... They made sure it didn't matter."

"You should have told the Enforcers as soon as you suspected, Father."

He nodded. And Pheon hated the swell of pride and warmth that spread through her chest. Such a small acknowledgement should not have filled her with joy.

"I will report back to them. We will find the answers."

Her father's touch on her shoulder was a cruel sensation. Too many things she had wanted, and now meant nothing.

Or meant all the wrong things.

"I knew I could count on you."

As soon as he dropped her shoulder, Pheon stalked out of the clearing, through the lines of trees and past the guards without looking at anyone or anything, except her way out.

"What are you going to do?" Nyami asked, as Pheon paced back and forth in front of the small pond. *Their* pond. She had decided the Enforcers could wait. Time was of the essence, and her blood hummed for revenge.

"I need to find her baby."

"And then?"

"I..." Pheon stopped pacing. "I don't know. I know what she showed me, but she might have been traumatized by having her wings cut off. How do I know she hasn't mixed up the rescue with the attack?"

"Do you really believe that?"

Pheon locked eyes with Nyami and shook her head.

"She was strong, mentally. Her body was so broken, slowly tortured. But her mind..."

Pheon didn't want to be caught up in all this. She just wanted to do her job, take pleasure in Nyami's body, and feel the freedom of the sky above the trees, alone and free.

"You are stronger than him, Phe. You always have been. Why do you think they fear you?"

"They fear me because I'm different."

"They fear you because you are stronger."

"Is that why you are with me?"

"Oh..." Nyami swayed a little back in the water, a single foot breaking the surface and causing small ripples to grow away from it. "I'm with you because you are a damn fine lay."

Pheon laughed out loud, causing a few shuffles and squawks to call out from around them.

"I'm not that strong, Ny."

"We are opposites. Trust me, I know these things."

"You are not weak."

"No, but I am predictable, a product of my bloodline. I am cold and water; I am the unknown luring you to your demise."

"Yes." Pheon's lips curled up at the corner. "Yes, you are."

"Trust me."

"I do."

"Good. Now trust yourself."

Pheon didn't say anything. Instead, she took up her pacing once again.

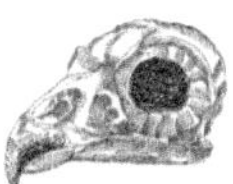

They were easy to seek out. Each Hunter had their own unique scent woven through the metal and fire they carried. It lingered on their skin and transferred to every living thing they touched. The ones who had hurt Jia—the ones who had tortured her and ripped her wings brutally from her body—had a sweet scent beneath. It was almost as though they knew how to make flowers grow, how to tend to the nature they killed with each Sprite they stole from. And now they were stealing from Fairies.

Pheon had always feared the Hunters would learn about the other creatures in the woods, other magic they could harness for themselves. But the Fairies were across the river; they were low on that list of worries. They didn't need her, or any other Enforcer's, protection. At least, they hadn't before.

These thoughts ran cyclical through Pheon's mind as she slowed her pace along the branches. She stopped when the clearing came into view below. Hunters rarely looked up, but she hadn't survived this long by making assumptions.

The clearing was half-filled with a white and brown caravan, a fire pit surrounded by several plastic and metal chairs.

A campsite.

Pheon shook her head back and forth. This wasn't a normal Hunter's base. Those were small strips of canvas, blended into the surrounding trees and shrubs. There was never a fire.

Focus!

Closing her eyes, she blocked out the sounds of the birds and the rustle of the trees. There were no larger animals nearby, no scurrying beneath the shrubs. The scent of the Hunter was over everything in the camp ground. Even the birds were higher up, closer to her than usual.

A boy, dancing at the edge of manhood, stomped out of the caravan, the door he pushed open slamming against the metallic wall beside it.

"Why do we have to keep the thing alive? It won't shut up!" he called behind him, as he slipped behind the tree where Pheon stood, zipped down his pants and began to piss against the trunk.

The sound that had followed him out of the caravan touched Pheon's senses. A babe. A Fairy babe, scared and hungry and so very angry.

He wanted the child killed.

This one would be all too easy, but that didn't mean Pheon couldn't enjoy herself.

The rush of blood roared in her ears, and her breath quickened. A flick of her tongue wet her smiling lips, and with a breath of a laugh, easily mistaken for a gust of wind, she landed behind the pissing boy. He turned, dick still in his hand.

"Big man, killing innocent babes."

"What the—?"

His words were cut short by the base of Pheon's palm slamming into his nose. Not quite hard enough for the cartilage to pierce the brain.

Pheon smiled. She had never seen herself during these moments, but whatever it was that contorted her face created the same reaction in every Hunter she found. Fear and limpness overwhelmed them, and then the instinct to fight for their survival. A few tried to run, like her latest hunt. There was a different kind of fun in the runners.

But she knew he would be a fighter, and just as stupid. Fighters dispelled any guilt she might have felt at ending a life. Not that there was much guilt for these beasts. She only ever killed the guilty, and this boy reeked of murder.

Damn! Sounds were coming behind her and she didn't have time to play. *Pity.*

He opened his mouth to say something, perhaps to call for help. But with another strike, harder this time, she snapped the cartilage into his brain and what was once a growing Hunter, became nothing more than a meal for the animals.

"Where the hell are you, boy?"

The words were gruff and annoyed and Pheon forced the smile from her face, focusing on the job.

She had to know how many more were in there, and there was nothing like discovering a corpse to have everyone rush out to see the tragedy of another, even one of their own. With an intentional scuff of her bare feet on the fallen debris of the forest floor, she jumped back up into the tree, scurrying quickly to her former position.

It didn't take long. Three more hunters stood around the dead body. They looked left and right. One even looked up. Pheon was out of sight, but she saw the chestnut brown eyes of a girl, still years from womanhood, looking up at her.

Families.

Nyami's information had been correct. Though the Sprites were rarely wrong with their intelligence of the forest, Pheon had still hoped.

Her stomach churned at the idea of Hunting together as a family. Even the Witches refused to allow the children to learn any of the darker teachings until they had reached maturity, and they shared the original bloodline with the Hunters.

But even Witches knew the value of life.

"I told you, taking babies is wrong." The girl spoke out the words in a choked rush. For her voice, she received a backhand from the man and a scowl from the woman.

What a delightful family they are.

"Go shut the kid up, and I'll take care of this."

The woman and girl scurried back away to the clearing. The shrill cries became louder and more insistent. It was a smart child, giving her such a tangible indicator of the enemy location.

"You shouldn't have touched the mother," Pheon snarled from her branch, before she jumped down.

"I was hoping I would be the one to kill you."

Pheon lifted her eyebrows as they circled each other. "Me?"

"The freak they let grow up. He told me you were off-limits, but he'll get over it when I tell him it was your life or mine."

"It is your life or mine. But seeing as I'm far more keen on my own, you won't get to tell him anything."

"Bloody half-breeds," the man muttered, and in those words, Pheon's last hope was shredded, her fears confirmed.

She knew the truth, though deep down she hadn't been able to convince herself Jia was wrong.

Leaves and dirt flew up into her face, taking her by surprise. There was a sharp sting in her right shoulder that turned her away from where the man had been. She spat out the forest floor debris in time to see the Hunter slip back into the caravan. Looking down, she saw the handle of a knife sticking out of her.

Her growl rumbled from her stomach, up her throat and over her lips with skin-blistering heat. She reefed the blade from her body and threw it down into the earth. Blades were a Hunter's weapon. She barely registered the sting of the wound as she followed the screams and bellows.

He rushed back out of the caravan, the screaming child in his arms. Behind him, both the woman and the girl looked on, fear and blood smearing their faces. Had he hit his own companion to take the child? Yet the Fae and Sprites were called animals and beasts.

Focusing on the woman and the girl, Pheon spoke as gently as she could while the rage bellowed up inside of her.

"Run while you can. Never step foot in my forests again."

The woman ran, but the girl stood frozen and trembling. Pheon didn't care. She would do what needed to be done, in the girl's sight or not.

"I will kill it."

"It?" Pheon hissed, as she stepped closer, but stopped once the man lifted a second blade, a twin to the one she'd discarded. He pointed the tip toward the child's head.

"Why are you keeping her alive?"

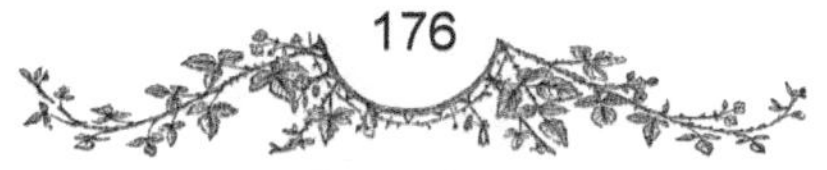

"You really are as stupid as he said."

Don't flinch.

"Perhaps."

"Half-breeds have regenerative properties."

"And?"

"And wings can be taken and crushed, and they just grow back. And since we learned that ground wings are the most potent of ingredients, what's more valuable than a regenerating half-breed?"

"Grinders..."

Pheon couldn't hide her own frustration. She knew about the regenerative powers. Her wings had grown back after she tried to hack them off, only succeeding in destroying the right one before she passed out from the pain. She had woken days later, two strong wings on her back. It was all falling into place, and that place was a sickening pit.

"But he's not happy with you." She redirected her anger to where she needed it, for now. "You touched a pure Fairy."

"Meh." He shrugged. "What's a man to do when profit is staring him in the face?"

"Exactly."

Pheon smiled as she ran toward the man. The knife in his hand pulled away from the child and aimed at her. But he was too slow, and she knocked the blade to the ground with ease.

"Stop!" he screamed as he fell backward, the child rolling from his arms.

"You were never going to kill her when it wouldn't profit you until her first wings sprouted."

"Please!" He choked around her fingers as they squeezed his larynx. "We can make a deal! We can help each other out."

She eased her fingers off his throat, the heat raging inside of her, building as her breath became more ragged.

"I'd rather be ripped to shreds by hounds."

Her hands moved to cradle his skull in her palms and her thumbs pressed into his eyes. He screamed and bucked beneath her, pulling and

scratching at her arms. Harder and harder, she pushed against the resistance until finally, with an audible pop, blood and ooze seeped out, running down over her fingers.

He screamed the kind of scream that filled nightmares.

Behind her, something shuffled—movement and the screams of the child—but she wasn't done yet with this creature, this inhuman monster, this *Grinder*. His hands lost strength and she thrust him to the ground, his babbling filled with incoherent whimpers, shock and pain.

"You deserve this punishment. Fae kind will have their vengeance on you."

"Please…"

The whimper behind her was ice water thrown over her head. Pheon turned, no longer concerned about the Hunter who sobbed and drooled, hands covered in blood and tears. He would wait. He was no threat anymore.

Before her stood the girl, the child clutched to her chest.

"Let her go," Pheon growled.

"I didn't know. I didn't even know you were real." She bounced the child in her arms, a second nature that intrigued Pheon despite herself. "But please, don't kill him. He's my father."

"He's a monster."

"Yes." She nodded, bottom lip trembling. "But he's harmless now."

"He doesn't deserve to live."

"Perhaps not." She took a step closer. She was brave for a Hunter's spawn. "But do you deserve more blood on your hands?"

Pheon cocked her head. She had interpreted innocence in the plea for his life. Now she saw the spark in the swirling, brown color of the girl's eyes. They were not as young as she'd first thought, but still not quite a woman.

She looked down at the babe in her arms. "What happens now?"

"I kill the bastard behind your daddy's orders."

The girl held out the baby and Pheon took the child in her arms. The crying stopped, and Pheon bit back the scoff that tried to escape.

"You have a minute. One minute to run before your camp is destroyed."

The girl didn't hesitate. She turned and ran. The numbers were slow as Pheon counted in her mind. Eyes closed, she let the anger and fury of her life overflow from her. The child trembled in her arms but did not cry out.

As the minute passed, Pheon opened her eyes, and screamed.

The flame that burst forth burnt its way up her throat and over her lips. She screamed a river of fire as the camp went up in flames.

When the fire died from her mouth, she collapsed, breathing heavy, the child safe in her arms.

But there wasn't time for rest yet.

Standing, Pheon held the child tight as she walked away from the charred clearing behind her.

The Fairies were about to learn of the new power in their midst.

The Lost

By Angèle Gougeon

"Stop daydreaming, boy."

"Sorry, Uncle Hep."

Rory reached down for the last bag, heaving the flour with a grunt. He shouldered it through the back door with a curse, tripping over the warped steps, then headed for the basement larder.

"Watch your mouth!"

"Yes, sir."

Rory made a face and stomped down to where the air was cooler. The faint magic of the cooling stones cast a pale light through the dusky shadows.

"I told you to turn on the light," Hephaestion's voice called down. "Going to break your damn neck."

"Sorry, Uncle Hep."

Rory dumped the sack, biting back another curse when the top seam burst, spilling flour across the floor. Wincing, he turned to the steps, but his uncle was already gone, footsteps thudding overhead further back into

the bakery kitchen. Rory dragged the sack against the nearest cupboard, then hastily swept up the spill, patting his dirty hands against his thighs.

"What's taking so long?"

"Coming, Uncle Hep!"

Rory bound up the stairs, toes catching at the top, making him step twice to stay upright. He ignored his uncle's sigh, feeling a flush spread across his cheeks. He'd grown a foot over the last two weeks and his uncle said it was his height making him clumsy as a newborn colt. Rory just hoped it stopped before he tripped right down the stairs.

"Go open up, would you?"

Hephaestion gestured, dough flying off the end of one finger. The dark circles under his uncle's eyes seemed a little better, he thought.

Rory tried on a smile that felt wrong on his face. "Yes, Uncle."

The front of the bakery was narrow, kitchen door hidden by a minor glamour, and back wall filled with rows of display shelves, enchanted glass casting a faint sheen in the morning sun. Rory touched a finger to the activation rune on the side wall behind the counter. The warm mage lights sprang to life. With a few more steps, Rory unlocked the front door, then busied himself making sure the freshening and warming charms were working properly on the shelves.

Sticking his head through the glamoured doorway, he caught his uncle staring fixedly at a spot on the wall. "We're out of carrot loaf, Uncle," he said.

Hephaestion grunted. "Thanks, boy."

He blinked down at his flour-covered hands. The dough looked overworked.

Rory hummed, pulled back into the shop as the bell over the door sounded, and pasted a smile onto his face. "Good morning, Mrs. Telpin!"

The wizened woman hobbled towards the desk, throwing her purchases on the counter as though settling in for a long stay. Rory's smile stretched, even as his stomach dropped.

"I was hoping for your uncle," she said, voice grating like a bowl full of rocks. She reached into her pocket for her pipe and ashweed. "I wanted to offer my condolences."

Her eyes glinted with the strike of her flint. Rory might have believed her, were he ten years younger.

Rory's smile felt like the baring of teeth. "He's very busy, unfortunately, Mrs. Telpin. I'm terribly sorry."

"Yes, yes." The old woman patted at her other pocket. "The poor dear. What a shock. We were all so overcome with the news."

She swept a coin onto the countertop, snatching a wrapped package of rock candy. Surely it would crack the few remaining teeth the old woman had left. Uncharitably, Rory rather hoped it did.

"And you?" she asked, mouth twitching at the corner.

Rory slipped her coins into the warded coin box beneath the counter. His cheeks hurt. "Ma'am?" he asked.

She reached out to pat the hands he'd unthinkingly spread atop the counter. "How have you been coping, darling?"

"As well as can be."

"As good as your mother, your aunt was," the old woman pressed. "What a horrible loss. To lose her in such a—"

"Thank you," Rory forced out, smile unchanging. "We appreciate the sentiment."

Mrs. Telpin's twitching mouth stilled. Her shoulders drooped with disappointment. The bell over the door dinged, heralding the hurrying form of Mr. Brook. Mrs. Telpin hastily grabbed her bags, hobbling to the side, then out the door when Mathew Brook sneered at her, coins already dropping into Rory's hand. The young man efficiently handed over three custard tarts and a loaf of rye, like clockwork.

"My sympathies to the family," he said, through his large, brush-like moustache, nodding his head once, then heading out the door.

The bell dinged and he was gone.

Rory's uncle swept his head through the doorway's illusion like he was a macabre hunting trophy, neck sprouting from the center of a non-existent lamb meat pie. "Is the harpy gone?"

"Yes, sir."

"Soul-sucking ghoul," his uncle muttered.

"Yes, sir," Rory agreed, and Hephaestion snorted something that might've been a laugh, if his uncle still had any humor left.

"Good lad," the man said, and withdrew.

Rory straightened his shoulders, stretched his smile, and set his spine.

It was going to be a very long day.

"Good afternoon…"

Rory stuttered to a stop as he turned from restocking the sweet buns at the sound of the bell. Horrifyingly, he felt his cheeks burn red.

Jeric Farrower, the apothecary's grandson, gave him a kind smile. His blond hair flopped over his brow, falling into pale blue eyes. Several months older, he was already sparsely sprouting at the chin.

"How are you doing, Rorick?"

Rory licked at dry lips. He tried to muster up a less false smile. "As well as can be," he got out, which was rote at this point in the day. He'd never had to repeat himself so many times before.

"I was very sorry to hear of your aunt's passing," said Jeric, voice hushed. "It's good to see the shop open again."

"It's good to be here," Rory croaked.

The kindness in Jeric's eyes was almost too much to endure, always so honest and earnest in a disarming sort of way. Rory's heart beat a tattoo against his ribs. Self-consciously, he dusted flour off the front of his vest.

Jeric finally came close enough to lean against the front counter. Rory caught the whiff of lemon balm and ginger. "Grandpa forgot lunch again," Jeric said. "Are there any pies left?"

"Of course." Off-balance, skin prickling, Rory nearly dropped a beef pie on the ground, before setting it on the counter with shaking fingers. He couldn't force his eyes higher than Jeric's chin as he asked how many he would like.

The sound of the bell was almost a relief.

"Good afternoon…"

For a second time, Rory came to a stop, blinking with wide eyes at the stranger standing in the bakery doorway.

"Sir," he said.

Jeric turned with mild interest.

The man was dark-haired, skin as pale as the young Miss Ivey's—Jeric's long-time love interest, much to Rory's consternation—with piercing grey eyes. He seemed ageless in the same way as Wizard Waylon down the street, who never looked a day over twenty-five despite being born two hundred years ago. Mouth a thin line, the man regarded Rory with an intensity that set his skin crawling.

"Sir," Rory said again, then turned to get another meat pie, carefully wrapping both in butcher's paper before taking Jeric's coin.

"Alright there?" the other boy said, quietly, something cautious in his eyes.

"Yes, thank you," said Rory.

Jeric nodded, then hurried around the man and left the shop. It immediately felt colder with him out of sight. The world much emptier. Rory dragged too-thick air into his lungs, stitching his courage back together. "How may I help you, sir?"

The man glanced at the door, frowning.

Slowly cautiously, he stepped nearer to the counter. His eyes flickered over the shelves. There was something off-putting about his stillness. Long fingers came up to clasp against his front, thumbs brushing jacket buttons that shone gold. The stitching on the material was fine, silk thread that caught the light with an indiscernible pattern when he moved. Rory tried not to stare.

The man blinked. Like an inspection had been passed, a smile flickered over his lips, head tilting in a way that set his long hair slithering over his shoulder.

"A dozen honey pastries," he said. His voice shivered its way down Rory's spine, making his shoulders go taut.

Rory grabbed the sweets, as carefully and meticulously as possible, if only not to raise his head.

"That will be seven coins, sir," he whispered. His voice felt like it was trapped behind his teeth.

Long fingers crept into his down-turned vision, pushing seven coins that weren't of Isle make. Delicate flowers twisted up the outer sides of the thick silver and Rory looked up, surprised, jaw open in protest.

His mouth went dry at the sharp smile directed his way.

The man left while he was still trying to remember how to breathe.

Rory stood near the base of a tall oak, grief growing a little larger in the center of his chest.

He shouldn't be here.

There was the tang of old magic in the air, wild and dangerous, leaving zings of faded lightning across the skin. Between the trees, the ground was a large, bare circle, earth burnt to remove blood and bone. The nearby vegetation lay shriveled and limp. The bark on the nearest trees sat scorched.

There was a smell of burnt sap and sage, as though Wizard Waylon had tried to purify the incident from the very loam and clay itself.

Rory pressed trembling fingers together, feeling nauseous.

Stories about the state of Aunt Eileen had already made the rounds, but Uncle Hep hadn't truly explained what the village defenders had found. Rory didn't need his uncle trying to protect him anymore. He wasn't a child. He was old enough.

A branch cracked and he flinched, looking around with a lie ready on his lips.

No one was there.

Uneasy, Rory silently turned to creep back to the forest's edge, and then into the village. He didn't need witnesses to his stupidity.

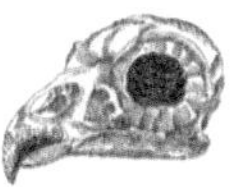

"Ah, Rory!"

Wizard Isaiah Waylon turned from his work station, glancing in surprise at his large pendulum clock. His hands were covered in a gleaming, viscous red liquid. It was also spilling onto the ground at his feet.

"Lunchtime! Did I order something?"

"No, sir," he said.

"Ah…"

Puzzled, the wizard turned to clean his hands on a rag already smeared with uncountable stains.

The wizard's work station was near the back of the store, in a shallow pit with a drain. Thankfully, the numerous herbs and potions dangling from the ceiling kept the space from smelling too peculiar, though Rory had once visited when the man was working with a stink crab and had to immediately leave to vomit in the street.

"What can I do for you, Rory? Does your uncle need something? Did one of the shop's mage lights fail?"

"No, no," Rory insisted. "I… I, um…"

He studied the shelves against the walls. Statues, necklaces, and far too many books. There was a table full of hunting orbs against the entrance window and he cut a look at the wizard, biting his lip so hard that he was almost certain it was bleeding. Feeling a flush of irritation, Rory closed his eyes, took a breath, then stared up at the man.

"I was wondering about my aunt, sir."

Isaiah blinked, nonplussed. "Your aunt?" Then, he frowned. "Ah… Your aunt."

The wizard stared down at his fingers, wiping carefully into the wrinkles of his middle knuckle.

"Your uncle hasn't told you."

It wasn't a question, but Rory still said, "No, sir."

Gently, and apologetic, he replied, "You ought to speak with your uncle, Rory. I won't go against his wishes."

"But it's too painful for him to talk about!" Rory argued. "He won't tell me! I deserve to know what happened to her."

His jaw clenched. Unexpectedly, fury rose like a tide. His fingers tightened so far that his bones ached.

"Rory..." the wizard grimaced, looking away.

"You saw her. I know you were there. Your magic is all over the site where they found her."

The rag fell from Isaiah's hands. The next second he was shaking Rory's shoulders. "You were in the forest? Rory! It's *incredibly* dangerous right now. You can't—"

The front door opened.

Reluctantly, Wizard Waylon released him. "Promise me you won't do anything so foolish again, Rorick Hanover," he said, voice low and hard.

Rory swallowed, heart thudding and blood rushing through his veins, but he couldn't bring himself to agree.

"Isaiah!" Mr. Alpon called, from just inside the doorway. "Your missive said my order was ready?"

"Ah, yes." Waylon's smile didn't reach his eyes. "This way, please, Charles."

When Rory reached the door, Wizard Waylon was bent over another table in his workspace, explaining a brightly glowing stone to Mr. Alpon with a serious expression. Quickly, Rory reached out and snatched one of the hunting orbs. Then, he fled the store.

It wasn't stealing.

He'd return it later. He would.

He promised.

Rory rushed into the back alley—he'd already been gone longer than he'd wanted—and then through the back door of the bakery, tripping on the uneven doorjamb. Carefully, eyes on the doorway to the front of the shop, Rory shoved the orb between two rolls of parchment and twine in the far reaches of the wall cabinet.

With a quivering breath, he stepped through the door's glamour, praying his uncle wouldn't see the guilt on his face.

"There you are." His Uncle looked tired. Rory hoped Mrs. Telpin hadn't been in. "Did you eat?"

"Yes, sir."

"Hmm..." His uncle finished loading a fresh batch of braided herb bread onto a shelf, then sighed, looking at his nephew. "Thank you, lad."

"Uncle?"

"I know this hasn't been easy for you."

Rory ducked his head, insides twisting horribly. "There's no reason to thank me, Uncle."

His fingers still hurt. His chest felt oddly empty, like the flash of anger had burnt his insides out.

"You've let me hide away while you've dealt with the gossipmongers."

"I don't mind."

Hephaestion snorted in disbelief. "Then you're a better man than I."

Rory's cheeks burned. His eyes did too. He picked up the cloth and wiped down the counter to hide his reaction. The space was too narrow and his uncle's hip jarred him. The bell above the door chimed.

"Oh," Rory said, looking up. "Hello again, sir. What can we get for you today?"

The thin, pale man with the piercing eyes and the long, dark hair entered the bakery. He nodded, but didn't speak, still out of place in their small shop—foreign, with his rich clothing and elongated limbs and unnatural stillness. Rory wanted to be relieved that, this time, the man was staring at his uncle, but he wasn't. That gaze was a glacial thing.

"Who are you?" his uncle asked, rudely, and Rory startled.

Their customer's lips turned up at the corners, but there was nothing happy about it. The hairs on Rory's arms rose. With a lazy blink, he said, "The honey pastries again. Please."

Hephaestion bristled.

Rory pushed past him. Then he fumbled with the wrapping. The twine got stuck around his fingers.

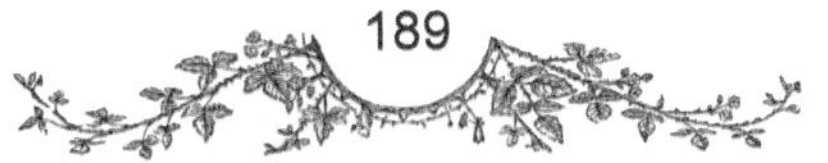

The silence stretched long.

"Here you are, sir," said Rory, breaking what felt like a taut wire.

Seven silver coins were pressed onto the counter.

"We only take Isle coins," Uncle Hep growled.

The stranger paused, staring at Rory's uncle with a thin kind of keen amusement. Then, he turned and left the shop.

He also left the coins.

Uncle Hep snarled a curse. Rory glanced at him, but his uncle was already turning toward the kitchen. "Stay away from him, boy," he warned.

"Yes, Uncle," Rory agreed, confused.

"And get me if he comes in again. I wish to have words."

"Of course, Uncle."

Rory watched him disappear through the doorway's glamour. When he glanced out the front window, the odd stranger was already out of sight.

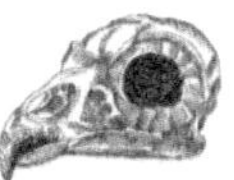

Rory frowned down at the hunting orb cupped in the palm of his right hand. It remained, infuriatingly, black.

Slowly, he moved along the edges of the burnt circle of earth. The magic had faded even further, but the spun-glass orb should have worked. There *had* to be some kind of print to mark the beast that had harmed his aunt.

Rory widened his search, stepping further away.

With a soft glow, grey wisps floated from the center of the tracking device to settle against the forest floor, illuminating the tiny tracks of a rodent that darted off into a charred bush. Rory's lips pressed together and he turned in the opposite direction.

There was nothing.

"What are you doing?"

Rory flinched. The glass orb crashed to the ground. Distantly, Rory hoped it hadn't cracked. His breath hitched as he turned, shoulders riding up towards his ears.

"Where did you come from?" he demanded of the pale, thin man with the fancy jacket. Then, he went red at his own rudeness.

"I saw a young man enter the forest and thought: how odd. The entire village is currently whispering of a danger between the trees."

Rory swallowed. His tongue felt thick in his mouth, barely fitting between his teeth.

Grey eyes shot to the black orb upon the ground. Long fingers reached down. Rory bit back his protest.

"Hunting?"

Rory didn't answer.

"For?" the man prompted. He rolled the orb in his palm.

"It doesn't matter," Rory rasped. "It didn't work."

Slowly, the man blinked. "Didn't it? And what does that tell you?"

A scowl crossed Rory's face. The man lifted a dark brow. He waited.

Rory huffed. "The prints were burned away by Wizard Waylon's magic."

"Unlikely." The man looked pointedly unimpressed and Rory had to glance away. That anger seemed to be crawling back. Irritation ripped up his rib cage, fuelled by the hitch of his lungs. "This orb," the man said, rubbing a thumb against the glass surface, "was made to track animals."

"Yes," Rory agreed, shortly.

"So," the man said, leading, "if they do not show the prints you expected, then..."

Rory went hot. Then, exceedingly cold.

He stared at the burnt earth beside his feet, the large circle, the place where the carnage had once lay. He felt numb.

"Then it wasn't an animal."

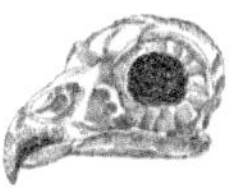

Rory slammed through the front door.

The house was dim, with a faint, closed-off, dusty smell. The windows

and shutters were all closed, with light coming only from a flickering down the hall.

The shock had worn off somewhere between the town square and old man Laurence's place. Then, determination had set in.

Mouth thin, Rory marched down the hall, coming to a stop in the small drawing room. His uncle sat, drink on the table, eyes glassy and expression broken. He looked up at his nephew, and Rory wished the man didn't look quite so pathetic so that he could keep on being angry.

He fell into the opposite seat, absently tracing over the circle burnt into the old wooden table from one of his aunt's dinner pots.

"You were out late," Hephaestion said.

Rory crossed his arms and breathed through his nose.

His uncle drank, again, large body listing to the side. "Not getting into trouble, I hope."

"I want to know what happened to Aunt Eileen."

Hephaestion reared back, choking in surprise. "Boy—"

"I deserve to know," Rory pressed. "I'm old enough. Why won't you tell me?"

The flickering mage light cast dark shadows across his uncle's face. Rory didn't think his cheeks had always looked so hollow. "Your aunt's memory deserves better."

"Please."

Hephaestion shook his head. His shirt sleeves had been pushed up to the elbows. The patches in the material rumpled oddly, material too thick.

"Uncle..." Rory pressed.

Hephaestion exhaled with a shake. "We knew they would come, eventually," he said. "Whether it took one year or sixteen."

Rory scowled in confusion.

"We were so young and foolish. And I told her... I told her not to go into those woods."

His uncle's drink sloshed over his knuckles, spilling across the uneven slats of the table. His cheeks glistened in the light, and a horrible sort of shame rose up in Rory.

He swallowed hard, throat thick with something he couldn't describe. His chest felt too full. His fingers clenched at the fabric at his knees, so taut his whole hand hurt. After a moment, Rory rose and tugged the mug loose from his uncle's grasping fist. Then, he pulled at his uncle's large shoulders.

"She never listened," Hephaestion said.

He swayed and, with some surprise, Rory found that he was the one wrapping an arm around his uncle's shoulders, tall enough that he had to stoop.

"You need to sleep, Uncle."

Hephaestion's eyes closed against the tears on his cheeks. "I knew it wasn't safe."

Rory led him to his bed, pushed him flat, and patted the quilted blanket up to his chin.

"Don't go into the woods, boy. You have to promise. You promise me."

"Of course," Rory whispered, "I promise."

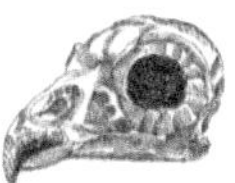

It was bad luck that Uncle Hephaestion was in the front of the bakery when the man came back.

Scowling, Uncle Hep braced his palms on the counter. "We don't want your kind here."

"Uncle Hep," Rory exclaimed, shocked.

"My kind?"

The man's tone was polite, but his grey eyes gleamed, sharp, and his lips twisted up into a smile that stole all the apologies from Rory's mouth. His teeth looked sharper, somehow, and when he tilted his head, the tiny point of one ear pushed through his dark hair.

All Rory could hear was the rush in his ears. With stunned eyes, he could see his uncle's mouth still moving, but he didn't hear a word.

His arms rattled with the force of Uncle Hep's palm slamming onto the wooden counter. The fae's smile widened, eyes cold cold cold. With an

almost mocking bow, he disappeared out the door and sound came rushing back in.

Beside Rory, Hephaestion trembled, bone-white fingers gripping the counter, breathing hard and cursing under his breath.

"Uncle?" Rory dared to ask.

Hephaestion turned wild eyes on him, jabbing a finger into his chest. "Don't you get involved with the fae, you hear me? They'll bleed you dry, just because they can. They killed your aunt, boy, and they'll kill you too."

Then, still breathing like a dying bull, he stumbled into the back, through the glamour, and the shop fell into an uneasy silence.

"What was that?" Rory asked the empty room.

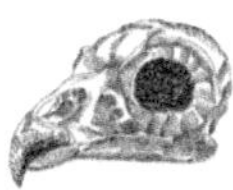

"My uncle thinks the fae killed my aunt."

"Your uncle," the fae repeated, flatly.

He stood with arms crossed, standing at the border of the bracken forest. He'd been waiting, as though summoned. Rory's pulse thundered in his throat.

"Was it?" Rory demanded, that familiar anger surging.

"Why would the fae kill your aunt?"

"Answer me. Yes or no."

"What reason would anyone have to kill dear, sweet Eileen?"

Rory's hands turned clammy with fear. His throat went dry. He fought the urge to step back. "Was it you?" he whispered.

His skin felt tight. His eyes burned. Faster than he could blink, a long finger touched his cheek, feather-light, and he jerked away, terrified beyond reason.

"I would never hurt you," the fae gently said. Then, interrupting before Rory could do more than open his mouth and stutter, his hands spread wide and he said, "I've been searching for a lost soul."

Rory licked at dry lips. "Who?"

"A child was bargained, many years ago. A deal was struck. And a deal was broken."

Rory shook his head. "I don't understand."

"A couple came. Broken-hearted. A child, they asked for. A child they would give in return. A deal struck."

"You're speaking in riddles."

The fae stepped forward, and Rory stepped back, pulse in his throat. "Am I?"

"You're here for a child."

"I'm here," he said, "to bring a lost child home."

Rory tripped on a root. "You mean a...a changeling?" he breathed.

The fae paused mid-step, a small smile twisting his lips. A pit grew in Rory's stomach. It trembled and surged and threatened to swallow him whole. He shook his head. His thin voice came out wretched.

"Why are you telling me this?"

"You already know why."

Rory did.

The clarity was a grisly, horrifying thing. Denial sat on the tip of his tongue.

But...

But.

"What do you want?" Rory asked in defeat, facing the cruelty head-on.

"My only wish is to bring my stolen son home."

"Why did you do it?"

Hephaestion looked up from the kneaded dough. There was flour on his face again. His apron was crooked. "You're late."

Rory remained silent, staring.

Hephaestion dusted his hands. A frown joined the wrinkles on his brow. "Boy?"

"Why did you do it?"

"Do what?" The man pulled down an oiled bowl. He kneaded the dough once more, then put it in and covered it. "What happened to you? You look terrible." The corner of his mouth twitched. "Run into young Jeric again? One of these days, the blood won't run back out of your cheeks."

Rory's jaw clenched in anger. The betrayal was a thick sludge, travelling up to where his eyes stung. It coiled in his belly, squirming like a living thing. Nausea rose in his throat.

"What was it you said? They'll bleed you dry? Just because they can?"

Hephaestion stilled. "I did," he growled. "And I'll have no talk of fae in this shop, boy."

"Because you're afraid. Because you broke a deal."

The man's eyes widened.

"You and Auntie Eileen went to the forest. You found a faerie ring. You spoke of an ill child. You proposed a trade. A son for a son."

"Boy..." Hephaestion croaked out. He staggered forward.

"You lied."

Large fingers curled around Rory's shoulders, digging in and trembling.

"You didn't have a son. Your wife was barren. So you stole theirs. And you ran."

"How do you know this?" Hephaestion's voice was a hiss.

"Were you ever going to tell me?" Rory asked.

Hephaestion shook his head, but not because that was the answer. His horrified eyes narrowed, a darkness that gave Rory pause.

"With me, boy!" Hephaestion snapped.

His fingers encircled Rory's wrist like a vice. With a lurch, he tugged him out the back door. The shop's rear alley was empty, the early morning quiet and chill. Rory tugged against the grip, feeling his skin bruise. Hephaestion slammed through the back of Wizard Waylon's magic shop.

"Isaiah!" he yelled.

Rory scrabbled at his uncle's fingers.

"Hephaestion?" Waylon asked as he appeared. "Rorick?"

"He knows!"

The wizard's expression went flat. Rory groped at the hand on his wrist, panic chasing away the tar in his chest. He couldn't get enough air.

"You knew?" he whispered.

Wizard Waylon didn't seem to hear. "And?" he asked, brow arched high.

"Did the binding break?" Hephaestion demanded. "How did that fae bastard find us? Make another one! Do it in iron if you have to."

Isaiah blinked at Rory as he struggled, considering. "That could kill your nephew."

Rory jerked back. He tried to escape. His uncle's grip remained strong.

"That monster killed Eileen. I will never give him what he wants." Uncle Hep stared at Rory. Then he scowled. "Do it."

"Uncle Hep!"

Hephaestion dragged Rory towards Wizard Waylon's work space. The wizard sighed. "Perhaps a memory charm as well. You will not want anyone knowing what we've done."

Rory fought and begged as Hephaestion forced him down onto the cold metal table. "If he lives," he agreed.

Wizard Waylon leaned forward, a bottle of iron powder in hand.

Rory screamed as he burned.

My Beloved

By Chris Bannor

"This is the third raided village we've found," Tallen said, kneeling beside the burned corpses. It was no funeral pyre, just a pile of bodies left to warn anyone that came looking.

His mentor nodded. "The raiders are taking a clear path south. I don't think we need to worry about them turning around and attacking Redhills, but I'll feel safer if I see they've passed the Summerflood River."

"The messengers we sent should have warned the closest villages. Hopefully, they listened and fled, or have a powerful defense."

"We have enough trouble without borrowing theirs."

Gavin's eyes continued to search the ruins of the village. There was no sign of life, but the man didn't relax. Neither of them had since they got word of the raids.

"We should push on," Tallen suggested. "There are a few hours of daylight left and we can make it to the river tomorrow if we keep going."

Gavin nodded. "I don't want to sleep in this place anyway. This land is rotting, and the dead have eyes."

Gavin had always been superstitious, and while Tallen didn't share all the same beliefs, he knew enough to respect the dead. This area was fae ground as well, and no one wanted to get caught in their games. The old women in Redhills had a saying. *Steer clear of the fair ones, lest they turn your heart to bleeding and your eyes to the dark.*

He had no intention of finding out how true it was. He had his own reasons to avoid any creature of magic.

10 years ago, Tallen had stumbled into Redhills village. He'd wandered from place to place, traumatized by an attack on the royal family. The castle had fallen, and King Cecil of Dasmar had claimed Asmian as his own.

Gavin had taken Tallen in when he revealed he was the son of the butcher and seamstress who had taken employment in the king's court years before. Gavin had let him heal, in body and heart, then taught him to hunt and track. He was an accomplished hunter now, and he and Gavin were well-liked in Redhills for their ability to keep everyone's bellies full.

If the raiders turned back though, a tight belt in winter would be the least of their worries.

They left the ruined village behind and detoured around the hills. They could see the stones surrounding the tops and neither would risk a fairy ring. They traveled by light of a full moon, and when they were tired, they took shelter under the boughs of a tall pine. It was the rainy season, and the air was damp with it.

When they woke, they ate out of their bags on the road. It had drizzled some time before they woke, and even though it was light, they were drenched long before midday.

"When is King Cecil going to stop this?" Gavin grumbled, as they found the wreckage of a wagon.

They couldn't stop to bury the dead, but they pulled them under the cart. They'd burn the bodies on their way home, if it was dry.

Tallen didn't think much of the king, but he usually bit his tongue around others. Alone with Gavin, he could speak his mind.

"If he could, he would. This kingdom has been falling since the day he took the throne. Anyone who thinks otherwise is in his pay or burying their head in the sand."

Gavin looked around before he nodded. A habit from the village. You never knew when someone was listening and would send word to the king's ears.

"At least the roads were safe with King Ashford."

Tallen didn't need to chime in to hear Gavin's opinion of kings, past or present. There'd been no love for King Ashford before his death. He had been a strict ruler, too concerned with rules and the dictums of court. He wasn't lenient, though most claimed him to be fair if you followed the word of the law. He turned his eyes from starving farmers who couldn't pay taxes, and lost the heart of the people long before his death.

Under Cecil, the people had thought they would be happy. No ill word ever came to them of the king from a neighboring kingdom. When he took Asmian, they learned the brutal truth. No ill word came because no one dared to speak out. If there was a well-to-do family in your village, they took the king's coin. Everyone else was ground down by taxes and tithes.

The sun was almost to the horizon when they reached the last village before the Summerflood. Wilford was set high on the hills looking down at the river, safe from the yearly flooding. It wouldn't matter this year though. The village was a cemetery, filled with the dead.

The buildings were half-burnt, flames put out by the rain before they could consume it all. Tallen and Gavin went from house to house, pulling the dead into a central building. They could give them the pyre the earlier dead had been denied.

"The Gods will end their suffering and take them to the Peaceful Valley," Gavin said softly, as he stuffed dry hay under the floorboards.

Tallen was accustomed to the sight of the dead—he'd be a poor hunter and a worse scout in these days if he couldn't take it—but this pyre pinged at things in the back of his mind he didn't want to remember.

"I'll find more kindling," he said, walking away from the building.

Down the main street was a barn where they'd stored wood and grains for sale. The barn had been missed in the destruction, the sole, untouched survivor standing sentinel. Tallen pushed the door open and found bundles of kindling at the back. He hefted two on his back and turned towards the door when something pulled at his foot, and he fell. He scrambled backward and rolled so he could see his attacker. Hidden behind a stack of hay bales, an old woman lay bleeding and white-eyed on the floor.

"Grandmother?"

He took a deep breath to still the beating of his heart. She hadn't made a noise and she was still, though her milky gaze met his with unnerving intensity.

"Are they gone?"

"The raiders have passed through already," Tallen assured her. "My friend and I came scouting from Redhills when we got word of the attacks. You're safe with us."

She closed her eyes and a rattling breath followed. She wasn't long for the world, and Tallen felt shame at not being able to offer much comfort. "What can I do to ease you, Grandmother?"

"Water," she mumbled.

He felt a fool for having left it with his pack at the burned inn. It had been easier to move the bodies without the burden of his pack, but he knew better than to leave it once the heavy work was done.

"Let me get you some."

Tallen walked through the yellowed greenway, but a clamor and scream broke the unnatural silence of the decimated village. As Tallen tried to pinpoint the source, Gavin came crashing through a blackened wall. Glass and wood splintered around him. Tallen ran to him as a raider came through the hole in the building. He was taller than Gavin by a good foot and held a sword in hand. Tallen was too far away to stop the fatal stroke, but Gavin countered with his hunting blades. The thrust missed its mark, but pinned Gavin through the middle. Gavin's move unfooted the raider, and he fell forward. Gavin's other blade met him, sinking into the man's heart.

Tallen threw himself at them, pushing the bigger man off Gavin. The raider was dead weight, and it took Tallen a moment to free his mentor.

"Gavin, what do I do?"

Gavin was bleeding out from multiple wounds. Even if that didn't take him, the stomach wound would do him in. There was no healer here to save him, no priestess of the gods to perform miracles.

"Tallen, get out of here. There may be more hidden that we didn't see. You have to run."

"If he wasn't alone, his partner would have come to defend him already," Tallen said, grabbing a cloth sack they'd used earlier. He pressed it against Gavin's stomach, trying to see where the worst of the immediate damage was. "He was probably a deserter, following behind for whatever spoils he could get."

There it was. A gash on Gavin's upper thigh. His pants were slick with blood, but it wasn't flowing too fast. In other circumstances, he would think it good news, but he'd seen too many animals bleed out. He recognized lack of blood pressure. He closed his eyes and bit back his tears as he tried to think.

"Tallen, get back to Redhills. Let them know they're safe from the raiders. That was our mission."

"They can wait for news until I get you patched up," Tallen lied. There was no patching this up.

"Don't be afraid of the world, Tallen," Gavin said.

"Stop."

"You hide in my home back in the woods. You hide behind fake smiles when we go into town. I don't know what you hide from, Tallen, but it's time to stop. Time to fight for whatever is in that heart of yours."

"You don't know what you're talking about," Tallen said, as he found his canteen and put it to Gavin's lips. It was only then he remembered the old woman, waiting. She'd have to wait longer. "I've never hidden from a fight in my life."

It was a lie, but not one Gavin could know. Tallen had run from one fight, long ago. He'd vowed, once Gavin had taken him in, that he would never do it again.

Gavin coughed up the water and pushed the canteen away. Tallen steadied him, but there was nothing he could do for the man who had taken him in and raised him. The man who had taught him what it was to be a man in this world.

"Take a rest," he said softly. "You just need to let your body heal. I'll get you stitched up better than ever. You can barely even see the scar from the last one I did, right?"

Gavin smiled and blinked heavy eyelids. "Aye, you managed that, okay. Not sure there's anyone could stitch this up without leaving a nasty scar though."

"Just try me then."

Gavin sighed, but the breath shuddered and Tallen rested his hand over Gavin's heart. He felt the last rise of his chest and lowered his head, tears burning his eyes. He didn't hold them back. Gavin had trained him, taught him, raised him in every way that mattered. His real father certainly hadn't taught him how to survive in the world. Gavin had taken him in without question.

For years, Tallen had followed in his footsteps, learned everything he could, and did his best to emulate the man he wanted to call father more than any other.

He didn't know how long he sat at Gavin's side, but a chill crept up his spine, and when he opened his eyes again, the world was dark. A door slammed somewhere behind him, and he turned, expecting an attack. Nothing came forward though, and he realized it was just a strong wind blowing. His eyes turned down the path, and he remembered the old woman again.

He doubted she was still alive, but he had to check. His first mistake of the day had been to leave Gavin and let himself get distracted by the old woman. His latest mistake was forgetting her in his grief.

He wiped his face with his sleeve, but he could see the ash of the village smeared on his clothes and knew his face would look monstrous now. He grabbed his canteen and walked down the path to the barn where he'd left the old woman.

"Grandmother?" he asked.

The door creaked open, and he could barely make her out in the back corner. The moon was almost full in the sky and the broken rafters let enough light to find her by.

"You returned to me," she mumbled. "Almost too late."

"I'm so sorry. There was...a raider. A fight." It was all he could say, but she looked up at him with a knowing expression. Those white-coated eyes seemed to understand what he wasn't saying. "You wanted water. I brought you some."

She'd crawled out of the hay and was lying on the floor now. He propped her up gently and set the canteen to her lips. He let the water trickle out slowly and she drank what water remained. When she was done, he set her down onto her back and made her as comfortable as he could on the cold floor of the barn.

"I know the truth," she said, as she closed her eyes.

"What truth?"

"The words came long ago, but maybe it's not too late. Even if I didn't speak them at the time, may they come true now."

He watched as she opened her eyes again, but the white was replaced by a pulsing blue. He startled back, landing heavily on his ass as he scrambled away from her.

"The spider protects the throne. The realm betrays the king.
The ethereal crown once withered, regrows within the ring.
The hunter stalks the rainbow, to find the web of lies,
Old friends will be united in a kingdom full of eyes.
Death will have its fill. Freedom will be found.
The kingdom will be restored, when compassion is finally crowned."

He listened to her words and felt a stone drop into his stomach. He had always been good at puzzles, and this was easy enough to read. The spider and the hunter were plain to his eyes, but the rest?

It was an old prophecy, so the realm betraying the king could mean the way the people had prayed that King Cecil was a better man than King Ashford or his heir, Prince Ainsley. The rainbow had to be Sunlit Castle with its stunning, stained glass features.

But who would be united? What old friends? Could it be…? Could the spider have truly survived?

"It can still be restored, right?" He rushed back to her, looking into blue eyes that didn't seem to notice him. "Please, how can I make it right?"

Her eyes closed, and Tallen shook her, gently at first, but with increasing force until he was sure there was no waking. She was gone.

He was left alone in the world with her words. He'd never seen prophecy before, but everyone knew what the stories said. The blue light, infusing the seer with their sight, before stealing their vision. Few prophets lived long after they spoke their words. This woman must have been well-loved in Wilford, and well cared for over the years.

"It's not possible," he said, as he backed away. He kept moving until he ran into a wall of hay. The bale at his back supported him and he dropped his head back, trying to think. "He died. He died because I ran. I should have protected him." He pulled his knees up to his chest and dropped his head. "It was my duty to protect him."

He could remember the day, every detail, to a fault. The invasion of King Cecil of Dasmar. The castle in chaos. The invaders looking for Prince Ainsley. How the Prince had been with the seamstress and her son, and she'd hidden them in the courtyard together. How they'd been found, and he had run, leaving the other boy behind to suffer his fate at the hands of the invaders.

He shook his head, pushing the memories away. He'd spent years being better, learning to be the man he should have been that day—even if he'd just been an eleven-year-old boy. Was this a chance to right that wrong? Could the other boy still be alive?

His head swam with the implication of the old woman's words. Could they change things together? Could they save Asmian?

His head ached with it, almost as much as his heart. He stood slowly, legs shaking but steady as he reached his full height. Before he could plan his next step, he needed to complete the work he and Gavin had set out to do.

He placed the woman's hands over her heart and picked her up carefully. He trudged through the night and brought her to the building with the rest of the dead. He didn't have it in his heart to add Gavin to the pile. He set the building alight, saying a prayer to the Gods that the souls meet their journey's end at the Peaceful Valley and those who had been lost found their guides to return them safely.

As the pyre lit the night sky around him, he left and found a wooden table. He stacked wood around it and packed it with kindling to make a proper fire. He placed Gavin on it, but not before he took his mentor's possessions. He'd return them to the village once he made his way home, except those that were his by right of love.

As Gavin's body took flame, Tallen stumbled into a splintered doorway and slid down. Tears filled his vision and he wept openly until exhaustion took him. He dreamed of the long valley that Gavin would cross and begged his mentor to wait for him, but Gavin had laughed at him.

"Soon!" He pointed towards a house at the clearing in the woods. "I'll be waiting. We'll be together soon, son."

Morning found Tallen on the road towards the Sunlit Castle, the ancestral home of the Kings of Asmian. Tallen had to find the boy he'd left behind. If he was still alive, the trail began at the castle. He thought about returning home first, to give word to the people of Redhills, but he moved onward instead. He would send a messenger when he reached the next village, if he could.

If the prophecy still held true, he could turn the tide of evil that had befallen Asmian by undoing the mistakes of his past.

The day was long, and rain threatened, leaving the bleak grey of the world to seep into his joints and remind him of wounds long-healed.

He slept wet and cold under the shelter of a pine, but the great branches couldn't stop the water that seeped into the ground, nor could he make fire from wet branches.

Miserable and hungry, he ate on the road again, trying to put as many miles between himself and Gavin's death as he could. Gavin had taught him to blame the man holding the knife, and he knew he could get vengeance for his mentor at the castle. Those raiders were the king's responsibility, shirked, and he would see something done about it, once he fixed his mistakes.

When he grew too tired, he stopped and rested, but he and Gavin had been traveling the world for years, sometimes hunting for food or scouting raiding parties, or taking travelers safely to the next village. He was used to a long day's walk, but by nightfall, he was tired of the rain. There was no respite from it, and he shivered under his soaked clothes.

Morning gave him sunlight for a few hours. He was dried and warmed, but by midday, the rain fell again. Before evening, he began to look for a place to shelter. He needed a warm fire tonight. He turned off the main road when he found an area of rocky hills and caves. He passed on two before he noticed one higher than the others. He found a path that took him to the cave entrance, but darkness fell as he climbed.

He reached the cave and found light already spilling from the entrance. He hadn't seen anyone since he'd left Wilford, and he pulled Gavin's blades to protect himself from whatever was in there. It could be just another traveler like himself.

He walked into the cave mouth and found a man sitting beside a fire. Two conies roasted over it and the smell had him licking his lips. He and Gavin had always eaten plainly, but this smelled good enough to set before a king.

"Do you have a place for another at your fire?" He kept his hands at his sides, weapons down, but easily visible. He didn't want a fight, but the other guy should know he was ready for one if it came.

The man turned and Tallen gasped.

"Fae..." he whispered.

The creature smiled, warm and inviting, as he gestured towards his fire. "All are welcome here, friend."

Tallen watched the skin around burnished, gold eyes wrinkle ever so slightly as the fae's smile grew. His dark hair hung loose down his back and Tallen had never seen anything he wanted to touch more. He gripped the hilt of Gavin's blades tighter.

"Forgive me."

He bowed his head slightly, but kept his eyes on the fae. He had always been told these lands were fae territory, but in all his years he had never come across one. He knew what they said, but his tongue was dry in his mouth and all etiquette fell from his memory. He began to back away, but the fae moved faster than he could track, and a hand was wrapped around his elbow, pulling him closer.

"I have offered you hospitality, and on such a horrid night. Would you say no?"

"No, of course not," he assured. He wouldn't dare. He had a debt to pay, and he couldn't allow a stupid misstep with a fae to stop him. "Thank you for the offer."

The fae led him back towards the fire and Tallen sheathed Gavin's knives before he sat on the stone floor. The fae sat between him and the exit, but there was nothing he could do. Even if he had that advantage, he wouldn't make it out into the night if the fae wished otherwise.

"Please, eat. I would be a poor host if I left you hungry while I dined."

"Is this fae food?" Tallen asked.

The fae laughed and it felt like silk had slithered over his skin, leaving pleasant goosebumps all over his body.

"It's simple cony; nothing from the fae-realm. Do you think I have come to travel the world just to lure unsuspecting humans to their demise?"

"Have you?"

There was a light in the fae's eyes, and Tallen couldn't look away from it.

"No. I have no intention of harming you."

Tallen nodded. The fae didn't lie. No one believed them, but they

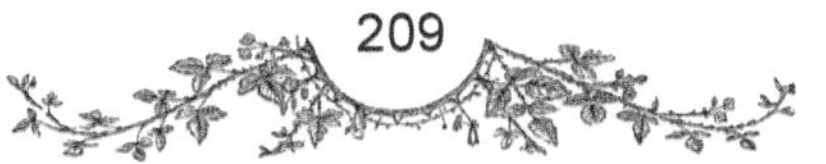

didn't lie outright. So, he didn't plan to harm Tallen. It wasn't exactly reassuring, but the fire was warm, and the food was tempting. The fae took his silence as consent, took a cony off the fire and set it on a rock before him to cool.

The fae took the second cony off the fire and placed it next to the first, moving closer to Tallen. "Do I get to know your name, sir?"

It was dangerous to give the fae your name. In the wrong hands, a name gave power. For Tallen, his name could unmake him. He was in a position of advantage though, because while Tallen was the name he had lived with for ten years, it was not his original name. His current name held little power.

"I'm Tallen," he said, as he warmed his fingers by the fire. It was warm enough now that he dropped his pack and shed his wet outer layers.

He looked at the fae and the man had his head tilted to the side, grin still in place. "You can call me Wynham."

"Is it your name?" Tallen asked. He realized his words too late, but the fae didn't take offense.

"It is a name, and you may call me it. That's enough for tonight, isn't it?"

Tallen nodded, grateful for the reprieve. When the fae pointed to the food before him, Tallen took it and didn't complain when he was given a reason to keep quiet. Gavin was the only person he'd ever felt comfortable talking to, even after all his time in the village. He couldn't leave the fae without giving offense, but he could keep his mouth shut and do his best to get out without any more trouble. Perhaps the fae would leave when Tallen proved to be uninspiring.

He ate quickly, washing it down with stale water from his waterskin. Days of travel behind him, a warm fire before him, a world of grief and anxiety pressed into him. As he stretched out, he felt more tired than he had in years. Since the days he'd been on the run and had stumbled into Redhills.

"No harm will befall you tonight, Tallen," the fae said softly. "Sleep well. You have a long road ahead of you."

Tallen woke the next morning, stiff from sleeping on the cold, stone floor, but he'd slept deeply. He sat up and looked. There was no sign of the fae who had visited him the night before.

"Well, that's taken care of then."

He was pleased Wynham was gone, but surprised. His father had always said people exaggerated the stories of the fae to explain their own weaknesses, though the villagers had been adamant about the dangers they posed. He could now say that his father had been right.

Probably the first time in his adult life he'd thought that.

"Awake finally?"

Tallen startled as Wynham walked into the cavern.

The fae smiled. "Did you think I was gone?"

"I did," Tallen said, as he grabbed his cloak and began to dress for the day's travel.

"You'll go without food?"

"I've imposed too much, and I have a long journey ahead. A walking breakfast will do me fine." Tallen checked his bow was still strapped securely to his pack, then pulled it onto his back. He let his fingers drift over Gavin's blades, strapped to his thighs. "Thank you for the company and the care, Wynham," he said, stiff with long-unused formality. "May the road you seek guide you safely."

He didn't wait for a response, but left the cave and stepped out into the morning light. The weather had cleared, and he took a deep breath. It had been years since he'd run from the castle. It was time to start the journey home.

"I suppose I'll have to see this all the way through." Wynham joined him outside the cave. "Shall we begin?"

He didn't look at Tallen, but at the surrounding land. It was a beautiful view of the Summerflood River valley, but Tallen had little interest in the scenery.

"What do you mean?"

"You are obviously on urgent business. I will join you."

"That's not necessary."

"Perhaps, I rarely come across urgent business though, and I have a desire to learn more about you, Tallen. You hardly spoke at all last night. How could I end our relationship in such a way? Yes. I have decided I will join you."

"I don't have time for this, Fae." He was being rude, and he knew it, but Wynham seemed to take the whole thing as a joke and Tallen had never been involved in anything more serious. He had a chance to change things, to make right the sins of his past. "What do you really want?"

Wynham regarded him without the wicked smile, and the light in his eyes grew darker. "I want only to accompany you on this journey, Tallen. I have no other desire."

There was a world of lies behind the fae's eyes, but none on his lips. Tallen didn't trust him. He might not mean Tallen harm, but he certainly wasn't there to help. The fae never did anything without motive or cost.

"I can't stop you from traveling, Fae. But I head to the Sunlit Castle, and King Cecil is no friend to your kind."

"King Cecil is a friend to no one that isn't willing to enrich his coffers," Wynham said. "I'll take my chances. If the road becomes too troublesome, I'll take my leave. You don't need to worry about me, Tallen."

Tallen decided not to answer. Instead, he began the trek that took him back into the valley and headed west.

They traveled for three days with no adventures. Tallen steered away from any signs of villages, and Wynham warned him when travelers walked the same path. Tallen quickly learned that having a fae with him made the road easier. He didn't trust him, but when he set out snares they were filled, and they didn't lack for fresh berries and fruits along their path. He didn't know if the fae had the power to grow them, or if he could find them where no one else could, but they made quick time without having to worry for food.

Wynham didn't ask him to talk, which surprised Tallen since he'd said his reason for following had been to get to know him. Instead, Wynham spoke softly of the world he'd seen, and of the beauty of the fae-realm. Sometimes, he would sing in a tongue Tallen had never heard. The stories moved his heart more than he wanted to admit. Wynham, with his intense eyes and mischievous smile, moved him more than he wanted to admit.

He didn't trust the fae, Tallen reminded himself, but he had to admit he was a pleasant traveling companion.

"There is a place, not far from here," Wynham said, as they passed through the lower hill regions. "It wouldn't take long to reach, and there are healing springs."

"Healing?" Tallen was skeptical, but Wynham hadn't led him astray yet.

"The hot springs are filled with waters from the fae-realm. Such places are rare in Asmian. It would be a shame to miss them when they wouldn't delay our journey more than an hour's time."

"Alright. Lead the way."

Wynham smiled broadly at him and Tallen couldn't help but return it. Wynham began to sing a bright, festive tune. Tallen felt his steps were lighter for hearing it, and he looked away as Wynham's smile grew.

The weather held clear as Wynham brought them to the healing springs. A system of caverns burrowed through the hillsides, but Wynham led them unerringly down into the maze to the springs.

"We can make camp in here," Tallen offered, as they entered a fair-sized cavern just outside of the smaller chamber that held the spring.

"Leave me to it." The fae removed his pack and set it on the floor. "You should enjoy the water while you can. The aches and pains of the last few days will leave you entirely."

Tallen eyed him a moment, then shrugged as he tossed his pack to the floor. His entire life he'd been told that the fae were terrible, horrifying creatures. Wynham was going out of this way to prove the exact opposite. He was courteous and considerate, and he shared his joviality freely. He was nothing like Tallen had been taught.

He left the cavern and walked into the chamber with the hot spring. He stripped out of his clothes and slipped into the water. The heat was divine, and he could feel the stress of the last few days melting from his shoulders. He dunked his head under the water and scrubbed at his scalp, coming up for a breath before doing it again. When he was done, he found a natural shelf along the spring wall. He leaned back against the warm rocks and closed his eyes.

He must have fallen asleep. Awareness crept up on him gently, with the warmth of the water against his skin and a familiar voice singing softly. He slowly opened his eyes and watched as Wynham rose from the spring. His long, dark hair trailed into the water and danced on the surface like ink. The fae was turned away from him and Tallen couldn't help but admire the width of his back and the strength of his arms as he pulled his hair to the side and wrung it out. The movement drew Tallen's eyes to three ugly red scars across the otherwise perfect expanse of Wynham's back.

He stood up and moved a step closer, but Wynham turned, letting his hair loose to cover his back again. Tallen looked up and was surprised by the shadowed look in his eyes.

"You were asleep," Wynham said.

"I was."

It was a stupid answer, but his tongue was tied, and his brain was caught trying to keep his hands from reaching out. The fae was beautiful beyond measure, but this unbound creature before him was intoxicating. It was dangerous, this desire to touch.

"I should get out," he said quickly.

He scrambled out of the spring and grabbed his clothes to dress in the other chamber. As he pulled on his underclothes, he realized the fae had washed everything. A fire burned at the other end of the cave where Wynham's clothes were already set out to dry. Tallen set his outer layers there as well and pulled on his remaining clothes. Food was resting on warm stones and Tallen felt guilty that he'd slept while Wynham had taken care of the chores for the night.

He stretched out on the warm floor and had barely settled before Wynham came back. He wore loose white linen pants and a tunic. His hair dripped down his back and Tallen turned his eyes away from the revealing sight.

Wynham approached with the rock he'd used as a plate and handed it to Tallen. He came back a second later and sat next to him. Tallen wasn't sure how to react to that, but Wynham ate silently and Tallen felt himself relaxing more in the fae's presence. When their meal was done, Tallen cleaned up to atone for his earlier nap.

"Are you feeling better?" Wynham asked, when Tallen came back.

Tallen nodded, though he'd barely thought about it since he woke up. "It truly is a healing spring. I haven't felt this healthy or rested since... Well, long before I started this journey."

"Speaking of your journey, we'll reach the castle soon. What are your plans?"

Tallen wasn't sure he wanted to talk to the fae about it, but there was no one else to discuss it with. The man had been a good traveling companion since they'd taken to the road together and though he still didn't trust him, he was beginning to feel that Wynham had at least earned a little faith.

"It'll sound crazy to you, I'm sure, but when I was in Wilford, an old woman spoke a prophecy. She said it was old, but that it might still come true. I'm going to the castle to find someone I thought had died more than ten years ago. I think if I can save him, then maybe I can stop the curse that's fallen over Asmian."

"That's a tall role for a tracker from a small village."

"Maybe," Tallen said. "But I have to do it. When I get to the castle, I have to find a way into the prison."

"What do you hope you can accomplish, Tallen? Is this prophecy really worth the tortures King Cecil will put to you if you are caught?"

He didn't want to talk about this, and the fae's questions were frustrating him, but he tried to answer calmly. "Ten years ago, I forgot who I was.

When Cecil's army swept into the castle, they killed anyone that might be royalty. I ran and saved myself, leaving another behind to die. If I do nothing else, I *will* regain my honor."

"Cecil's prison won't be easy to access. What if you die in this attempt?"

"Then at least I'll die doing something right!"

He got up and stormed away, walking through the tunnels until he came to a place he didn't know. He crossed his arms over his chest, feeling the ache of that day all over again. He had grown used to it, but the old woman's words had reopened the wound. He took a deep breath and tried to still the racing of his heart. He knew the right thing to do.

"Tallen, you aren't on this journey alone."

Wynham's voice was soft as he approached. Tallen felt the gentle sweep of the fae's hand across his back, before he rested it on the nape of his neck.

"Why are you here, Wynham?"

"I only want to see you reach your journey's end. Whatever you need of me, I will see you through it."

"You barely know me."

"So few men are bound by their words. They speak lie after lie, deceive others almost as much as they deceive themselves. I know you hold secrets, but there is honor in you that few men attain these days. Nobility rests on your shoulders and I would be at your side to see it."

"I'm not noble."

Wynham pulled Tallen around and they were face to face, too close for comfort, but not close enough for Tallen's desires.

"You are. I can see that in your heart, clear enough."

Wynham moved closer, his hand on Tallen's hip as he leaned into his space. He could pull away, but he'd been alone for too long. Even with Gavin, he'd felt a distance because of the secrets he kept. Here, with Wynham, he felt as if someone finally saw him for who he was.

When Wynham's lips grazed his, he didn't move away. He leaned into the kiss, opening to him as the kiss deepened. Tallen slid his hand into Wynham's hair and clenched his fingers in the silken strands. Wynham pressed him closer against the wall of the cave, his own hand reaching under Tallen's tunic. Tallen moaned at the touch and Wynham pulled away, just enough to rest his forehead against Tallen's temple.

"We should take this back to the fire," Wynham whispered.

"Or the hot spring," Tallen offered.

He felt Wynham's lips split into a grin before the fae took him by the hand and led him quickly back the way they'd come.

Tallen woke the next morning with Wynham's arms around him and a deep-seated contentment he hadn't known in years. He looked up at his lover and pressed a kiss to his lips. Wynham smiled, though he didn't open his eyes.

"We could stay in this chamber forever," Wynham offered.

"Eventually we'd need to leave for food."

"Perhaps I'll just eat you."

Tallen laughed, but he leaned on one elbow and looked down at Wynham. "You are a fae. It's quite possible that was your plan all along."

Wynham was the one that laughed then and his mirth was contagious. Tallen took a deep breath, then settled back into the fae's arms.

"We'll reach Sunlit Castle tomorrow. After that, after I see this done, I'll come back here with you. I have no reason to return to Redhills. I'll follow you, wherever you want."

"You would?" Wynham asked.

"I will. If you want me to."

"I want that. More than I can tell."

"It's settled then. When this is finished, we'll come back here to rest, then we'll go wherever you want."

Wynham turned him onto his back and kissed the rest of the words from his mouth. Thankfully, he had already planned a late morning start.

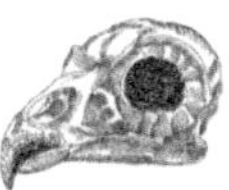

Sunlit Castle was everything Tallen remembered. Stained glass walls decorated the upper levels of the castle and cast colored lights across the city as the sun rose in the sky. It was magnificent, and Tallen's heart ached in memory of the time he'd called the castle home. Thankfully, King Cecil hadn't destroyed the glass when he took the castle.

There were other changes Tallen could see in the city though. The streets were dirty and in ill-repair. Guards were posted at every major intersection.

He watched as a guard beat a merchant when he asked full payment for a piece of fine silverware. People all around turned their eyes and lowered their heads. King Cecil might have secured the castle, but the people hated his rule, even more than they'd hated Ashford's.

Wynham walked beside him, face hidden in the deep hood of his cloak. Tallen had no idea how people overlooked him, but Wynham reminded him.

"I'm fae. How poorly do you think of me, that I can't perform this little act of glamour?"

Tallen smiled back at him. "Perhaps you've put a glamour on me, so I no longer think of you as a fae."

"What do you think of me as then?"

"I think of you as mine. None of the rest matters, so long as you're mine."

"So long as your heart beats, I will keep it as I keep my own."

Tallen turned away before Wynham could notice the grin on his face. When he did, he noticed the guard he was looking for. He elbowed Wynham to redirect his attention. "He's the one the innkeeper told us about."

"I don't think this is the best plan, Tallen."

"If something goes wrong, we meet back at the inn."

Tallen walked away before Wynham could reply. He followed the man into a congested street. A street performer was attracting a crowd and Tallen moved closer to the guard. The performer spit fire above the crowd and as the guard cheered with the rest, Tallen made his move. He bumped into the guard and reached for the keys he'd seen him slip into his pocket earlier. With hands that could pluck a fish from a swift stream, he lifted the keys and tucked them into his pouch in a heartbeat.

"Watch it, vagrant," the guard grunted.

Tallen bowed his head, mostly to hide his smile. "Begging your pardon, sir."

He made his way back through the crowd, only to see another half-dozen guards coming his way.

"Hold it right there!" the leader barked. "You think we can't spot a thief in our own city? Turn out your pockets."

Tallen held up his hands, ready to comply, just as the fire-breather let out another gust of flame. He twisted back into the crowd, scattering onlookers, and burst out the other side, into the nearest alleyway. For all the years he'd been gone, the city streets hadn't changed, and through twists and turns in the side streets and back alleys, he found his favorite hideaway, where the guards would never find him.

He tried not to think about the boy who had shared in his adventures. All he could do was try to make that right.

He cursed his luck and, even more, cursed that Wynham had been right. He made his way back around the city until he reached the room he and the fae had rented that morning.

He was pacing the floor before Wynham appeared in the doorway.

"Where have you been?" he demanded.

"Were you worried?"

"Of course! Cecil hates the fae. If you were caught—"

"Good thing I *am* fae then. None of them could catch me."

Tallen shook his head as he sat at the small table and tried to think. He'd been unable to do anything but worry until he appeared. "I got the keys, but the other guards spotted me," he explained. "If they figure out that I took them, they'll be on high alert."

"I don't think they'll figure it out."

Tallen looked up at the mischievous tone in Wynham's voice. "What did you do?"

Wynham pulled his hand out of his pocket and dangled a flowery handkerchief before Tallen. "I might have replaced them with something… convincing."

Before his eyes, the handkerchief turned into a familiar bundle of keys, then back again.

"How did you…?" He shook his head before Wynham could answer. "Of course. Fae. Tricksters. Scoundrels."

Wynham laughed. "I am all of the above. Though I would prefer another epithet."

"And what is that?"

"Beloved?"

Tallen stood and kissed the fae quickly. "Do you doubt?"

Wynham brushed the back of his fingers over Tallen's cheek. "I love. What lover doesn't want to hear such words from their heart's desire?"

"Tomorrow, when this is all done, I will spend the rest of my nights showing you just how loved you are."

"We could start tonight."

Tallen laughed as he was swept into another kiss. And into bed.

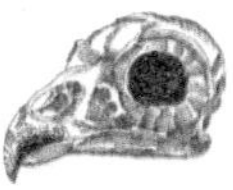

Everything had gone according to plan. Tallen was able to sneak into the castle's lower levels through little-used passageways that had been blocked since before Ashford had died. Wynham stood behind him, but the fae had little power here. The prison levels had too much iron and he was weakened.

Tallen had argued for him to stay behind, but the fae refused. One thing Tallen had learned was that he couldn't argue with his lover.

Tallen watched as the guards passed. He took a deep breath and steeled himself for the next move. He crept out of this hiding place and down the hallway to where the prisoner was held. It was an old cell, rusty and damp. As a child, he'd been terrified of these cages, but his father had made him walk the halls.

To learn to be a man.

The stolen keys clanked as Tallen opened the lock. He pushed the door open and turned his eyes to the huddled figure inside.

There was little light from the outside, just a small window that gave the barest illumination to the dark corners. Sitting on a dirty bed of hay was a young man. He was bone thin, face scarred and covered in filth. He sat with his back straight and his shoulders high though. He was regal, no matter the conditions he'd been thrown into. He was everything Prince Ainsley should have been.

Tallen felt tears fill his eyes as he looked at the man who had once been his only friend. "I thought you were dead," he whispered. "I thought they killed you in the courtyard. I would have come sooner if I had known."

The man's eyes widened in understanding. "Ainsley?"

Tallen sobbed as he ran to the young man. "I let you take my place in this cell, and bear my name, but it should never have been yours. I'm sorry, Tallen."

"So, you were right."

He turned to find a guard with a knife to Wynham's throat and the king's bodyguards striding into the cell. "Wynham!"

King Cecil appeared, and looked around in disdain. "We kept him for years, watching. Waiting. The fae said prophecy was not yet done with Prince Ainsley. Little did we realize, we had the wrong man all this time."

Tallen—Ainsley, the name he'd given up so long ago—looked at Wynham and he could see the truth in the fae's eyes. "You knew?"

"I told you I could see the nobility in you. The old woman's prophecy was just a retelling. The original vision belonged to the fae. To me."

"What do you want from us?" the real Tallen asked.

"The fae said the prophecy wasn't done, so I did the only thing I could. I kept you as bait, hoping the real prince would return someday. Now, I'll kill you both."

"You don't need to do this," Wynham said. "You can just keep them locked up. The prophecy does not say they have to die."

King Cecil laughed. "I'm not a fool." He raised his hand and motioned with his finger. The guards in the room began to move forward.

"Tallen, you need to make a break for it," Ainsley said, as he kept himself between his friend and the guards.

"Ainsley, you're the prince. You're the true ruler of Asmian. I'm just the seamstress's son. You should have left me here."

"No. You were my closest friend and I won't let you die here."

He pulled the blades from the sheaths on his thighs and prepared to fight.

"Don't! You can escape! Leave me!"

"I won't!"

"Tallen!"

Wynham's scream cut above their argument as the king's guards attacked. He could hear Wynham struggling against his captors, but he couldn't turn to look at his lover. He pushed Tallen back against the wall and as the guards rushed, he evaded their blows. The space was too close for longsword work, but his shorter blades bit deep as he slashed into two guards in one magnificent circle.

From the corner of his eye, he saw movement. A guard had passed him, sword poised to pierce Tallen's heart. He spun and ran the man through before he could attack. The guard toppled, taking the blade with him, and he fought on with the very last gift Gavin had ever given him.

It was a fierce struggle, and Ainsley felt the sting of the blade more than once. Blood trickled down his thigh, and his left arm was little more than dead meat. He fell to his knees, too weak to fight, or even to stand, and felt a blade drive through his back.

The world slowed. The pain stopped. The world darkened and spun as Tallen hit the hard floor of the prison cell.

"Ainsley!"

Tallen, his oldest friend, who'd suffered in his place and never betrayed his escape, slid to a halt next to him and cradled his head. Ainsley could see the guards around them, standing back, bewitched by Wynham's magic, as the fae took his hand. But he had changed, no longer covered in the dirt of the castle's decrepit halls, but as pristine and beautiful as he had been when they woke together the first time.

"Wynham?"

"You have done what needed to be done."

"You knew all along that I was the prince. Why did you let me lie?"

"Prophecy is never easy to understand, even for those who speak it."

"You said I didn't have to die."

"It was one outcome."

"And you came to stop it?"

Wynham kissed his brow and there were tears in his eyes. "No. I came to witness. The kingdom has held its breath for too long, waiting to see which side would win this war. Waiting for a prophecy to be fulfilled."

"Was my father really so evil that you came to watch me die and see Cecil take his place?"

"No." Wynham kissed his lips and Tallen could taste his tears. "King Ashford and King Cecil showed how corrupt human hearts have become, but your sacrifice has stirred the hearts of fae. We won't allow it again. When your heart stops, my kind will hear the call. We will rise, and we will take this kingdom as our own."

"And what of this? What of us?"

The words were lead on his tongue, but he had to speak them. Tears leaked from his eyes, and he didn't try to check them. Wynham had destroyed him completely and he deserved to see the ruin he left in his wake.

"You have taught me what no vision and no amount of watching the human world could. I have loved you, and I have been loved. I will take the care of your people into my heart, and I will be just and kind. I will sacrifice for them, just as you have for the boy you thought dead."

"Save him, Wynham," Ainsley whispered, as his lover ran his fingers over his cheeks. "Save them all. Please. Be good to my people. I wish I had listened in the cave. I...I wish I had stayed there with you and given up this idea, but..."

"We both know you couldn't have," Wynham said, as he kissed Ainsley's lips. "But I would have stayed with you as long as I could."

Ainsley felt the life draining from him, but he was warm. He could almost feel the hot springs and his lover's embrace calling him.

"Call me by my name," he asked. "Just once. Let me be the person I was supposed to be."

"Prince Ainsley," Wynham whispered. "Goodbye, my beloved Ainsley."

WILD

BY MORGAN ELEKTRA

I don't make wishes anymore, but if I did I would only need one. I would wish us anywhere but there that night.

The summer of 1997 was a dream. The weather in upstate New York was hot and perfect. Phoebe, Billy and I snuck out of our respective windows and spent all the hours from midnight to dawn cruising back roads in the dented, green Dodge Dart Phoebe inherited from her grandfather. We puffed cigarettes like Victorian chimneys and sang loudly to Live and Concrete Blonde. Sometimes we would pull off the road into an empty field, lie back on the still-warm hood and watch the stars.

That's where all the really important moments happened; the conversations about the teachers we hated and the classmates we loved, our hopes and fears and plans for the future, what we'd do when we finally got through this one, final year of high school.

It's where Billy confessed the things that happened at home when he acted 'too gay', and Phoebs and I held him while he cried. Hot metal burned the backs of our thighs while Phoebe railed against the limits of her small body and our small town and the small minds of the people who lived there. I poured out every doubt about myself that huddled in the dark corners of my mind to those two while contemplating Orion's Belt.

It was our ritual. Better and more powerful than any of the sweat lodges and harvest dances Grandfather had dragged me to every summer since I'd begun to bleed.

Any other night...

Though I guess the whys don't matter to anyone but me anymore. It's what happened after that everyone always wants to know about. It's what *you* want to know. And I suppose I'm finally ready to tell it all.

Not that you'll believe me.

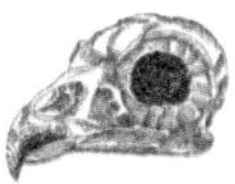

Phoebe practically thrummed with nervous energy when she picked me up. She tapped her ringed fingers against the steering wheel in a rapid, pattering rhythm—*tun-tun-tun-tun-tun-tun*—as she waited impatiently for me to pry open the finicky passenger door.

"Hurry, Ellie," she said, eyes glittering in the dark, lips trembling in a smile. "Come on."

I slid onto the cracked, black vinyl of the front seat, pressing into Billy's side. He threw one thin arm around my shoulders and the other around Phoebe's, but before either of us could speak, Phoebe gunned the engine. The light from my front porch filtered through the trees, casting wavering shadows over her angular face.

She chewed her lower lip and pushed a strand of red-gold hair behind her ear. She'd added another piercing, a jade hoop, on the upper curve just that week.

"I need to show you two something."

Her voice, normally full of sharp humor, was hushed. Billy and I nodded without speaking, each of us hearing the quaver. Eagerness or fear, I've never been sure. Maybe both.

Phoebe drove with purpose, music on but turned low. She'd chosen David Bowie, which meant Phoebe had been to visit her mom. She always said there was something about the songs on *Aladdin Sane* that soothed her after listening to her mother's broken rambling.

I leaned my head against Billy's bony shoulder, the clean scent of his deodorant wafting up from the warm, slightly musty fabric of his flannel shirt. He propped his chin on my head, humming along to 'Lady Grinning Soul'.

Thunder rolled in the distance, faint and grumbling, as Phoebe navigated down roads that were little more than narrow strips of smooth asphalt crowded on either side by woods thick with trees. The sharp scent of sap drifted in through the open windows as we sped toward our destination. In the dark, with the trees streaming past and the road unspooling like a grey satin ribbon ahead of us for what seemed like forever, it felt like we were flying.

My body was heavy and my head slightly floaty with exhaustion by the time Phoebe turned off onto a rutted, dirt road. The forest drew back like a curtain until the trees were a darker line against the black horizon.

Tall, dry grass brushed against the sides of the car, filling it with the sound of rough-throated whispers. I shuddered at the eerie noise and reached to turn up the music, but Phoebe stopped the car before I could.

The only sound in the silent night was the ticking of the cooling engine. Phoebe slid out of the car a second later. She left her door open and didn't look back at us as she spoke.

"There are flashlights in the glove box."

She waited for us just ahead of the car, in the middle of the bright cone of light cast by the headlights, pacing back and forth. I stared out the windshield at her, watching her worry the silver rings on her thin, white fingers while she studied the tree line. Billy opened the glove box, remembering to knock his fist against it to pop the latch when it stuck.

"You have any idea what this is about?"

I chewed my lip, tasting blood. "None."

He handed me one of the flashlights, his grin crooked. Moonlight glinted off his glasses.

"Guess we'd better go find out then."

I still don't understand how he could be so endlessly optimistic. No matter how dark things got, Billy still smiled. Still joked. Even blackened, his hazel eyes held hope.

Phoebe's soft voice carried on the light breeze, drifting back to us like sweet opium smoke. "C'mon."

Billy slid out the driver's side, casting a glance over his shoulder at me. I sighed, my lungs tight with unease. He just shrugged and turned toward our friend. I switched off the headlights, throwing them both into faintly moonlit darkness.

We followed her, like we always did. Billy and I had been friends since preschool, but ever since that day in junior high when we'd met Phoebe, we'd been drawn into her orbit. Satellites to her tiny, brilliant sun.

Twigs crunched beneath our feet as we trudged through the dense woods, the spicy scent of crumbling bark, moss, and leaf mold rising around us with each step. It was silent but for the sound of our passage, the high whine of insects, and the occasional furtive rustle of some small animal in the underbrush. Sporadic flashes of lightning were the only illumination, apart from the thin beams from our flashlights. The moon didn't penetrate the thick branches.

You're no doubt wondering why we followed her, no questions asked, into a dark and unknown place. I probably would be too, if I were in your seat and you in mine. But only if I didn't know Phoebe like you don't know her.

She was unlike anything that tiny town had ever seen.

Short—barely five feet, even at seventeen—thin, sharp-featured, strange, charismatic, and so pale she seemed to glow. Her hair was the thing people always remembered about her. Her step-mother called it 'strawberry blonde', but it wasn't.

It shone like strands of gold set on fire and fell in soft, silky waves down her narrow back. And it almost seemed to float around her, to move even when she was still. She rarely wore it down, because people she didn't know or like would often just come up and run it through their fingers or squeeze handfuls and stare at her with glittering eyes like they wanted to snatch it off her head.

Like I said, the hair, you noticed right away. It's only once you got past it—if you got past it—that you saw her eyes.

They were sort of green and sort of blue, like the color of the water in those ads they show you for tropical vacations, the ones with white sand and a perfect sky and water so clear you can see all the way to the bottom. Phoebe's eyes were just like that. Crystalline and serene.

My father's been to one of those beaches before, and he said you had to be careful because the clarity of the water could trick people.

"When you can see the bottom like that," he said, "sometimes your brain thinks it must be close. You might not realize how much danger you're in until you're already out too far."

Phoebe's eyes were just like that too.

So, we followed her. We always followed her. Every time she said "I have the best idea!" or "This is what we should do..." we did. Even if we were terrified—like the time we got lost hiking Quarry Mountain—or angry—when that substitute teacher, Mrs. Bromley, slapped Billy for pointing out she was wrong about what year Martin Luther posted his little Dear John to the church—or emotionally exhausted from listening to our parents fight all evening, like I was that night.

Phoebe led with purpose, sometimes straying to one side as if to check we were on the right path. Not that there was any path I could see. But her steps never faltered. I linked my arm through Billy's and we stumbled along together, sharing the light and a little warmth.

Though it was still summer, the night air held a trace of autumn chill and I'd only worn a long-sleeved t-shirt.

The rain started sometime before we got to the creek, but the trees were still so close and thick that we stayed dry. The steady sound of it spattering against the leaves over our heads was hypnotic. Between that and the hushed sound of our breathing, I felt lulled into an almost waking sleep, broken only by the occasional stray, cool raindrop that slipped through the canopy to trickle down the back of my neck.

Phoebe still hadn't told us where we were going. She didn't even look back to make sure we followed. Her lithe form wove through the crowd of dark tree trunks and grasping, pricker-fingered bushes with the ease of a dancer. She swayed, her arms occasionally stretching out to her sides to brush against rough bark or glossy green leaves. Every once in a while I heard her voice, drowsy and honeyed, though I couldn't make out her words.

My breath tripped when I realized she was singing softly. Not Bowie, or anything else I recognized, but a lilting melody that made my skin tingle and my heart flutter too fast.

It began to thud against my ribs like a trapped bird when she reached up and undid the tie in her hair, tossing it into the darkness and letting the shimmering silken mass cascade down to the small of her back.

Strands sparked in the glow of our light, and each flash of lightning left an after-image of writhing, reaching copper tendrils on my pupils. My belly filled with greasy dread.

Beside me, Billy shivered, though it really wasn't that cold. His lips brushed my ear as he leaned close to whisper, and his voice sounded almost as groggy as I felt.

"This is not good, Ellie."

I nodded. I knew he was right. I could feel it too, the darkness a heavy hand pressing down on us. My chest hurt with it. The air was too thick, like during the height of summer humidity, only cold.

Every breath was like breathing underwater.

Still, neither of us stopped walking or called out to get Phoebe to stop. And when we reached the creek, swollen with the rain that fell now in steady sheets, we both pulled off our socks and shoes, rolled up our jeans, and waded across. The water was biting cold and the rocks on the bottom were both sharp and slippery. Phoebe glided across as if she were on a smooth floor. Billy and I clung to each other for balance and nearly ended up going under more than a few times.

Though not deep—*you might not realize how much danger you're in until you're already out too far*—the current was swift and pulled at our legs, trying to trip us.

Still, we followed her. At that point, it felt inevitable.

Just beyond the creek, the land began to rise in a steep bramble-covered incline that we had to pick through carefully to avoid being scored by the wicked thorns.

It seemed at the time like it took us hours to reach the clearing, but the prosecutor says it's only a mile from where Phoebe parked the car. A twenty-minute walk. He timed it and presented survey maps and everything, so I suppose it must be true. At least, on any other day, it might well be. But that night, nothing was as it seemed.

The first hint I had that something was wrong—really wrong and not just odd—were the mushrooms. Just as we crested the hill, the rain stopped abruptly and a line of mushrooms greeted us, knee high and nodding in the wind. They had thick, pale, waxy stems and huge, liver-red caps speckled with brown dots that looked like rot.

They shone in the moonlight with a greasy sheen and exuded a musky, mineral sort of smell that made my skin feel too tight and my stomach turn. When I glanced at Billy, his face was flushed and his narrow shoulders hunched. He avoided my gaze.

We both paused, but Phoebe stepped between two particularly fragrant and grotesque specimens as if nothing was out of the ordinary.

"This is it."

I turned to Billy, my light trained on the rocky ground at his feet. He gave me a look I couldn't read, his fingers so tight around his flashlight that the bones of his knuckles pressed pale against his skin. His face was white too, the faint light casting sharp shadows under his cheekbones. The bulb flickered, and for just a moment Billy's thin throat seemed topped with a grim-faced skull.

My heart swelled behind my ribcage and clogged my throat.

"Maybe—"

My voice gave out, the half-whispered word almost inaudible even to me. I chewed my lip. I wanted to turn back then. Desperately. Panic set my limbs twitching. I thought about simply leaving. Running away.

But Phoebe was already in the clearing, staring up at the suddenly cloudless sky, and as I hesitated, Billy edged between the frightful fungi and joined her. Once they stepped onto that patch of abnormally perfect grass, I was lost. I couldn't leave them.

I brushed one of the disgusting toadstools as I slid over whatever boundary they marked. It smeared my jeans with milky, viscous goo. When it soaked through the damp, worn denim, it made my skin tingle and burn. I scratched at my thigh.

"Phoebs."

My voice cracked with trepidation. She stood in the center of the clearing, head back as she stared up at the star-strewn sky.

"This is where it happened."

Billy played the beam of his flashlight around the clearing, illuminating the lush, dark green grass. Unlike the wildness of the woods, the clearing looked groomed, like someone had recently mown it.

The grass was nearly a perfect circle, I realized, surrounded by the ring of those hideous mushrooms.

My heart trembled in my chest.

"Where what happened, Phoebs?"

"My mother." She spun in place, arms out, head still tipped back, like we used to do when we were kids. Make yourself dizzy and then you fall down and it feels like the ground is rocking beneath you. "She used to come here. She told me."

Billy darted a wide-eyed glance at me.

"Phoebe," he began, gesturing at me with the flashlight, urging me toward her.

I moved closer, reaching out to take her hand. She stopped spinning. Her fingers were cold in mine. I squeezed them.

"You saw her today?"

Phoebe folded to the ground gracefully, legs crossed. She nodded.

"She wrote me, said she was finally going to tell me the truth."

I exchanged another tense look with Billy. Marianne O'Hara had been in an institution since Phoebe was six. I didn't know exactly what was wrong with her, because Phoebe didn't like to talk about it, but I knew she'd tried to hurt Phoebe.

Billy bent his thin frame into origami on the ground beside her, gripping his ankle in one hand.

"The truth about what, Phoebs?"

She stared out into the rustling woods.

"Everything."

The soft, eerie, sing-song cadence of her voice echoed through the dark forest and skittered up my spine. She smiled at me and butted her shoulder against Billy. Billy glanced up at me, the fingers of his left hand white-knuckled where they curled around his ankle. His eyes pled with mine.

"Come sit with us, Ellie."

With a sigh, I sank to the grass. It was soft, cool, and damp under my butt. I tucked my chin against my shoulder, trying to ignore the way the mushrooms smelled and the fact that the sky above us was a crystal clear hole in the heavy cloud cover.

Phoebe hummed softly under her breath and turned her face up to the sky as if the sun were shining and she wanted to bask in it. I reached out to twine my fingers with hers, running my thumb over the heavy silver ring on her left index finger.

"What'd your mom tell you, Phoebs?"

She lifted our joined hands and pressed them to her lips. They were a warm, satin shock compared to the chill air, the sensation making my belly twist and go heavy. I pressed my knees together as I felt the reverberation of her humming against my skin. She spoke against my knuckles.

"She used to meet my father here."

Billy cocked his head, brows flicking upward.

"Here? Why?"

I snorted at the disbelief in his voice. Looking around, I felt my own credulity strain. Woodland trysts were one thing, but this place was just creepy. Phoebe smiled, eyes distant. She pulled her hand free from mine and turned off the flashlight Billy held. The loss of even that small bit of illumination made the surrounding woods seem darker.

Phoebe wrapped her long arms around her shins. She rocked a little, in time with her soft humming.

"It's much more beautiful at night. I was here before I came to get you guys and it wasn't nearly as... Hmmm."

I wished it was daylight then, with a passion that shook me. Surely, if the sun was shining, the strange mushrooms and the eerie silence and Phoebe's odd behavior would seem silly. I glanced at Billy, but he watched Phoebe, head cocked and mouth open a little. I waited for him to speak, but he was silent.

Or not exactly silent. I became slowly aware that he was softly singing along to her humming.

I wanted to run again then, but the muscles in my legs were water and my hands felt rooted to the ground. I dug my fingers into the grass. It was too soft against my palm, almost like fur. I shuddered.

"Phoebs... Bills..."

Phoebe touched her fingertips to her lips.

"He's beautiful. So beautiful that she didn't even know his name when she let him kiss her."

I twisted the slippery grass between my fingers. It struck me suddenly that Phoebe wasn't talking about her dad. Not the one I knew. Mr. Hopkins was handsome in a gruff, beefy, gym teacher kind of way, but no one anywhere would call him 'beautiful'.

If it hadn't been Mr. Hopkins that her mother had met here, though...

"Who, Phoebs?"

She turned to me, a stray beam of moonlight flaring in the treacherous depths of her blue-green eyes. Behind her, Billy kept up his soft singing. I wanted to shove him and tell him to stop, not to encourage her, but I couldn't move. Phoebe smiled.

"My real father."

Of course, I knew that's what she was going to say. What else? But the words still struck me like a blow to the gut.

There had always been talk. Adults whispered. Kids teased. Phoebe looked nothing like her broad, florid, brown-haired, brown-eyed father.

She didn't even have the same last name. No, she was an O'Hara, not a Hopkins.

I asked Phoebe about it, when we first met, but she said it was a tradition in her mother's family. It originated in what her Irish grandmother called 'the old country'.

"Female offspring are always named for their mam's line," Phoebe said, quoting her Nannie O'Hara word-for-word.

When I heard Phoebe's words that night, I wondered fleetingly if that was just an excuse because Mr. Hopkins didn't want to give her his name. Now, I know better.

Whether he wanted to or not, there was no way he would ever have been allowed to claim her.

Phoebe still talked, but I couldn't follow her words anymore. My head swam and little colored lights flared before my eyes. The scent of the mushrooms grew stronger, became sweeter. Thicker. I could feel it coating the inside of my throat with each gasping breath I took.

The night seemed suddenly warmer, humid, bringing sweat on my upper lip and under my arms.

Billy was still singing, louder, and I thought I heard music drifting to us from out of the trees. Not normal music though. Nothing like what we listened to while barreling down back roads in Phoebe's Dart. This was something else. Something tinkling and jangling. Oddly catchy and yet discordant. Like funhouse music.

My feet twitched. I felt the urge to get up and dance. To throw my arms up in the air and spin. A laugh bubbled in my chest, pressing against my throat until it hurt to hold it in. And yet I swallowed it back, because it didn't feel like mine.

It felt like I imagined being drunk would feel. Or drugged.

I smoked a joint once and the feeling was similar to the detached dizziness I felt then, only that night it was tenfold.

The colored lights brightened and the music grew louder. Phoebe stood, pulling Billy to his feet. They danced together, feet kicking out, laughing.

"He's coming!" Phoebe called. "I can't wait for you to see!"

She spun Billy in a wide circle. I shook my head to clear it, but it only made me woozier. Billy reached down for my hand, but I still couldn't lift it from the grass. The line of skin on my thigh where the mushroom had brushed me burned.

In the woods, I glimpsed dark figures, heard the shifting of feet. Something snorted and blew, and it sounded huge. Branches broke as it drew closer. Eager whispers rose over the music, twisted through it.

My skin felt cold, though the night had grown even warmer. Beads of sweat trickled down my throat from under my hair.

Thunder rolled in the distance, but it seemed to go on forever. It took my sluggish mind entirely too long to realize it wasn't thunder at all but the thud of hooves.

"Horses..."

I mumbled the word, my tongue thick and numb. I blinked up at Phoebe. She smiled down at me, her teeth white and gleaming in the dark. The corners of her mouth seemed sharp, stabbing up into her pale cheeks.

"He's bringing the Hunt, Ellie! I asked him to take us away with him. All three of us." She pulled Billy into a one-armed hug. "I'd never leave you two."

Billy threw back his head and laughed, moonlight gleaming off his glasses, cheeks flushed with happiness. But my heart was concrete in my chest. I tore my fingers from the grass finally, though it felt as if my skin was being sliced away by tiny swords. Rivulets of hot blood dripped down my wrist as I reached for them.

"We should leave."

My fingertips brushed Billy's arm. I tried to curl them around the fabric of his shirt, but Phoebe pulled him back into her arms.

"We will, El. As soon as my father gets here."

Billy turned his head, frowning over Phoebe's shoulder. "Did you hear that? It sounds like...bells."

It was only then it occurred to me that Billy wasn't seeing and hearing the same things I was, because I had been hearing the bells for... Well, I can't really say how long. Time was funny that night, like I already told you. But I'd been hearing them for a while.

Phoebe smiled that too-wide, slicing smile again.

"He's here!"

And she was right. Something had definitely entered the clearing with us. Power slapped me down against the ground like a hand swatting a fly. All the air rushed from my lungs. My lids peeled back from my eyes until I couldn't close them even if I wanted to—and I did, desperately.

The colored lights that had been dancing between the trees coalesced into a pupil-lancing brightness that brought tears to my eyes. It was beautiful and terrible and hurt so bad I wanted to scream, but I had no breath. I strained toward my friends, desperate to reach them, unable to move.

Billy fell to his knees. He was weeping, but unlike me, he wasn't in any pain. No, the look on his narrow face wasn't anguish; it was adoration.

The shadows I'd seen flitting from the corner of my eye, dancing among the trees, were visible then too. They took the shape of humped, gnarled, brown-skinned beings with black eyes, sharp yellow teeth, and long, many-jointed fingers tipped with jagged black claws.

My vision blurred and it seemed as if they faded into the forest, became part of the trees, their arms and fingers the branches, their twisted bodies the trunks. Then they were once again separate entities, prowling the edges of the clearing like dogs waiting to be given the signal to hunt.

Phoebe laughed, the sound musical and beautiful, but so cold I cringed against the hard ground.

In the midst of that brilliant light were other things too. Enormous horses, backs twice as high as my head, that pawed the earth with hooves as big as elephant feet, striking red sparks from the stony ground. Great cats with teeth like scimitars and eyes that glowed like embers. And tall, lithe beings with long, silken hair that moved as if it were alive.

Like Phoebe's.

One of them stepped forward, lifting a pale, slender hand to halt the others. His hair was smooth and golden, his lips full and red as berries, and his eyes faceted crystal. The scent of the mushrooms bloomed wet and mineral around me as he drew closer. Fire burned through my blood, settling a low, molten throb between my thighs.

I couldn't take my eyes off him. Somewhere nearby I heard Billy moan. Phoebe's voice caught. She was speaking, but the words made no sense to me.

My skin tingled, every hair on my body vibrating. The pain of being crushed against the ground was distant compared to how wonderful it felt to have him near. Even the trickle of my own blood soaking into the ground made my breath catch in pleasure.

I ground my teeth against the twisting ache in my chest when he parted his perfect lips and spoke.

"Daughter," he said to Phoebe, his gorgeous face serene. "I have come as you requested. Who have you brought with you?"

Phoebe clasped her hands together, beaming as if she couldn't hear the displeasure dripping from his every word.

"They're my friends," she said, dipping her head at Billy. She glanced around, her brow furrowing slightly when her gaze landed on my prostrate form. But she was smiling again when she turned back to Him. "I can't leave them behind."

He frowned at her, and I screamed at the pain that lanced through me. Behind him, the host shifted and murmured.

"Hmmm."

He purred the word, head cocked as he studied Phoebe. Then his jeweled gaze slid to Billy.

He beckoned Billy forward with the flick of his fingers. Billy stumbled to his feet and lurched toward him, tears streaming down his cheeks. He was smiling as Phoebe's father—and that's surely what he was, because seeing them side-by-side the resemblance was undeniable—plucked his glasses off and tossed them away.

He took Billy by the chin with elegant, tapered fingers and lifted his face for inspection. He stared into it for what felt an eternity, my breath rattling in my lungs as I waited for him to do...something.

His laugh was deep and rolling, sharp, and shocking. Like lightning and thunder at once. He brushed one of those thin fingers down Billy's flushed cheek, drawing a line of red.

Billy barely had time to gasp before he dragged that cutting finger over his throat.

For a heavy, frozen moment, nothing happened. Phoebe's father spun Billy away from him with the shove of one hand. Billy's hazel eyes, still full of hope, blinked and then widened as his neck opened in a grim, red smile.

Blood poured down his chest, soaking his shirt. He turned to reach for Phoebe, spraying warm blood across my upturned face. It stung my eyes and filled my open mouth with the taste of pennies. I wanted to look away, but I was still frozen.

I watched as Billy's knees gave way, spilling him to the ground near my feet without a word.

"Billy!" Phoebe stepped toward him, but her father caught her shoulder.

"I have done you both a favor, daughter. Believe me. He was too fragile. He would have broken."

She whirled on him, and I thrilled to see my Phoebe back. The one who kissed me and gave me my first taste of sweetness. The one who once shoved Billy's father out of the way when he asked her why she came by to visit 'the little queer'.

"He's not… He's my friend! I told you I couldn't just leave them without so much as a word! You said you'd take us with you!"

His golden brows rose. He sighed, the sound a sensuous breeze.

"Such foolish sentiment. You asked me to take you away. I agreed to come back, to show you the door. But there are rules. You are my daughter. I said nothing of them."

His lip curled as he looked at Billy's crumpled form. So far he hadn't even glanced in my direction. I was glad, as much as my skin seemed to thrum with his nearness.

Phoebe's determination flickered in the face of his derision, making her look much younger than her nearly eighteen years, but then she squared her shoulders.

"They are part of me. They're mine."

My heart both swelled and quaked at her words. What would he do when challenged? More tears trickled from my burning eyes, slipping down into my ears. Billy's blood had begun to dry, tacky and itchy, on my skin.

"They are nothing to me," Phoebe's father sneered.

Phoebe's eyes narrowed.

"Like my mother was nothing to you?"

His hand flew out, quick as a striking snake. The crack of his palm meeting her cheek was loud. The blow sent Phoebe flying, tumbling through the air. Her small body thudded to the ground beside me, her pale cheek crimson as a sunrise when her eyes found mine.

She bled from a gash on her forehead, just below her hairline. I watched it drip down to pool beneath her cheek as we stared into each other's eyes.

"I'm sorry, El," she whispered, her breath hitching. "I thought—"

"Get her up."

Her father's voice, sharp as a knife, cut her off. Long-fingered, white hands curled around her shoulders, her arms, and lifted her from the ground. Phoebe kicked and cursed as several of the other tall, beautiful beings carried her back into their terrible throng.

They hoisted her onto the back of one of the big, brutish horses. As I watched, they tugged her legs apart and forced her to straddle the beast's wide body. My heart pounded hard enough to hurt at the sight. The second her legs touched the horse's black-haired hide, Phoebe stopped thrashing. At least, her lower half did.

She shoved the men away and tugged at her own thighs, but her legs didn't budge. She yelled at her father, words I couldn't hear, but he ignored her.

His eyes, irises so pale they almost blended into the whites, finally fell on me.

I tried again to move, to pull myself away. I would have crawled if I could, but my muscles were still locked as rigid as stone. I could only stare up into his perfect face—beauty is too tame a word for what he had—as he stood above me and stared down.

He cocked his head, sending a cascade of golden hair over his shoulder.

I hadn't noticed before that moment what he was wearing. Even then, it was only a faint impression of a dark blue, velvet tunic and ebony...not quite pants. More like tights, but thicker. Leather boots hugged his legs to the knee. He looked vaguely like something out of a medieval painting only...more. I wouldn't have been surprised to see a crown on top of his head.

In fact, the exact opposite was true. My eyes and heart protested the lack.

I wanted to scream. Cry. Worship him. Die.

Fear and longing twisted within me, sharp and cutting.

And then he smiled.

"Interesting," he said, tapping a finger against his red, red lips. "You see through the weaving."

The words made no sense to me, but his regard burned me, like being kissed by the sun. I writhed against the cool grass, that pulse in my belly beating slower than my heart. Behind him, the beasts shifted. The other pale, beautiful men murmured. I could still hear Phoebe shouting and pleading. I wanted to look for her, but I couldn't shift my gaze away from him.

He narrowed his eyes slightly, studying me as he had Billy.

Agony slashed through me like knives stabbed into my brain over and over. My vision went grey. Though my hands and feet stayed pinned to the ground, my spine bowed up hard enough to crackle. The top of my head touched the grass.

Again, his laughter rolled through the clearing. The pain faded away then, and the pleasure came rushing back, so heady it turned my stomach. I sagged, waiting for the cut of his fingers, but it didn't come.

Instead, when I managed to open my eyes and blink through the tears, he extended a hand to me.

"Come, little beauty. Stand."

Whatever had been holding me down was gone. My body felt strangely light, as if I'd drift up into the sky if I didn't hold onto the Earth. I clawed my bleeding fingers into the grass, pushing them down into the cold, wet dirt below.

He laughed again, head thrown back, throat rippling with sound.

As if it belonged to someone else—him, perhaps—my body pushed up until I was standing before him.

I had always felt gangly and tall next to Phoebe and Billy. Though Billy wasn't anywhere near as short as her, he was still only 5'8, whereas I was nearly six feet. But trembling in front of Phoebe's father, I felt small. He towered over me, his slim form reaching 6'8, at least.

His hand came up to cup my cheek. I flinched, expecting the touch to hurt, for his skin to be cold after the way he'd treated Billy. And Phoebe.

But it wasn't.

His fingers were warm satin as he stroked my face. They wandered over my eyebrows, the thick, wiry blackness of them seeming to fascinate him. His hand drifted back to my hair, combing through the ebony strands that, in addition to my copper skin, had earned me the nickname 'Native Girl' at school.

My heart beat so quickly it vibrated in my chest. I panted, tasting the salt of blood and tears on my lips. The musk of the mushrooms was so thick it filled my nose, but I could still smell the herbal spice of the forest, and something else...like a hint of smoke.

I waited, staring into those eerie eyes, for him to kill me as he had Billy. Or perhaps for him to order I be taken, like Phoebe. I couldn't tell if the feeling that sparked in my belly at that thought was more dread or desire. My knees shook.

His hand fisted in my hair, tugging me upwards until I stood on tiptoe, bringing my face closer to his. His breath washed over me, sweet, cool and faintly citrus, like lemon ice. I shivered, hanging from his grip like a kitten even as the pain radiated from my scalp, down my spine.

"Please," I managed to whisper. He once again raised those pointed, golden brows.

"Please what, darkling?"

My tongue twitched in my mouth, because I didn't know how to answer. But then words slid up from deep in my gut, and I parted my lips to let them out. They took wing.

"Please, let me go."

The murmuring behind him grew louder, angrier. His horde of men and beasts didn't like my request. But he smiled. It was like Phoebe's smile, the too wide, too toothy, too sharp one. Only more.

"I will," he said, still grinning.

One of the beautiful, dangerous men gasped, "Sire!" But he held up his free hand as he lowered me back to my feet. He didn't release his hold on my hair though.

"Tonight will be a treat!"

He called the words back over his shoulder without looking away from me.

He lowered his face close to mine, eyes sparkling like diamonds with vicious glee. He brushed his lips along my cheek, the corner of my mouth, making the skin there tingle and buzz.

Fresh, hot tears dripped off my chin as waves of ecstasy rolled through me, curling my toes. It was pleasure like I'd never felt before or since. Thinking about it now still makes me weep with gratitude and despair in almost equal measure.

Then he breathed in my ear, his fiery tongue flicking delicately against the sensitive lobe.

"I'm giving you a chance. A small one. If we catch you, you're mine. And not just for a night, darkling. I could play with you for eons."

Teeth grazed my jaw briefly before he flung me away from him. I stumbled, skidding and sliding down the side of the hill, taking out one of the meaty, fleshy mushrooms as I fell.

Glancing over my shoulder, I saw him raise his arm above his head. Behind him, horses reared. Monsters shrieked. Men cheered. Phoebe screamed.

He called after me.

"Run, darkling! Run!"

I did.

I tore through the woods with the sound of his company chasing me, tears pouring down my cheeks. The forest, hushed but for the sound of my panicked flight and the following horde, seemed to conspire against me.

Branches scratched my face, thorns plucked at my clothes. I fell more than once, though I practically flew back across the creek without touching the water. Rough stones seemed to rise up out of the ground to trip me.

I ran blindly, careening off tree trunks. My hair caught on their jagged bark, pulling. Roots wrapped around my ankles.

No matter how fast I ran, the scenery didn't seem to change, as if I was on a treadmill with the landscape scrolling by me on a loop. Every inch of my skin felt abraded and bruised, throbbing with blood and stinging with sweat.

The muscles of my lungs and legs burned with effort. I sobbed, wanting to give up, but the sound of the hunt never faded or faltered. It only grew louder.

Every time I stumbled or snagged, I expected him to be on me, plucking me up onto the back of one of the great horses.

He called after me, his voice teasing, the certainty of my capture in every ringing syllable.

I prayed, out loud, wishing I had listened to my grandfather's stories about the gods of our people. About raven, the trickster whose wings were as black as my hair. But I hadn't believed, hadn't ever wanted to be the 'Native Girl'.

"I will put you in such pretty chains, darkling!" His distant voice slid over my many wounds like a barbed caress, soft as a velvet tongue and then biting with sharp teeth.

Once, I thought I heard Phoebe, tears in her voice, urging me on.

My feet tangled, sending me sprawling, but I clawed my way through leaves and dirt, dragging myself forward. The jingle of a harness made me scream. I grabbed at a branch, felt it cut into my skin, bringing fresh blood. I pulled myself to my feet.

Run. That's all I could do. Keep running until I couldn't anymore.

Less than a mile from the car to the clearing, the prosecutor said.

Twenty minutes one way. But it had been just before midnight when Billy and I followed Phoebe into the woods, and the sun was spilling over the horizon, all pink and orange, when I threw myself into the driver's side of Phoebe's car and turned the key in the ignition.

I don't know if I was still hearing the hunt or only imagining the tinkle of bells and the raucous calls that promised me an eternity of pain. Or pleasure. Perhaps both. My arms shook with fatigue, relief, and a shameful flicker of disappointment as I spun the steering wheel in a wide arc and bumped back down the dirt track to the road.

David Bowie's rich voice spilled from the speakers, bringing fresh tears to my eyes. No more 'Aladdin Sane', now he sang of painting mornings of gold while honey-hued rays pierced the horizon as if by his command.

By the time I reached the Sheriff's station in town—bruised and covered in Billy and Phoebe's blood—the sun had fully risen.

So, that's what happened that night.

The rest is what you'd no doubt expect. The cops took me to the hospital to have my injuries checked out. The doctors insisted on head scans and psych consults because they thought I'd lost my mind. They eventually ruled me sane and fit to stand trial and that was that.

I know you won't believe me any more than the police, or my parents, or my lawyers did. It makes much more sense that I'm a psycho who lured my two best friends out into the woods, slit Billy's throat and did who-knows-what to Phoebe, hid her body and refused to tell anyone where it was. That I concocted this whole unbelievable tale of monsters to cover up my own guilt.

That's what the jury thought, in the end. They believed the testimony of the experts about the wounds on my hands and supposed argument—over what they never did say—and shipped me off to this place, the oldest women's maximum security facility in the state, built before electronic locks and modern conveniences.

I'll be here for the rest of my life.

I've found some comfort inside these crumbling, grey concrete walls and metal bars, weeping bloody rust from beneath a thin veneer of white paint. Whatever he was—and I have my suspicions—he is, I am sure, a creature of the wild places, and the only green here is the mold growing in the grout between tiles in the showers. Still, I watch the edge of the woods outside, and at night I listen for the jingle of bells.

I try not to dream of his perfect face, and I pray to the old gods of Grandfather's tribe that he won't find me again, because I suspect he could if he wanted, and this time I wouldn't get away. This is why I don't file appeals or fight for parole. Here, I am surrounded by people and thick walls and iron bars.

And I read somewhere they can't stand iron.

ABOUT THE AUTHORS

CHRIS BANNOR

Chris Bannor is a speculative fiction writer who lives in Southern California. Chris learned her love of genre stories from her mother at an early age and has never veered far from that path. Her stories have been published in over two dozen anthologies and range from horror and science fiction, to fantasy, romance, and steampunk.

www.chrisbannor.com

NEEN COHEN

Neen Cohen is an Australian Sapphic Speculative Fiction author. She lives in Brisbane with her partner, son and fur babies, has a Bachelor of Creative Industries from Queensland University of Technology, and is a member of the Springfield Writer's Group. She's had a multitude of 'day jobs' to pay the bills but her heart has always been in the art of marking dead trees with squiggles of ink and graphite.

When she's not running after her son, spending time with her partner, or working at the current 'day job', she can be found writing while sitting against a tombstone or tree in any number of graveyards. She's also discovered a new found passion for throwing sharp objects at thick pieces of wood (knife throwing and axe throwing) and tries to squeeze at least 30 hours in to each day because sleep is for the weak.

Check out Neen's latest misadventures - https://linktr.ee/neencohen
Or you can find here below:
Facebook: https://www.facebook.com/neencohenauthor
Instagram: https://www.instagram.com/neenauthor/
Twitter: https://twitter.com/CohenNeen
TikTok: @neencohen
YouTube:
https://www.youtube.com/channel/UCYBopH46A62LJzihXf4JHUg

Georgia Cook

Georgia Cook is an illustrator and writer from London. She has been published in such places as Baffling Magazine, Luna Station Quarterly, and Vastarien Lit, as well as shortlisted for the Bridport Prize and Reflex Fiction Award, among others.

She has also written and narrated for the horror anthology podcasts 'Creepy', 'The Other Stories', and 'The Night's End'

She can be found on twitter at @georgiacooked and on her website at https://www.georgiacookwriter.com/

Morgan Elektra

Morgan Elektra writes dark fiction, paranormal romance, and erotica for those who, like her, are in love with the dark. When not writing, she can be found in a book or volunteering for her local LGBTQ+ center. She currently lives near Savannah, GA with her husband and their cat Harlequin.

www.bymorganelektra.com

K. B. Elijah

K. B. Elijah is a Brisbane-based speculative fiction author whose work features in dozens of anthologies about the mysterious, the magical and the macabre. Her own short fantasy novellas with twists, The Empty Sky (collection), Out of the Nowhere (collection), Whispers in the Dark and Metaphoria, are available now. Join her on Instagram @k.b.elijah for book reviews and upcoming stories.

https://www.facebook.com/KBElijah
https://www.amazon.com/K-B-Elijah/e/B07Z1D3HPF

Angèle Gougeon

Angèle Gougeon is a speculative author from Manitoba, Canada, with short stories published in literary magazines and several anthologies, as well as a dark Gothic Paranormal novel published with EDGE Science Fiction and Fantasy Publishing. With a long love of all things fantastical, this ace couldn't resist taking part in this incredible collection of lgbtqia+ stories about the fae.

https://www.amazon.com/-/e/B01BHPHNII

S.O. GREEN

S.O. Green (they/them) is a genre-fluid writer and editor living in the Kingdom of Fife with husband, John. Author of the post-apocalyptic novelette, Sin Chaser, published by Eerie River Publishing, as well as over 80 works with imprints including Dragon Soul Press, Black Ink Fiction and Nordic Press. Simone also won 3rd Place in the British Fantasy Society's Short Story Contest 2018. Writer, vegan, martial artist, gamer, occasionally a terrible person (but only to fictional people).

Website: https://thebasementoflove.blogspot.com/
Facebook: https://www.facebook.com/thebasementoflove
Twitter: https://twitter.com/SOGreenWriter

DONNA J. W. MUNRO

Donna J. W. Munro teaches high schoolers the slippery truths of government and history at her day job. Her students are her greatest inspiration.

She lives with three cats, a patient, fur covered husband, and her encyclopedia son. Her daughter is off saving the world.

Writing is Donna's painful passion, and her pieces are published in Nothing's Sacred Magazine IV and V, Corvid Queen, Hazard Yet Forward (2012), Enter the Apocalypse (2017), Beautiful Lies, Painful Truths II (2018), Terror Politico (2019), It Calls from the Forest (2020), Gray Sisters Vol 1 (2020), Borderlands Vol 7 (2020), Pseudopod 752 (2021), and others. Check out her first novel, Revelation: Poppet Cycle Book 1.

www.donnajwmunro.com
@DonnaJWMunro

McKenzie Richardson

McKenzie Richardson lives in Milwaukee, WI. A lifelong explorer of the dark corners of imagined worlds, she has spent the past few years chronicling her findings. Her horror and dark fantasy can be found in several Eerie River anthologies, including Dark Magic and With Bone and Iron.

Her storytelling and poetry can also be found in publications from Iron Faerie Publishing, Black Ink Fiction, and Nordic Press.

McKenzie currently works in a public library, doing her best not to be buried beneath an ever-growing TBR list. When not writing, she can usually be found in her book hoard, reading with coffee in hand and a cat on her lap.

Facebook: facebook.com/mckenzielrichardson
Instagram: instagram.com/mckenzielrichardson/
Blog: craft-cycle.com

Frank Sawielijew

An eccentric Russo-German author with Bulgarian roots, Frank Sawielijew loves to forge fantastic tales set in strange, imaginative fantasy worlds. Due to his love for the pulp classics, he often combines fantasy and science fiction in unorthodox ways. He writes in both English and German and had a handful of his short stories appear in various anthologies since 2015. He has also written professionally for the video game industry. When he's not working on anything, he wastes his time watching campy 1980s B-movies, taking long walks through nature and playing Thief, the best game ever made.

www.isfdb.org/cgi-bin/ea.cgi?240679

WYNNE F. WINTERS

Wynne F. Winters has been known to dabble in the fantastic and the macabre, sometimes at the same time. She's been published in several horror anthologies, including Daughters of Darkness, Black Rainbow, and the dark fantasy anthology With Blood and Ash. She's also been known to post stories online under the Reddit username u/firesidechats451. If you're interested in hearing her controversial tea opinions, being regaled with grisly true crime details, or finding out when a new story of hers is up, you can follow her on

Twitter @WintersWynne.
https://twitter.com/WintersWynne

More from Eerie River

Eerie River Publishing, is a small independant publishing house that is devoted to releasing quality dark fiction books and anthologies.

To stay up to date with all our new releases and upcoming giveaways, follow us on Facebook, Twitter, Instagram and YouTube. Sign up for our monthly newsletter and receive a free ebook Darkness Reclaimed, as our thank you gift.

https://mailchi.mp/71e45b6d5880/welcomebook

Interested in becoming a Patreon member?
Patreon membership gives you exclusive sneak peeks at upcoming books, early chapter releases, covers art as well as free ebooks and discounts on paperbacks.

https://www.patreon.com/EerieRiverPub.

ALSO AVAILABLE FROM
EERIE RIVER PUBLISHING

NOVELS
Miracle Growth
Storming Area 51: Horror At the Gate
In Solitudes Shadow
Dead Man Walking
Devil Walks in Blood
SENTINEL
A Sword Named Sorrow

ANTHOLOGIES
Of Fire and Stars
Monsters & Mayhem
AFTER: A Post-Apocalyptic Survivor Series
Last Stop: Horror on Route 13
It Calls From The Forest: Volume I
It Calls From The Forest: Volume II
It Calls From The Sky
It Calls From the Sea
It Calls Fromt he Doors
Darkness Reclaimed
With Blood and Ash
With Bone and Iron
Forgotten Ones: Drabbles of Myth and Legend
Dark Magic: Drabbles of Magic and Lore

COMING SOON
It Calls From the Veil
Nothus
Infested
Shade of Night
Path of War
Void

www.EerieRiverPublishing.com

An Eerie River Dark Fantasy Series
WITH
BLOOD
AND
ASH
T.M. Brown
David Green
Crystal Lynn Hilbert
Joel R. Hunt
Michael D. Nadeau
Rose Strickman
Wynne F. Winters